THE SOLDIER A NOVEL
R.C. Binstock

Phillip's insular life borders on self-exile. He lives in the woods of New Hampshire in a centuries old farmhouse. He does not simply prize his privacy, he insists on it – until a female relative arrives. He has offered the young woman a temporary haven trading labor for room and board. Instead of resenting the invasion, Phillip finds himself liking it, and her.

But how alone has he really been? How isolated is his existence? A woman prowls the grounds. A soldier of a war fought long ago dreams of home. Lives, past and present, flow together in mystical fashion, amplifying one another's conflicts, joys, desires. They inform Phillip's life and art, infusing his isolation and imagination.

Ann Beattie has lauded R.C. Binstock's writing as "serious and often radiant." The *Boston Globe* cited his last novel as "a work of genuine moral imagination." The *Los Angeles Times* called it "expert and moving."

R. C. Binstock is the author of *The Light of Home* and *Tree of Heaven*. He lives in Cambridge, Massachusetts.

Fiction
272 pages, 5 1/2 x 8 1/4
1-56947-059-6 $24

Cosmic romance and ethereal reunion mark the second novel by the author of *Tree of Heaven*.

National Advertising
Advance Reading Copies

 British, Trans., 1st Ser., Dramatic:
Smith/Skolnik Literary Management

the
SOLDIER

Also by R. C. Binstock

The Light of Home (stories, 1992)
Tree of Heaven (novel, 1995)

the
SOLDIER

r. c. binstock

Published by
Soho Press, Inc.
853 Broadway
New York, NY 100037

Library of Congress Cataloging-in-Publication Data

Binstock, R. C.
  The soldier / R. C. Binstock.
      p.   cm.
  ISBN 1-56947-059-6 (alk. paper)
  1. Authors, American—New Hampshire—Psychol-
ogy—Fiction. 2. Man-woman relationships—New
Hampshire—Fiction. 3. Family—New Hampshire—
Fiction. I. Title
PS3552.I57S65   1996
813'.54—dc20   95-26356
                                              CIP

Manufactured in the United States of America
        10 9 8 7 6 5 4 3 2 1

For my sister Lynn and my brother Ben

and in memory of Myra Louise
my cherished friend

part

I

Every heart has its secret
sorrows which the world
knows not, and oftentimes
we call a man cold when he
is only sad.

—HENRY WADSWORTH
LONGFELLOW

When Phillip opened the door for Jennie it was October, and the wind was blowing. Behind her he saw his trees, partly red and partly gold—he got to look at them each time he went through his front door, it was one of the best things about the house—and the hill just beyond, and the blue sky. It was late in the day but the time hadn't changed yet and the sun was still high, casting a brilliant light on everything. What am I doing at my desk, he thought, I should be out enjoying this, but then she smiled and he remembered she was there.

"It's good to see you," he said.

"You too," she said, and he peered at her face. It was pretty and open and he couldn't help seeing his aunt's face in it, his uncle's as well but particularly his aunt's because he'd known her and could remember her when she was almost this young and the resemblance was very strong. The girl's nose was a reflection of her mother's and father's both—broader than one and slightly shorter than the other—and her hair was like neither's, and he wasn't sure where her high forehead could have come from, but most of all she reminded him of Carla. They say you can live forever, he thought, and here was the proof right in front of him. Seeing her look that way made him feel old and a little afraid.

"Well," he said. "Welcome. Are these your only things?"

"Yes. This is all of it for now."

In the hallway Phillip waited while she pulled off her jacket and then took it and hung it in the closet. In his view it was too slight for New Hampshire, even in October—she would have to get a real coat soon—but he knew this was a fashion among people her age. As she straightened her clothing and bent to remove her boots he thought: she's lovely, and I'm sure she doesn't know it. It was the kind of human shape that made him wish he were a painter. He felt the crestfallen panicky longing that always came in the presence of something beautiful and he wanted to warn her to take care, that some day she might be like everyone else, but he knew she wouldn't hear.

"I can't imagine living in a place like this," she said, looking at him, her hands on her hips. "It's almost like heaven."

"No angels here, believe me," he said. He lifted her pack and handbag. "Will there be more coming later?"

She looked puzzled, though he thought it an obvious question, and shook her head. "This is all I've brought," she said. "All I'm bringing." She watched him for a second more. "I have lots of money, Uncle Phillip. I'll buy whatever else I need." To unfreeze the moment—he had nothing to say—he gestured down the hall toward the rest of the house, and after a pause she went ahead. "I do have lots of things, I'm not ascetic," she said. "But they're all in storage now. I didn't want to be burdened."

Or to commit yourself, he thought. Easy come, easily gone.

When they stepped into the living room he could tell she was charmed. It was a fine place, he knew, a treat for most visitors, with the view through the big window and the carefully collected furniture and the paintings and sculptures and strange little objects. The rest of the house was dull by comparison. It was his outer pride, this room (and of course the land itself, the trees and stream and the hills all around); for him there was his work and his satisfaction in it, balancing the discouragement he felt about the way things had turned out—no wife, no child, not much in recognition beyond the invested royalties off of which he lived and the rare invitation to speak somewhere, or to sit on a panel—but that was nothing he dared share and so his boast was his living room. The implications of this, of what the room might stand for or reveal in summation of his nearly fifty years, he tried not to pursue. When people came he sat them on the couch and entertained them, and if they tried to talk of his books or of him he drew their attention to some artwork instead, some curio, to the sun falling behind the mountain or the stars or the wind.

Her eyes were bright as she turned to him. "Can I sit in here?" she asked. "You don't work in this room, do you?"

"No," he said. "You can stay here as often as you like."

She drew a long breath and took the center of the couch. Her smile was warm and though he knew to call it gratitude—he hadn't seen her in over ten years but had agreed to her spending the winter in his home, in fact had suggested it himself—it felt instead like praise. And he found that her approval pleased him, pleased him deeply. This was bothersome, so sudden and so contrary to what had become the basis of his life, that it couldn't have upset him more had she pulled her shirt over her head or hurled a carving through the glass. In his house three minutes and he wanted her to like him!—that was what had happened. It brought strong second thoughts.

"I'll make you some tea," he told her, setting her bags on the floor. "And we'll get you something to eat." He stopped. "I assume you like tea?"

She half rose and put out her hand. "Not yet," she said. "I've just barged in on you. Sit down and let's meet each other. Get to know each other, I mean. And then I'll make myself a snack—I didn't come here as a guest."

Carla's daughter, he thought. Without a doubt. He nodded and sat a little stiffly in the big brown chair, across the coffee table from her.

"You seem hesitant," she said. "If you've changed your mind I'll understand."

"I was working," he said. "It always make me this way."

Her hand went to her mouth. "I'm sorry. I didn't realize."

"How could you?" he asked. "We'll sort it out soon enough but today was unavoidable. You had no way of knowing." She sat there looking disturbed. "No harm done, Jennie," he said. "I don't mean to aggrandize myself. Look, if I couldn't have afforded the interruption I wouldn't have answered the door."

She smiled back at him then, timidly. "I walked here

from town," she said. "I guess I didn't consider your not being here, or not letting me in."

"You walked from town?" he asked. "All eight miles?"

She nodded. "I loved it," she said. "It was fun."

As he studied her—in response to his silence she was looking around the room, gazing briefly in one direction or another before moving on, and the sunlight played in her hair—he became aware of her beauty all over again. It was like a change in the evening sky in the springtime, or some subtle shift in an orchestra's intent; what was at one moment merely true became at the next unbearably lovely, overwhelming, impossible to believe. The shock faded quickly but the quality remained, like a single pure tone, and he was bitterly jealous: she had more beauty about her, just sitting there, than he would be able to create in his cramped and cluttered study if he lived another fifty years.

" 'Uncle Phillip,' " he said. "It's a little strange to be called that again. After so much time." He sat and watched her carefully, as if she were a deer surprised at midnight in his pasture, as if she might run. "No," he said gently. "I haven't changed my mind."

The volunteer is lost. He admits this to himself and feels better. He is lost and he's alone, more alone than if he were the last man living, the last in Tennessee, because if he does meet someone odds are he'll have to hide while they go by. His face and hands are filthy, his vision blurred by fatigue, his gut long unsettled from whiskey and bad food and fear. The day is warm and still. He has no hope of finding his fellows, no idea even of the most likely direction; it makes very little sense for him to stay where he is but he has no good reason to move from the spot.

He is failing in his duty—there are others counting on him—but he suspects it soon won't matter.

He checks his kit for the hundredth time: water, biscuit, balls and powder. What else does he need? They are between him and his regiment, he guesses, between him and safety, but if so he could turn and head north and never meet them. He could steal some clothes and lose his gear and walk the miles until the river, and cross it, and keep going after that. The moon is near full for travel by night if need be. He could live off the country and keep moving toward home. He could get clean away.

It's as good a place as any, he decides. He looks up into the treetops, listens harder to the wind; he lays his pack and weapon on the ground.

As they sat and faced each other—it was awkward, he found, it seemed much too familiar, but he told himself she lives here now so you might as well relax—he decided that he'd been right in the first place, about her face. It was pretty but no more. And he'd been wrong about her form; while it was perfectly appealing, what any young woman might want, he very much doubted if it could be mined for aesthetic treasure. The effect, though surely real, was in some combination of things, and it went beyond her body alone, far beyond it; it was the physics of her skin and hair and irises and the bends at her waist and knees, yes, but also some incumbent quality, some self-aware decision, a way she chose to be.

He breathed long and deep, although she didn't seem to notice. In his discomfort, his restlessness, he recognized the frustration of not understanding, all mixed up with the fierce resentment of his unfulfilled desires. Why would you want to recreate what she is, or even to know where it comes

from? he asked. What kind of foolish conceit is that? What
she is, is—a human being, part of the natural world, which
black words on dry paper are not. Stop confusing things.
You ought to be able to distinguish by now.

"Uncle Phillip," he said again, into the quiet of the
room.

She nodded. "It's what my mother calls you."

"Yes. Even though she's my aunt."

"I think she wished you were our uncle," said Jennie.
"Because we hadn't any others, really."

He knew this was true and he remembered fondly her
older sisters calling to him, calling him by that name as he
stepped out of their father's yellow Beetle in the driveway,
as he waved to them from the side of the swimming pool. He
remembered with pleasure and joy. But the title seemed part
of an ancient past, irresurrectable, and it was jarring and
almost offensive to hear this graceful young woman use it.
He had wanted to be their uncle and their brother as well
but it had entirely to do with the fact that they were children,
which they weren't anymore, and the affection involved had
been something of which he was no longer capable in any
case; she was now where he'd been then and he was somewhere else entirely. If he saw Amy and Emily now—if he
saw them at five and two, or eight and five, running toward
him across the field to lead him home for dinner—he would
turn his back, take off the other way, disintegrate in sorrow.
He wondered if they'd talked to Jennie about him and realized they must have; she would hardly have come without
first asking questions. But the thought of this discussion
made him feel even less like her Uncle Phillip, not more,
and farther away from her sisters too. It occurred to him then
that not once since the phone call from her mother had he
even tried to remember how Jennie had looked when he'd

seen her last. He'd thought of Carla—Carla of twenty years ago—and briefly of Amy, but that was all.

She had risen and was walking around, examining things. Her hands rested comfortably on the backs of her hips. He was considering both her movements and the things she chose to study when she turned around and blushed.

"I'm sorry," she said. "You seemed distracted and I didn't want to bother you. I was just looking."

He'd been staring, he knew—first he'd forgotten her and then he'd stared, as if she were amateur dramatics in town—and had finally managed to make her embarrassed. He tried to rise above himself and soberly shook his head. "I'm the sorry one," he said. "I know I'm being rude."

She stood before the bookcase for another moment, her cheeks pink, her eyes on the carpet, then shook her head just as he had.

"I think this may not have been a very good idea," she said. "I'm just realizing how ridiculous it was of me to force myself on you."

"Not at all," he said. "I wasn't forced. I invited you."

She smiled, a smile different from all her smiles since she'd arrived. An older smile. "I know you did," she said, "but I'm worried about why. I'd prefer that you not be generous to me against your own better judgment, or against your own interests. And I'm getting the feeling I'll be in the way." She searched the room for the route to the door. "I think I'd better leave you alone," she said, starting for her bags.

With a quickness that amazed him he was on his feet to stop her. He put a hand on her arm.

"Jennifer, please," he said. "I'm very glad you're here and it will do me a great deal of good."

She watched his face, the smile half gone.

"I believe that now, this second, as I'm standing here,"

he said. "I really do. But that doesn't make it easy to get used to." Still she watched him. "I live alone, you know, and you've been here all of twelve minutes, and the fact that it unsettles me, that I chose to interrupt my own work and answer the door and then behaved badly as a consequence, doesn't mean I'm unhappy about it." He paused. "Or that it won't work out for both of us."

"That's true," she said.

"Please don't go," he said, thoroughly ashamed of himself. "We'll talk it over." She nodded—she looked as though she didn't want to speak—and he felt a vast relief.

His hand was still on her arm, he noticed, and he pulled it away as if she'd burned him. They were looking into each other's eyes and for a moment before he shifted his gaze—for the shortest of moments, for a part of a second—he felt owned by her; he felt dedicated. He felt both greedy and frightened and he recognized (from a distance) a loss of control.

Enough already, he thought as they stood there—enough preoccupation with her looks, her age, her feelings, her blood, her flesh and her presence. You don't need any new obsessions or secrets. You don't need any heroes. This is just a young woman who reminds you of your aunt. She's here to work and to help you work and having made the decision to allow that you're stuck and it *will* do you good so try to be strong, if you can, try to be calm. Try to get a grip on what's really important, for once in your dreary days. You are not mooning now over your pretty girl cousin, not now or any other time, you are writing a book. A better book than the last one. If you want to imagine her admiring it, you can. But leave it at that.

*   *   *

"I wonder how Phillip is," Jane said to her brother. she stood almost in the middle of the main shed, surrounded by full or partly full baskets, her long brown hair streaked with gray, her tall rubber boots (she'd finally bought a new pair) gleaming green in the sunlight that drifted through the door. "I wonder if we have enough Northern Spy." When he turned he could see only part of her clearly, the section from her calves to her throat; her ankles and feet were hidden by baskets, her head in shadow. She held a clipboard in front of her but no pencil or pen. Her hands gripped its top edge—gripped it tightly, he noticed—and he guessed she was probably looking at nothing and thinking of something far away, as she seemed to be doing very often these days.

"I don't know that it would be possible to have enough Northern Spy, darling," he said, grunting a little as he tried again to shove the spare generator the last inch into its usual spot. "There isn't any call for 'em. When was the last time you sold even one?"

"This afternoon," she said without moving.

"I don't know how much would be enough," he said, "except maybe none. None would be enough." Seeing that the machine was finally butted against its column—he'd somehow moved it three or four feet, all told, though it had felt like pushing a wall—he stood to his full height and mopped his forehead with a cloth.

"Oh Bill," she said from her shadow. "You're so smart." She coughed, and then moved entirely into the light. He saw she was wearing her glasses. "It happens I have a letter here from someone looking for Northern Spy."

"I'll bet you do," he said.

She sighed and stared out the door. "He got them here last weekend. I made him up a bag of antiques, and Northern's the one he likes. But he doesn't know what it's called."

She turned to him and for a moment the sun was reflected by her glasses—or was it focused?—right into his face. He considered her with affection.

"What about Phillip?" he asked.

"Nothing," she said. "I haven't heard from him in a while, that's all."

Bill waited. It was chilly—cold, really—in his part of the shed, and he had plenty of work to do. "You're not bickering again, are you?" he asked.

She looked to the door again, then back at him, as if deciding whether to walk away. He couldn't see her eyes behind the big shiny lenses. He knew he'd offended her but she just said, "We never bickered. That wasn't what it was." She drew a deep breath and knelt suddenly by the basket at her feet (he'd seen her do that and pass her hand over the red and yellow surfaces, for minutes at a time), then stood again.

"Anyway, do you want to hear it?" she asked.

"Hear what?"

"The letter," she said. "From the customer."

"Sure."

She laughed. "In case I misunderstood him." She looked down and he saw that it was open in front of her. Before she started she caught her breath.

Bill listened with arms folded. His sister read quickly but very nicely, he thought, very evenly and clearly, as if she were a teacher or a speech-maker instead of what she was. You'd sound good on the radio, he wanted to say, but he kept it to himself.

"Now is that a Spy, or is that a Spy?" Jane asked when she'd finished. She was smiling very proudly, as if she'd written it herself.

"You know," said Bill, "that's a pretty good description. A damn good description."

"It sure is," she agreed.

"Give me that part again."

" 'The apple in question is fairly large and symmetrically round,' " she read. " 'The color is pale, ranging from yellow to a deep pink, with a streaky low-contrast mottling, generally even over the surface; the white spots are small and few. The flesh is very firm and crisp, a yellowish white. The taste is tart (but not sharp) with a hint of Delicious.' "

He nodded. "You got it right. Northern Spy. Wow." He looked around at the crowded baskets. "Gonna send him some?"

"If he wants," she said. "He gave a number. I'll call."

He turned from her for a moment (she was staring off at nothing again and he realized it hurt to watch) but then turned back. "What was that at the end? About being jealous?"

" 'I envy you your stewardship,' " she read.

He laughed. "What do you think he means by that?"

She took a deep breath, folded the letter, removed her glasses, and walked away. "He means," she called, her voice getting lost in the spaces of the shed and in the thousands of gently curving fruits, "that we're blessed."

That very night (long time after sleep should have joined him) he found his hand, with a life of its own, grasping him tightly and speaking of Jennie. My god, he thought, what have I done?

Sutherland clings to a tree. In near distance the sound of battle. He prays wildly that it will come no closer, that it will pass away to the south, but hopes also for his chance. They want to kill him, he remembers; he grips the musket in his hand. He makes the effort to be ready. Ready to step away, to look, to raise the gun and shoot when they come smashing through the forest, through the brush, when they force their way into his clearing.

For a moment he is almost asleep. He reaches for the picture in his pocket, then for the book, then for the picture again, but each time something stops him. Even better to be still.

Above the gun he thinks he hears the horses, and the men. He believes he hears their cries.

chapter

2

November 4

Dearest Mother,

Here I am, in Uncle Phillip's house! It's a
lovely day, though pretty cold, at least it was when
I went walking this morning. I've gone out every
morning since I got here; I'm trying to make the
most of the season, as he warns me that the woods
get very difficult after a couple of storms. I'll probably have to buy some snowshoes, although there
may be a pair waiting for me in the attic over the
garage. (I can hardly wait to look through that collection. He showed it to me the day I arrived and
I saw some fabulous things. Most of it hasn't been
touched in twenty years.)

I'm sure you'll agree that our phone call last week was rushed and a little uncomfortable. I felt bad about that and rather than risk repeating it— I don't feel entirely free to use the phone here yet, not for any good reason but because I still see myself as a sort of intruder—I thought I'd write you a letter. I'd like to write more letters in any case. I had an interesting insight just after my most recent talk with Charlie, around the first of last month. I'd called to ask what he wanted me to do with his books and CDs and despite my best intentions he managed to drag me into one of those recrimination fests he loves so much. It went on and on. Finally I got so angry at him for being angry at me (what's the point of being mad at someone who's honest with you, it's not like he really wants me to sit there quietly hating him because I'm not elsewhere) that all at once, without knowing I was going to, I told him a few tough things, a few especially blunt things, and then hung up. It was wild! I mean, I was really flying blind, and I don't remember half of what I said. But I thought about it for a long time afterwards and came to the conclusion that I'm usually so ready to revise my own statements—so quick to take them back or change them, or even to stop before they're done—that I'd had to literally disconnect my ears to say what I wanted to say. I went back over as many conversations as I could recall and discovered that I hardly ever say *anything* important without some kind of qualification or adjustment. You've probably noticed this. I would never have described myself as confident

of speech but it upset me a lot to realize that I'm
so much the opposite. And it came to me all at
once that given my ambitions, in fact whatever I
might do, I've got to get over this.

So I thought I'd start by writing letters. And
not on any computer, either. Pen and paper for
me, so that if I do revise after the fact I'll be able
to look back and see that I did. And if I really
can't stand what I said in the first place—if I decide not to send it at all—I'll have to try to figure
out why before I start the whole thing over.

Not that there's anything wrong with editing,
you understand, but I'm beginning to see that you
have to say it first and then edit it later. After the
moment has passed. All the words are true when
they come out, really, just because something in
you needed to speak them; you can't judge them
as you say them but only after they're said.

I gather you've never been here so I owe you
a description. I don't think I'm going to tell you
all about it right away—I guess I'm not ready to
share it yet—but I will say that it's one of the nicest places I've ever seen. Really, anything would
be possible here. I feel such relief from all my
worries about the world, a false relief because all
that stuff is still happening everywhere else, but I
can't begin to say how soothing it is to be able
to forget about overcrowding and human dirt and
desensitization and the death of nature for days at
a time. Here those problems don't exist; we have
lots of room, everything's wonderfully fresh and
clean, nature is thriving, and there's so much
beauty in any given field of vision that you'd have

to be dead to be insensitive to it. Most of all it's the peace and quiet and the solitude, I suppose, precious things that most people don't get anymore and suddenly I'm drenched in them. They feed right into my heart, right into my brain. Even the loneliness. You and Dad taught me to appreciate such things and I've been so starved for them I couldn't possibly tell you. The city looks very different from here.

In fact it's a little frightening, the way I'm losing track of the rest of the world. The rest of my life. But why else did I come? Letting go was a part of it.

I'm even lucky enough to have work, of the kind that creates its own peace. As per our agreement I'm responsible for cleaning (fortunately I don't think his standards are high) and for dinner most evenings and shopping and errands and some outside chores as well, though I guess once the winter hits that will be mostly shoveling snow. Phillip—I don't actually call him Uncle Phillip, I'm sure you'll understand that it doesn't feel right—wanted to give me a week or two before I started with all this but I insisted that I begin right away. I think he feels sad about your daughter as his servant but I was able to convey to him that my living here would be, to me, an impossible imposition—exploitation, really—unless I gave him something substantial in return. And now I fond I wouldn't do without it for any reason. Yes, Ben Franklin and all you grown-ups are right: work *is* good for you. As long as there isn't too much of it.

Last week he put me on the phone with the woman who used to come out here, before she had her baby, so she could fill me in on everything she did. I could tell she was desperately curious to know who I was and why I was here. It was a problem I hadn't anticipated (can't imagine why) and I felt pressured because it was clear she was going to make something up if I didn't fill her in, and who knows what that would be. So I told her—I had reservations but I told her—what was more or less the truth: that I was a cousin of Phillip's with nowhere else to go and since I couldn't pay him rent I would be working for my keep. "He likes his privacy," she said with great doubt in her voice, clearly implying that we were headed for trouble, and I was so pleased that she didn't think I was sleeping with him that I led her on a little bit, I'm afraid, pretending to be alarmed, asking all sorts of questions about how to keep out of his way. I think I did a good job of satisfying her interest although I'm sure I left the impression that I'm a penniless orphan (hard as that must be for you to imagine, at least without laughing). Well, it makes a good story, and it isn't so far off at that— "nowhere else to go" means different things to different people in different situations, doesn't it? Meanwhile I'm glad to learn she thinks so well of Phillip that it never occurred to her to be concerned for me, just for him.

Even the cleaning (you know I dislike cleaning) is a pleasure because this house is so old and vigorous and sincere. It reeks of generations of life. I don't want to be sentimental but everyone

who's lived here has loved this house, you can feel
it the minute you walk in, and the changes he's
made—mostly opening up the first floor and add-
ing to the living room, including a huge picture
window—haven't harmed a bit of that. Before the
fact I probably would have been offended by the
idea of renovation but it's obvious he was right;
much better to have made it his own, like everyone else has (he tells me it was altered at least five
or six times before he got it) than to live with the
sense that it's inviolable, some kind of museum or
trust. We've all had enough of that sort of precious
nostalgic perfectionism, I think, the pretense that
anything old is intact. It was the kind of notion—
enlarging the living room—that is obvious after
it's done but takes a special sort of mind to see in
the first place. Phillip being a writer, an artist, it
doesn't surprise me that he could. It feels like a
writer's house.

He has all sorts of information about his relatives, mostly distant, who used to live here, he
says, and he'll find it for me when he gets a
chance.

I'm aware that one of my shallower, sillier
reasons for coming here (you probably saw this
long ago) was that I wanted to know how a "real
writer" lives, and I must say I find it very gratifying that Phillip matches my image so well. Just as
Judith (the woman in town) implied, he's an odd
and cranky person who has to do things in a certain way. It didn't take me long to figure that out.
He's also slow and a bit shy, at least so far, with
a tendency to lecture, though what he says is al-

ways of interest. That may not be the way he was when you knew him—probably not, I get the feeling he's changed—but now everything about him seems to express his basic nature as someone who lives inside. (This is what makes me feel like an intruder, you know. He's so *aware* of my presence, my interruption. I think I'd feel it standing with him on the street.) I could be making it all up, of course, painting him with my own fantasies, but I don't think so. At any rate I'm certain that he often doesn't speak when I expect him to, and leaves gaps in what he says, and almost radiates a sense of holding something back, and then suddenly begins to give forth at great length and with strong feelings about some topic that—as far as I can tell—is no different from the ones he let pass by.

He underestimates me, I'm guessing. He thinks I'm younger than I am. Normally, as you know, this would send me into a frenzy, but in these circumstances I happily tolerate it, or even accept it. For all I know he's older than I can possibly imagine so maybe I really am very young.

Our first encounter wasn't everything I might have hoped. He was at his desk when I arrived, he told me, and the doorbell took him away from it, and between his obvious disturbance and my own nervousness things got kind of out of hand. He seemed glad to see me from the first but seeing and welcoming are not the same thing. He was starting to make me feel almost guilty. So after some blundering around I got very brave, to my surprise, and very direct, and asked him to his face if we were making a mistake.

Remember back at the beginning of this letter (oh my god, I can't *believe* how long this is getting, I've been at it all afternoon) when I talked about always correcting myself? I guess the reason I brought it up was not to explain my writing instead of calling, or that stupid fight with Charlie, but because I'm still marveling over the fact that with Phillip on that first day I was somehow able to stop. I was. You wouldn't have recognized me. I told him I thought it probably wasn't a good idea for me to be here, that he probably needed to be alone, and then *I left it at that*. I actually shut up and allowed him to respond. I guess I'm learning after all.

The answer he gave in the end, by the way, was very reassuring, and though I can't help my instincts—walking around this place is something like passing through a penguin rookery or a forest filled with orchids, and it's impossible not to feel clumsy and out of place at least once in a while—I am essentially confident that he really does welcome me, that he's pleased to have me here. I'm not sure he knows why he is but he is, and that's enough. (And don't be embarrassed for me, Mother. Phillip and I were, a little, but it really was a brave and very useful thing I did. It helped us sort ourselves out properly, as Nina would say.)

After we had some tea—he was almost jaunty over "taking a holiday" from his work, as he called it—he gave me a tour of the house and

23

the grounds. Not the whole property, of course, he has sixty-seven acres, but the house and the garage and the area right around. There are some wonderful trees here, Mother. They're almost out of leaves but I can picture them in May. You'd want to start a garden first thing (there are so many places one could do it) but he hasn't any. Maybe I'll plant one in the spring, if I'm here long enough. If he doesn't mind.

The attic I was telling you about was the last thing we saw, and after we'd poked our heads up he started to say a bit more. He explained to me about getting the house—it belonged to a distant elderly relation on his mother's side, unmarried, and he was her only heir, though I suspect you know all that—and then giving away practically the whole contents to the people here who'd known her. I thought that was very clever, a way to make friends with his neighbors, but he said he did it because he couldn't have lived with her possessions, at least not happily. "Not," as he put it, "at that time in my life." After he'd moved in (he did keep some nice furniture, he may be strange but he's no fool) he discovered that he'd somehow missed that attic. He saw at once that there were things from the old woman's childhood, and her sisters'—they were listed in the phone book as "the Misses Yarrington," he showed me the page—and the way he tells it he could hardly stand to be near them. And it would have been awkward to haul out another load and invite everyone up again to pick it over. So the upshot is that he hasn't touched a thing in there since he arrived here over ten years ago. And from what he knows of Bertha Yarrington, he says, and her condition at the end, he doubts anyone else had for at least as long before that.

"I appreciate your showing me," I said, "because it seems to hurt you to go up there," and apparently he was shocked that I could see it so clearly. But instead of withdrawing like I thought he would he relaxed a little more and said that yes it was painful, very, and if I understood that he wondered if I understood why. To be honest, I don't think I followed most of what came next— not his fault, just that I was so unprepared—but he kept referring to the past and the distress he feels over it, and the tension that keeps him working. That writing helps him to relieve.

Does this sound like the man you used to know?

We haven't talked very much about his books. In fact we haven't at all. I'm afraid to say how greatly I admire them, for fear I'll sound like an idiot. And I get signals from him (it's amazing how much he can convey without a word) that he'd rather I didn't. If he feels like it he'll raise the subject himself, I suppose. Or I will, when I've got good reason. But it can wait another day.

As for my work—not the chores but the work I came here to do—there isn't any so far. I'm in no particular hurry. I gave up all sorts of other things to be here, a fair sacrifice on my part, and I expect to be rewarded for that, sooner or later. I'm also guessing that patience matters. Regardless, I think this will be my last reference to that part of it, at least for a while; I don't need you looking over my shoulder anymore and I'm sure you'll be just as glad to stop. (Don't deny it, Mother. I know you're there. I can feel you. You've been there for twenty-three years.) I'm done with being things, or trying to be things, or wanting to be things for other people. I'm even done with being things for myself. I can live here without needing to be anything, it's such a perfect place, and I'm wise enough to know what a blessing that is. Call it withdrawal—call it hiding, even—but don't call it discontent.

I'll close at last. Kisses to Dad. Answer soon.

Your daughter

chapter

3

The long retreat is wearying. They must keep up their pace, mere hours are life and death now; until they know for certain if the enemy pursues them no one can rest. He stares ahead at the endless column of dusty, dirty, bloody backs shuffling and limping before him, and can see without turning the sullen faces behind. Not one man, he knows, in a thousand has any desire other than these: that they be allowed to stop and eat and drink, or that the others come to kill them. No one wants to keep marching all night, not for any reason, not at any price. And many won't. They'll lie down groaning in the road or run and hide in the forest until the army has moved on. Had it been plain bad luck or even failure of nerve they might stay, might try harder to keep up, but once more it was

stupidity. The very simplest could see it. Stupidity beyond their imaginings, beyond their terrors. Most will
never trust their officers again.

Sutherland doesn't mind the stupidity as much as he
minds the waste. With every step he recalls that these are
minutes, weeks, months he can never have back. He
dreams of all he might be doing and begs them to finish it
quickly. Sometimes he thinks he would rather die now
than live another thirty years, knowing all the while that
he allowed his only treasure to be taken from him for this
ruined purpose. That he once believed in. Sometimes he
thinks he would rather lose an arm or a leg and go home,
just to be saved from spending his days with such a violent awareness of the time going past. Violent and venge-
ful; he hates calendars and newspapers and the weather,
anything that might tell him when it is, and his company
all know that to raise the subject with him means a fight.
Reading his letters from home he trembles and covers the
dates with his hand.

When he saw that dark-haired boy today—after their
cavalry had come through to clear the guns—he was
struck by the special status the mortal wound had be-
stowed, the immunity from age. It was a horrible wound
and it made him sick to look but from the chest up the boy
was exactly as he had been before the shell struck and
was fast approaching the point at which he would never
be anything else. Sutherland felt both envy and relief and
wanted to whisper something about it to the boy, something comforting, but as he knelt by the head, offering
water (grateful that the mouth wouldn't open because he
didn't want to see the liquid pouring out again fro somewhere down in the wound) he was struck by the impossi-
bility of beginning. He was at a loss for words. He

understood with sudden insight that it would hardly be a comfort, that time meant something only as it ran from you; once it had stopped you no longer cared.

"You're a handsome lad, aren't you?" was what he managed in the end. And he saw that it was true. The boy seemed to understand.

The very early mornings were the best times for Phillip. Not the most productive or the most rewarding or even the most peaceful, but the times at which he was closest to whole. At 5:30 A.M. there were no threats to him, as far as he could tell, not from outside or inside or the past or his future; not only was he intact but he could hardly believe that he would ever be otherwise. Usually he carried his fragility like a burden, like a bomb, fully aware that at any random instant some danger might come screaming down and break him into pieces. He knew he was rebuilt along delicate lines and while he valued the advantages this gave him as a writer and praised the good fortune that let him nurture it as he did, he respected the cost it imposed. The boundaries he stayed within and knew so well were more for self-protection than

they were the result of any limit to his range, and it sometimes troubled him to be doing (even to be subjected to) so
much less than might otherwise have applied, just because
he had to be careful. But in the hours around dawn this
sense of his own vulnerability slipped away and left him
alone for a time, or let him go free, not because he became
stronger or harder but because the world lost its will—its
capacity—to do him harm.

　· The morning gave this to him and also the setting: his
study, truly his. Its walls were lined with words and images
(postcards and photographs, quotes and excerpts he'd cut
out or typed up, maps and cartoons and other unrelated
items) and on some winter mornings as the very first daylight
came through the south window, showing everything in the
room to almost magical advantage, it seemed to him that
he'd made it into a museum of a sort, a museum of the moment—an exhibit showing Phillip as he was when he was
safe. He had many other reasons (including some he
couldn't name) for what he posted on his walls, but above
all there was that. It was a Phillip come clean. A person
making public what would be, in any other place, the deep-
est of secrets. It was only there that he referred to his
mother, for example, by hanging her picture near the window, only there that he admitted to frustration, to despair, to
jealousy, even to pride, by virtue of the statements he was
willing to make on the papers he taped to the wall. Since no
one else ever entered the room this arrangement did not
exist for anyone but him, but that was sufficient. He knew it
was there. It was a signal, a lifeline, a membership card for
the living race; in the very early mornings, resting in his
chair, he could look around and tell himself with confidence
that he had, at the least, what every other person had,
shaped and twisted though it was by his needless depriva-

tion, self-consciousness run backwards, strange longings no one shared. He could sometimes be an artist and a human being both, which was vital reassurance and gave him great comfort, and a hint of breathing space.

On this morning it was raining but he could do without the light. The taste of coffee, the warmth of his clothing, the prospect of a long day's work were enough. Seizing the moment as firmly as he could he allowed himself ease. His enjoyment, like his security, was a wholly private act, confined to one defined space and to a solitary condition (like silent prayers in a cell), but was nonetheless real for it. Confronted elsewhere with a video or description of himself simply sitting there, having such a fine time ten short minutes after dawn, he would have rejected it with conviction or even anger; it was so large a departure from, so much in contradiction of, the man he was in other circumstances, for instance going to the store or making toast in the kitchen, that it would have to be denied. But part of his happiness—the largest part—was that there could be no record, no recounting of these devotions. That was the virtue of being alone.

As the need to go to work began to worry his mood he looked around for recent pages and his pen. But then the faint sound of rain—he'd heard it first an hour before, lying in the dark, in the embraces of his bed—brought fresh distraction, and he turned to the window to see the water on the glass. What, he asked himself with sudden interest, was the feel of a rainy morning, two hundred and fifty years ago? What was the gist of it? You'd get wet, certainly that much was the same, but what about the rest? No umbrellas going by then, no swish of cars on pavement, no pavement at all in fact and no electric lights to shine off it if there were; the sound of the drops might be heard on your roof, depending

on its material, but elsewhere they would be quiet, most surfaces soft and absorbing. If you were near a pond or lake
you'd hear the rain on that, surely, and in the city there'd be
cobblestones and other hardnesses to strike, but in the main
it would be the same gentle apparition it was for him now:
muffled, dim, another form of silence really, not so very different from the day before.

And the disturbance involved. He wondered about that
too. Now it was simple or even petty, a predictable bother,
but in those days how might it affect you? How much would
you care? It was a complicated question he didn't know
enough to answer. The farmers would look to their crops, of
course, others might worry about falling ill, but there were
so many subtle factors, difficult to identify, in another sort
of life; all in all it was hard to guess, impossible really, what
it meant to wake up to the rain in New Chatham, New Hampshire such a long time ago.

He moved to the window to look out on the morning (on
a rainy morning much like the one he'd been imagining,
here in his notably unmodern world) and instead of seeing
damp colonists in muddy fields, easy as that would have
been, he found himself recalling vividly all the things he'd
just been wishing away: cars with bright headlights moving
slowly through the mist, windshield wipers, water rushing
down a storm drain, gleaming lights, terry towels, tomato
soup with crackers, boots and slickers and weather reports
on the radio. These came to him with a clarity and vigor that
surprised him, as did the aching affection he felt for them,
and he thought: ah yes, that was the purpose of it. Not history but me; not New Hampshire in 1740 but Bradley in
1955, a wet southwestern Connecticut town with a boy
named Phillip wandering around it. The weakened traces of
a prospect he sorely missed. A rapid but powerful anguish

passed through him, as cruel a punishment as if he'd been struck in the face, and though he shrugged it off (after brief confusion) he knew the process was complete, and had revealed itself to him: don't want what you can't have. All that you have is right here in front of you. The weather this morning is exactly what it is, not a bridge to anywhere, not an avenue—November rain and nothing more.

On the table by his desk was the accumulating manuscript; he turned to it with gratitude and relief. A thick bundle of notes sat inches away, notes he'd written to fix his thoughts more securely but hadn't looked at since because he was right in the middle of the very best stage, the easiest and most substantial: he knew who he was writing about and where they'd all begun and had suspicions of their endings, though he couldn't say for sure. He was just informed enough. One paragraph, one page, one chapter followed another without his really trying, and though each sentence held the threat (a very serious one) of error requiring correction, the sorrow of the wrong thing committed to the paper from which it was so hard to erase, it was such a blessing not to sit there and agonize about what to write next that he gladly accepted this risk. Later he would look at what he'd done and wonder if there were something else there, something much better, something he could no longer see because of what he'd put in the way, and that would be almost as bad as the pain of not having anything at all, but for now he was immune to both of these misfortunes because he was sure of what to do; three months in a year were like this for him, three months or maybe four, and they were the best months he had.

But confidence was a passing visitor at best. With regret he sent away his satisfaction, admitting in its place the nervous doubt that came to call. He couldn't have his cake and eat it too, he understood, nor be for long a man who had just written; even brief hesitation and he might find himself becoming a man who sometimes wrote. The only way to fend off that horrible fate was to write, again and again, all the time, the only reason being (pretension to art aside) that it gave him, in small doses, this lovely feeling of accomplishing something, of completion, of having scratched the itch he always wanted to scratch. It was a pleasure he could sample only briefly, an interrupted joy, but he drew from it his life.

His hand was on the computer's switch when he heard someone calling. It frightened him for a moment—terrified him—because he was so unprepared to be other than alone that he thought it must not be human. Or that a new and awful force had come to drastically change his life, an unlikely intruding event, a stranger who'd somehow approached. For an instant he saw a body lying broken on the drive or in the field, waiting for him, but he knew the sound had come from inside the house, from somewhere very near, and that its distress was not of physical harm.

Then he remembered Jennie. He waited and after a few seconds heard her voice again, raised in a peculiar cry or shout very different from her usual tones. She must be terribly upset, he thought, maybe homesickness of one sort or another, maybe some older misery, and his impulse was to leave her be. But this seemed wise for only a moment and most unkind after that; he reminded himself that she was all alone in an unfamiliar place, perhaps wondering why, and needed comfort rather than discretion. She's not much more than a child, he thought, she's younger than she seems. She's in your care. He knew that in some ways his house really was the end of the earth, far from anything that might soothe her, and that it was therefore up to him.

He went down the narrow stairs to the second floor. As he walked the long low hallway to her bedroom he heard her call a third time. He couldn't make out the words or even much about the feeling but what he gathered was enough to steady him. Unhappy she might be but not in truly desperate need. Not in need of him. Still, he'd come close enough for her to have heard his footsteps and to go now would be worse, much worse, than having stayed away altogether. It wouldn't do for her to feel deliberately ignored. He moved to the bedroom door, which was an inch or two ajar, and quietly knocked.

There was no answer from his cousin, no further sound, and the silence that settled about the house as he stood waiting was as deep and substantial as any he'd ever known it to hold, though full daylight had arrived. He regretted not having simply remained in his study but there he was. It occurred to him then—he knew it should have long before—that she'd been dreaming, talking in her sleep, and he was instantly sure that he would find her still dreaming on the other side of the door. He had a mind to turn and go but told himself again that having come all that way he had to finish what he'd started. With great gentleness, slowly, he pushed the door open.

Jennie lay on her side in the bed, facing him. The covers were well short of her chin and he could see her bare right shoulder, the straps of the white tank top she was wearing, the smooth skin of her neck and upper chest moving with her shallow breaths, her fine blond hair spread over the pillow. Through the window behind her (she hadn't drawn the curtains) there were maples visible, bathed in morning light, the long shadow of the house reaching halfway up their trunks. He heard the ticking of the clock. She was awake and watching him as he stood in her doorway, lying absolutely still but looking steadily at his face, and seemed much nearer than he knew she really was. For a moment he was almost overwhelmed by what he saw but he fought for control (this is someone in your care) and just managed to assemble the guise of his concern.

"You were shouting," he said.

She looked up at him, eyes clear. "Was I?"

He nodded. "In your sleep, it must have been."

She was motionless still but her gaze left his face—for the first time since he'd come—and then returned.

"I guess it was," she said. "I'm sorry if I disturbed you."

He shook his head. "Are you all right?" he asked. "I don't want to intrude."

Jennie stirred then, raising herself on her left elbow, her flesh shifting inside the cloth, and the sense of being where he shouldn't was so intense—flooded over him so quickly and completely—that he wanted to turn and flee. A tactical error, he thought, don't overreact, but the absurdity of being placed in such a situation entirely through his own free decisions alarmed him. If it happens once it can happen again; you'll have to make sure it doesn't. They watched each other in silence as the shadows crept down the trees. How did this come to be? he asked, not expecting an answer. What *is* she doing here?

"I'm fine, Phil," she said solemnly, at the very last instant, and then—as if remembering to appreciate her position—she smiled. "Thanks for checking on me though." She carefully pulled her right arm out from under the blankets and laid it on her hip, awkward and graceful all at once, and instantly he felt her presence even more strongly, as if she'd come impossibly close to him; he could almost sense her heat. They kept looking at each other (seconds stretching between them) until she began to blush, a very faint reddening, and her smile went away.

Go now, he told himself. This is when you should leave.

"You're very welcome," he said, "now I'll let you get some rest," and as he turned and closed the door behind him (the latch clicking into place more easily and definitely than he could remember any latch in his house ever doing) he understood that he was simply buying time.

chapter

5

Pulling off her pants in the dim bedside light, thinking ahead to her shower and wondering how hot the water was, Jane asked herself whether getting older wasn't just another way of getting tired. Everything goes in cycles, she thought, small ones inside larger ones and giant ones around those— no reason why weariness should be any different. Picking or sorting apples she was able one moment and feeble the next, just as she had energy in the morning that was gone by dinnertime; some weeks were better than others and some months too and even the years, at least in her experience, could be graded according to how vigorous she was in the course of them, whether each change of season brought renewal or a worn-out groan of dismay. And a life was just another unit of measurement, after all. She pictured a graph of enormous length with a dozen wavy lines on it, each moving up and down to show the rise and fall of her strength within a given period of time, and arching over them all a thick black curve with just one highest point, one slope up and one down, representing the majestic accumulation and dissipation of vital force through the course of her entire life, from the instant of her birth to the moment at which she would no longer have enough left inside her to draw a single breath.

It was a morbid topic, a queer one, but not so strange when you considered what she'd gone through that day, a series of incidents designated to demonstrate that she was not what she'd once been. She'd strained her back trying to lift a full basket, she'd been too slow to slam the gate before Pippin got through it and almost knocked down a customer, she'd tried to make friends with a nine-year-old boy and had come away shocked by her own naive confusion. And when Tom had again refused to get out of bed in the morning she'd simply let him be, instead of jollying him (or trying to) the way she usually did. All day long she'd felt inadequate to the task at hand.

Her balance had been seriously disturbed by all of this, she realized, more than she'd wanted to admit to at first, and her good nature too. As a general rule she didn't worry about getting older but when it seemed so emphatic—when it happened all at once—it was a frightening experience. She felt such treatment was unfair. She had no responsibilities other than her father and when her time came to be taken care of in turn (on some reasonably distant day, she hoped) Bill would do it, or if he couldn't it would be Betty and the kids. And Tom would have long since passed on. So the idea of decline (though she prayed for sudden death, with an apple in her hand) produced no anxiety in her, she accepted it gracefully in her opinion, and what she wanted in return was not to be baited or antagonized. It was a conceit of hers that she remembered, on occasion, to notice that she was older, and then forgot about it again; she sincerely believed that the Jane of age six was the same as the Jane of now, admitting all changes as nonessential, and asked only the favor of aging gently and in relative peace, in her particular way.

Standing on the bathroom rug she dropped her robe to the floor. As she studied her body in the mirror she thought: you haven't had much use from it. You haven't had much use. At once she wanted to slap herself; it was a contrary thought, almost insulting, because she got more from her body than any woman she knew of and always had. Even her brother had been heard to acknowledge that she liked work more than he did. But some failing or faultiness disturbed her as she looked and from her feet to her face she noted growing imperfection, visible or hidden, in almost every area until a wave of nausea passed through her, followed by anger, and she forced herself to stop. Enough of that, she thought, I know what you're thinking and it has nothing to do with you. Don't be such a bloody dupe.

She went to the tub and started the water to let it warm up, then turned to the mirror again and faced it squarely and bravely, her hands on her hips. This is a good body, she silently insisted, eyes passing over the rough and the smooth; this is a good life. There are lots of ways to skin a cat. It could have worked out differently but if it had you might be thinking all of this just the same, you might be standing here wishing for God knows what. Everything happens one way. Be content with what you've done.

The water was steaming as it ran from the faucet and loudly struck the tub's bottom, reminding her of its waste. She stepped in and pulled the knob up, flinching as the

41

spray hit her forehead and eyes. She felt briefly like crying as she reached for the soap because she was utterly unable to obey her own command; she liked what she had but still missed what she missed. I can regret being alone without condemning myself for it, she thought, only to find that even this gross distinction was beyond her and that they seemed like one and the same. The air was full of mist and she begged it to carry her off somewhere. A sob gathered in her until she bit her lip and scrubbed.

In an effort to forget she washed her feet and limbs with vigor and tried to bring back her thoughts of an hour or two before, closing the shop for the night. Her catalog—a someday project like anyone else's, she knew, like everyone else's, a silly notion with good sense in the middle of it, silly because while the idea was sound enough the execution might wait for a thousand million years—had been growing, developing, defining itself in her head for many months and at times she could picture it clearly. She was beginning to know the size of it, the cover art, the number and nature of the illustrations; she had even composed some of the text, to the point at which the urge to get to her typewriter (the ribbon needed replacing and you couldn't make a 9) was often very strong. She suspected she was running out of storage in her head. It's a lifetime of knowledge, she thought as she made the water very slightly cooler, two lifetimes including Tom's, the kind of thing that should be set down and preserved whether anyone wants to read it or not, and she knew (she always knew) that there was nothing really stopping her. Not inclination nor ability nor opportunity, nor even money; she suspected she could pay for the printing herself, if she had to, and when the shop closed after Christmas she would actually have the time.

There was a great deal to write, it was true, and this

gave her some pause. There was so much to make clear. To begin with there were terms; most people thought the word *antique* was funny when applied to apples, she realized, and some people even laughed, but nothing else fit. Every other label—*heirloom,* for instance, or *conserved* or *noncommercial*—was pejorative or false, and trivial to boot. Bad enough that people didn't know the word *cultivar* or recognize it as the botanical equivalent of *breed,* as the preferred formal version of the common word *variety,* but to say "antique cultivar" to a stranger at a party was enough to remind him that he needed another drink. Circumventing this required long explanation and either way people thought you were fussy and technical; there was absolutely no way to convey to anyone the simple beauty—the *majesty*—of an orchard full of antique fruits, the miraculous preservation of what was once daily life, just by talking about it. And that was why she dreamed of her book. Maybe it would be stuffy and boring, maybe she was a fool for thinking the topic was of interest to anyone but herself and a few other cranks (at least she didn't carry apples around with her like Avril and David) but she couldn't help imagining the glossy pages, with lovely pictures, with the names at the top in large and shapely type—Melrose, Jonathan, Spencer, Wolf River, Hubbardston, Opalescent—and the text to the side or on the facing page, the descriptions and the stories and details. If she got it right, people might understand. She saw her work not on coffee tables or even bedroom shelves but in library stacks all over the country, waiting for those who might come looking or just browsing, a dense and sturdy volume of irreplaceable information, all safely written down.

Don't ever be ashamed, she coaxed herself as she cautiously stretched her tender back under the warming spray. don't you ever be ashamed of it. These things were born from

love and hard work and without you they'd be gone in a
flash, as if they never were, like all the rest that's disap-
peared. No one would notice that the world had been
cheated; no one would care. Not that anyone has to care—
it's between you and yourself. The apples you save are
your own.

And that man, she reminded herself. The man who
wrote the letter. Don't forget him; *he* understands what
you're doing.

But the truth behind the catalog was that Jane loved
her apples—truly loved them with everything she had, eager
to see them in the morning and sorry to leave them at night,
grieved in winter and elated by the blossoms of spring—and
of that she *was* slightly ashamed. She'd wondered more than
once if a psychiatrist would find her attachment bizarre, or
worse yet fascinating. She found it bizarre herself. Most of
the time she pretended that no one had ever seen her holding them, caressing them, running her fingers and palms
over their smooth cool surfaces, pressing them to her
cheeks, but she knew (if only in passing) that this was ridiculous; of course someone had. Bill certainly, and possibly
Lois and one or two of the others, and for all she knew it was
the talk of the county. Still she could accept some minor
mortification on account of it because it was just who she
was, after all, no helping it, and because they all liked her
anyway, she was one of the best-liked people she knew.
Given that she was fifty and unmarried, living with her sink-
ing father and her shy younger brother, they would have gos-
siped no matter what, rotten things in all likelihood.
"Wonder if she talks to them, wonder if she sings them to
sleep"—embarrassing, yes, but still better than any number
of questions she could imagine. She knew how people were.

If she was a recognized lunatic at least she was a decent one, a moral one, an oddball with community respect.

And they weren't at all like people to her, really. It wasn't that way. They weren't symbols, they weren't a substitute for anything, there was nothing twisted or pathetic in her affection for them. She was a searcher and what she was after was beauty, pure and simple, something above and beyond the crudeness of human meat and daily life, and if she had the good sense and the good fortune to appreciate the glories of these living beings—God's creatures, as much as an eagle or a bear—and the way they'd been shaped and altered by women and men, the sweat and care expended on them, that made her different in a fashion that was fine and not tawdry. Some people followed mountains, some whales, some paintings; she followed apples. In her way she was an artist. It was the best of both worlds, she knew, when she lifted up a perfect shining pink and yellow fruit—both God and her ancestors resting in her hand—and she envied no one's passions. All she wanted for was company.

As she reached for the shampoo she felt herself begin to falter because she was suddenly aware of how the reverie that had unfolded at such length—the whole day, actually, with all its frustrations—pointed squarely at Phillip. Converged on him, more like it, narrowed down in concentric contracting rings to make her stare at him as surely as if her head were strapped in place and her eyelids held open. She was more sad than outraged to recognize her own vast conspiracy against herself, a lengthy and convoluted path to further heart-torture over him, nor just because he was still so inescapable (how long must she wait for relief?) but because she wished herself more straightforward, more efficient, less unkind. It wasn't interesting to her or in any way rewarding to spend a whole day working around to this same position,

the one she'd been in on and off for more than a year—it
was only masochistic. Of course he was at the center of everything that had happened, everything she'd been thinking,
but he always was, it wasn't just today; let him be constantly
with her in a less obtrusive way then, not coming and going
like a powerful tide, washing destructively over her mind
and her life. Let the thought of him make itself at home and
settle in. It was not a matter, at bottom, of acceptance or
even confession but of her threshold of pain; she was simply
tired of it all, of the drama and volatility, of hurting so suddenly and so sharply over him.

What was almost more annoying than the repetitive
ambush, her tightening throat and pouting lip—the familiar
heavy despair that made her want to sit in the tub and
weep—was that there was, as usual, nothing new for her to
learn. Yes, Phillip had understood about her passion; he was
the first and only person she had ever told it to who'd become more excited the more she'd explained. Yes, he'd truly
listened when she talked about it, and truly cared, and had
come walking in the orchard under the full moon to see
(she'd promised him) the apples glowing faintly in that gentle August light. She knew all that already, by heart so to
speak. He'd grasped more from the beginning than Bill or
even her father had in all their orchard lives, and she'd gathered—from this and so many other things—that he was the
man she'd been allotted, or granted, or assigned to, her part-
ner if anyone was ever to be. She had suffered horribly on
finding that he had no intention of giving up his solitude to
join her, nor of sharing at a distance, none even of continuing to bring her the pleasures of the flesh. Everything had
been wonderful—she'd been amazed and so happy—and
then he'd left her. Just like that. Like any other man or
woman, she supposed, for all his differences. She'd waited

nearly fifty years and he'd come and gone so quickly that she hadn't had the chance to have a single conversation with anyone, not one, about how deeply, how specially she'd cared for him. No one had even known that she did. It was better to have loved and lost, she was sure that was so, but as far as anyone except Phillip could tell she had never loved at all.

All of this was old news, however, ancient in fact, she'd ached and sighed over it for months, and though she knew better than to resist her own feelings they availed her nothing. It frightened her to think that she endured them over and again just to punish herself but she couldn't come up with any other reason. And this grim suspicion was abetted by the fact that she was still, after so much time, unable to be genuinely angry at him. She was certain this was wrong. She'd lived an isolated life and knew the limits of her wisdom but surely that would help at the least to start her on her way, on her way to not feeling so badly about him. If she could get good and mad. I get mad at Bill for leaving the refrigerator open because he read somewhere that all the cold gets out in the first five seconds, she thought as she rinsed her hair, I get mad at Pippin for chasing the ducks, I even get mad at Tom for being the tired old daddy he can't help being, so why not at this man? This thief? Why not at someone who comes to tempt me, to seduce me—to take advantage of me, wasn't it?, let's call a spade a spade—and then runs off with hardly a word? Why not at this hermit who thinks his next novel is more important than me?

But as hard as she tried to inflame herself against him it brought no fresh response, no new spark of condemnation; she didn't believe for a moment what she was thinking and she was still angry at her dog and not at him, still angry at her father and brother and her employees and her knitting

club and the extension agent and the governor but never at
Phillip, not at him, she couldn't be. The terrible, terrible
burden he'd brought was that her life was still richer—infi-
nitely richer—than it had been before he'd come, and when
God asked her at the gates (as she knew he would) whether
or not she was sorry she would have to answer no, whispering perhaps but certain of the truth, because she wasn't and
never could be. She was sorry but not that she'd known him
and loved him, her utter lack of regret was very clear, and
given the choice she would have it be so instead of wiping
it all away. She was sure he felt the same. He had blessed
her and she him and this was as clean and irrefutable as her
attachment to her trees and his to his pages, as the honesty
with which they'd spoken to each other, as the trust they still
had. It was the most difficult thing she'd ever done, to treasure him, but she would go on doing it. Anything else would
be wrong.

She looked down to find her hands on her breasts, holding and squeezing them gently, each cradled in each. She
couldn't help but smile, As she watched the droplets run she
felt a deep affection for them, they were so pleasing to look
at and pleasant on her palms, and so she moved her fingers
over their skin as she did with her fruits, felt them and
pressed them just as she did her Baldwins and Spies, and
though she tried to stop—though she wanted in some sense
to stop—there was no way she could. The water was still
warm and she had finally relaxed and the admiration she
now felt for herself, for her own form and being, brought her
fully to life. Her mouth opened wide to take in the damp air.
Not you, she thought, me, my pleasure, my time. Far from
imagining him there beside her she excluded him by doing
it, by touching her body, she sent him away, and she knew
it as her freedom and so kept on and on, ranging farther and

more quickly with each moment, glad the water was loud and the door tightly closed because she wasn't about to smother herself, wasn't about to hold back, and with glee she watched a picture of him grow distant and diminish, spinning, and then finally disappear. She almost laughed aloud but her breathing was too hard and her mouth preoccupied and she forgot him entirely as she attended to herself. She couldn't stop and didn't care and listened to the rush of the water and her blood and then it all poured over her just as the shower did, she felt it fall from head to toe, the rigid ache and release and the quiet shout that echoed off the tile, the faint bad feeling—guilt or even shame, she couldn't tell and didn't want to—all mixed up with her great joy, but more than anything there was relief. She leaned into the corner, in the mist and the spray, and felt her pulse slow down to normal. She was happy to close her eyes.

chapter

6

The Friday before Thanksgiving was fair and not too cold
and Phillip, feeling that he deserved it—or at least that it
was a suitable moment, a chance to pause before continuing—had almost decided to take the afternoon off and go
walking in the sun. He'd come to a stopping place and knew
exactly where he was and though far from certain that this
would still be the case when he started up again he found
that it was necessary, on occasion, to show trust in himself.
Having descended from his study to the first-floor landing
he couldn't decide whether to go back. He crossed the
kitchen to the window to check the outside thermometer and
look through the glass at the naked trees, to remind himself
of all he might enjoy by getting out of the house for a while.

He hated to leave what was going so smoothly but that

in itself was a reason to do it; overinvolvement was always a concern, at least for him, as much so as interruption or neglect. What counted was your record over time, he knew from long experience, not a specific piece of writing or a particular day. You had to accept it as it came. For several years he'd had Hemingway's line—about stopping too soon to leave something for next time—taped to his study wall, but he'd taken it down upon realizing that Papa had either been wrong or disingenuous; it wasn't a matter of actually having something left but rather of assuming that you would. Art followed faith, not the other way around. Often it didn't, of course, but you had to act as though it did, despite the pain of disappointment, because to behave in any other way was to ask for too much and risk far more serious punishment. Staying up all night furiously drafting three chapters was a destructive waste of energy—if the next refused to come. If you went calmly to bed, on the other hand, at a reasonable hour, with just one down on paper and two in your head, you might wake up having lost some or all of it but the process would start again sooner or later. Because you'd put yourself in its hands. You could count on the work if you avoided too much doubt.

In any case the time will come when you're not able, he told himself, to go out walking in the snow. Or walking anywhere at all. Then you can work sixteen hours every day but for now enough self-abuse for nobody's sake. Try to act like a full human being instead of an incomplete version of one.

He sat at the cluttered table, still undecided and annoyed with himself for it, looking at the cover of an old magazine and considering where he might go. After a moment he thought of the Saxonville logging road, a favorite route he hadn't walked in months, but to get there he would have to drive to Saxonville and Jennie had the car. She'd gone to spend the day in Williamstown, to visit the art museum, she'd said, and possibly to see some friends at the college. It was too bad because he really wanted to go to Saxonville, but it was also true that if she hadn't gone away—if he hadn't been aware that the house was empty and that he was alone—he probably wouldn't have left his desk in the first place. It was a largely unconscious expansiveness that had drawn him from his hole.

He sat comfortably unmoving in the old wooden chair, more relaxed on account of this new understanding, enjoying the idea of a truly quiet house and all his feelings about it. He knew he missed having the place to himself but to his ongoing surprise he wasn't unhappy. Jennie's presence probably had him working longer hours, which was useful, and more importantly her company had improved his disposition and contributed to his energy. Even his at times painful attraction to her was all to the good, he guessed, because it was a healthy tension, a strong and substantial (if often anxious) excitement that was driving out the usual neurotic stresses of his life. In a way it was fun. He knew he couldn't tolerate it forever, and once in a while it made him miserable, but sooner or later it would pass or she would go and it would no longer be a problem. He would remember it and smile. And in the meantime he was reassured by his desire and was even learning from it; when the book was done he would try to give attention to the possibility of becoming less lonely in some appropriate way. You're not young the way Jennie's young, he told himself—who is?— but you *are* young. You're only forty-six years old. You are still (this was amusing) in the prime of your life. There must be someone out there who would be glad enough to have you, and could stand the way you live.

As he glanced at the refrigerator Jennie walked in. She

was wearing her boots and though she had no coat she seemed dressed for the outdoors. When she saw him she smiled—a very nice smile, he decided—but then her face was overtaken by the diffident, slightly secretive look that he knew as an expression of discomfort.

"I thought you'd gone to Williamstown."

She smiled again, but in a more limited way. "I did— that is I started to—but I changed my mind. I wasn't in the mood." She looked at him. "I'm sorry, Phil," she said. "I see you need me out of here. I'll find somewhere else to go."

"Not at all," he said. "I was about to take a walk."

"I'm disappointed," she said. She stood in the doorway with her hands on the frame. "I was really looking forward to it, right up until the end of the driveway. Then I didn't want to go." Her shoulders had dropped and her lower lip was tight. He imagined he saw her left hand tremble, very slightly, as she took it from the jamb.

He watched her. "Go another day," he suggested.

She nodded as she sat down across the table from him. "I will," she said, "but it's a little upsetting"—not looking at him, her voice low, speaking quickly as if determined to finish—"to feel this way. I'm confused. I used to be the most social person in the world but now I don't want to see anyone at all. I can't believe how fast I've changed."

"It's probably not a permanent condition," he told her. "And there's nothing wrong with taking a break from your friends."

She raised her eyes and stared into his. "I'm not talking about my friends, Phil," she said. "I don't want to see any- one. Not even the guard at the museum. And it feels like forever." She looked away and carefully rested her forearms on the table's edge. "I don't want to deal with anyone but me. I want to be by myself."

"I still don't see anything wrong," he said.

"No," she answered, with a sadness that surprised him." You wouldn't. I've been trying to figure out why."

As she lowered her head onto her arms, her face turned toward the wall to her right, he was nearly overcome by her vulnerability and his own protective impulse. He wanted badly to give in. There—wasn't she asking him to take his hand from his lap and stroke her hair? Wasn't this a moment of great sincerity, the kind that called for demonstrations of affection and reassurance lest embarrassment or shame force an even greater distance than the one that had just been bridged? He didn't know what had bridged it (first they were simply chatting and then on the verge of embrace) but he couldn't pretend it hadn't happened and he knew he would have to do something about it. He wasn't a physical man, in fact months went by without his touching anyone except to shake hands, but he wanted to reach out for her. He pictured himself holding her. He felt urged on, even commanded—if it wasn't her purpose then why would she stay there like that, not looking at him, inviting the unlikely while she hid from his eyes?—and for a time he was in doubt. He was on the edge of a vast unmapped space. Then good sense (or something that felt almost like it) came rushing back, surefooted, and relieved him of his need.

"If my company," he said, "is something you want—I don't mind if it isn't—maybe you'd like to come for a walk."

"Yes," she said without moving, addressing the wall in a quiet voice. "I'd like it very much."

Then she raised her head at last, as if to promise him surcease.

*   *   *

It can't be true, she thinks. Someone like that here. So pretty and young and dressed so strangely. Where did she come from? Margaret, do you know her? Is she Alice's friend? I've never seen her in town.

Papa, are you there?

She stands lonely and silent at the edge of the lawn and watches them go into the woods. When they're out of sight she looks around the property. November, she thinks, and then with suffering certainty: November and I'm old. Not just older, *old*. I should be awfully cold standing here like this. Papa's been gone for years and years and so has Alice. And Margaret went six years ago June.

The man I know, she remembers. He gave away our things. He has the house now and lives alone in it, like me. But who is that girl? Not his family. What is she doing here? Why has she come?

What am *I* doing here? she asks in surprise.

She approaches a window and peers inside. The first thing she sees is a wooden mask from Africa hanging on the wall. She laughs—ha! ha! ha!, the long, loud donkey laugh her sisters always made fun of—but she can't hear herself. She puts her hand to her throat but can't feel her own flesh. Raising her fist to strike the glass she stops at the last moment, scared of doing damage, knowing it isn't her place. It wouldn't be right. And if it's true, she thinks, I can go down the chimney. Or even through a wall. If it's really true I won't need to worry. About anything. She resolves to take her time.

Moving south to the huge new window she examines what used to be the parlor. The wallpaper is gone and there are many odd things. It's peculiar to see the room displayed to the outside world this way; like sardines in a tin after you open it, she decides, or her blue and white doll's cottage. She's seen picture windows before but it's different in her own house, an old-fashioned house. Papa would have a fit, she thinks, but I rather like it. I'll bet it gives him lots of light.

Them, she thinks. I can smell her. The girl lives here now too.

She walks around the house to the door and sits on the step. She enjoys not being cold, not feeling the cold although she knows it is cold despite not feeling it. Through the trees to the right she can just see the road. They widened it in '56, she remembers, because Papa asked them to. He was still alive then. Alice was already sick.

Though the sunshine is weak and she has no skin she basks on the step, remembering the old days, remembering Papa. Missing him. He loved my laugh, loud and silly as it was, she thinks; he loved everything about me. He loved my sisters too. We were so happy here, the four of us, until my father died. So happy living here. We never needed to leave—everything was just so. We looked after every sparrow; we were friends with every stone, with every tree.

She drowses peacefully in the sun.

"The property line is just over that rise," said Phillip, pointing past some maples to a leaf-covered slope. "At least I think it is. It hasn't been surveyed in years." Hearing no response he turned to find Jennie standing several yards behind him on the trail over which they'd just walked, examining the lower branches of a spruce. She looked his way and then back to the tree, tilting her head and tucking her gloved hands under her arms, before turning and moving up the path to join him.

"I'm sorry," she said. "Walking with me is like walking a dog. I'm always running back and forth."

"I should be quiet and let you enjoy the woods," he said, starting forward again.

"Oh no." She took a quick step to catch up. "I didn't mean that at all. I want to hear about this place."

He glanced at her. "It doesn't matter where the line is," he said. "The neighbors don't care and the land isn't hunted."

They walked in silence until they came to a spot where thick mud on the left and a trunk on the right—recently fallen but long dead, the branches almost reduced to silvery stubs—forced them to pass in single file. He waited for her until she went ahead.

"I'll have to get Lem out here to work on this," he said.

"Who's Lem?"

"He helps with the property. Takes care of thing in the forest—like keeping this trail up—and some repairs at the house. Another inheritance, really; his family has always worked here. I could do at least part of what he does by myself but they need the money even more than I need the exercise."

"I could do it," she said. He watched the back of her blue coat, the same one she'd arrived in, still inadequate for the winter he knew was coming. "Not that I want to take the bread out of their mouths but I hope you know I'm strong and can do physical work."

"I assumed as much," he said.

"I'm only a girl but even so," she said. He could hear her amusement although he couldn't see her face. They were descending into the white birch dell, one of his favorite places on the property, and he hoped that she would be taken by it. As they came around the big moss-covered boulder, like the cursed head of a Norse god, the pale trunks were scattered in the sunlight before them and she stopped to look. The sight was even more affecting than in the summer, he knew, though not as soothing, because it was so simple, so plain: tall thin white trunks, brown leaves on the ground, blue sky above. He had always wanted a photograph but was afraid to try and get one, fearful that he might somehow worry the loveliness away.

"Anything that brought me out here would do me good," said Jennie, her voice quieter than before. "I could work with him."

Phillip started forward into the dell, brushing the sleeve of her coat as he passed. "I don't think you'd get along with Lem," he said. "No one does." She stayed by his elbow as they shuffled down the slope.

"This is a wonderful spot," she told him.

"I thought you'd enjoy it."

"Phillip," she said, "I don't want to be rude and I don't want to bring up any difficult subjects but I'm wondering what you live on."

He spread his arms wide, palms up. "fresh air," he said. She laughed. "And whole wheat toast."

They had slowed almost to a halt, and she stepped up on top of a small rock by the path. "All this land," she said, "and that big house to take care of. Lem and Judith Haas and the bills to be paid. You say your books haven't earned much but you don't have a job and you manage not to leave home for days at a time." She paused. "I find I'm getting very attached to your way of life and I want to make sure I don't have any illusions."

He looked up at her. She was almost in a prison of white. "So you don't get your hopes up?" he asked. "Or because you think I might be paying for it in ways you won't approve of?"

She shrugged, and shook her head. "Neither," she said.

"That is, I'm not sure." She jumped down. "I'm tempted to pretend it's some fabulous magic but I'd rather be grown up about it, I guess. Mostly I'm just curious."

At his gesture they started walking again. The sun shone down through the trees. "I've been ridiculously lucky," he told her. "That's all it is. Bertha left me some investments along with the house; they turned out to be quite valuable. Not a fabulous treasure but enough to renovate and still have some left over. And my very first book did sell pretty well—just by a fluke of timing, I think, I know my editor was amazed that so many people bought it—not wildly so but it produced a respectable return. And we sold a film option, though the film was never made." He turned and found her a few feet off the path, staring up at the old stone wall along the edge of the dell, but she looked back at him to let him know she was listening. "I've gotten pretty good at investing myself," he said. "Maybe it's hereditary. I managed to put those first royalties in all the right places. Blind luck, probably." He sighed. "Well, call it a mixture of skill and luck, and what with owning the house free and clear—it's just the taxes and maintenance and utilities, really—and never gong anywhere unless someone pays my way I have just enough to live on."

She came back to his side. "Nothing mysterious," she said.

"No."

"It must make other writers jealous."

"I think it must."

"You are lucky."

"I know it," he said. "That's part of why I work so hard."

As they walked on, leaving the birch grove and starting up a steep and rocky leg that became a swift water course when it rained—the traces of the stream were usually visible along the edges, and the stones were kept so clear of dirt by the frequent washings, in places, that they sometimes reminded him of an old cobbled walk—Phillip was preoccupied and a little amused by the fact that talking at length about himself was such a rare and notable event. When was the last time anyone had asked him about his finances, his circumstances? About any aspect of his existence? With the exception of Jane he couldn't remember such interest for a very long time. It just provided further evidence—as if he needed it—of the freakish and redirected nature of his life, and he wondered (not for the first time) if the peace it bought him might be gained in some other way.

"I admire that in you," said Jennie.

"What's that?" he asked.

"The way you work. So steadily and so long."

"I'm not sure it's something to admire," he said. "It's mostly that I don't have anything else to do."

She shook her head from side to side, her fine hair moving through space where it came out from the edges of her hat. "I don't buy that," she said. "It's a skill and it's one I want to learn. I've been watching and trying to figure it out." She wrapped her arms around herself and a crow called in the distance. "I think I'm beginning to catch on a little."

"You don't have much else to do either," he said. "Trapped up here with me."

"Listen," she exclaimed abruptly, her eyes on the ground a few feet ahead of her, walking with careful steps. "Would you look at some of what I've been doing?"

"Of course. I've been waiting for you to ask."

Her pace slowed a little. "well," she said, almost grimly—still looking at the ground—"it wasn't part of our arrangement."

"I think it was."

"We never said anything about it."

"That's true."

"You'd didn't even know I'd be trying to write."

"Why else," he asked, "would you have come to my house?"

At the top of the hill was a stretch he dearly loved. The ground was very rocky and clear of leaves and undergrowth, the trees closely spaced fir, and as the sandy way wove back and forth among them there was little to be seen but needles (green and brown) and solid timber and the sky. It was just a small hill but the setting made it feel as though the trail had climbed much higher, as though it might come to a cliff's edge at any moment, and he was grateful for the faint suggestion of being up in the mountains. It reminded him of hikes he'd taken in earlier years with his father and later with Probyn and still later with women he'd known, mostly Miriam but some of the others as well; it brought back a part of the pleasure they'd given him. Hiking was the closest he'd ever had to a hobby—his only real enthusiasm aside from art—and now his capacity to enjoy it was almost gone. He never went up a mountain anymore, hadn't in years. This little piece of his property, like a movie set on a studio lot, served instead to bring him once in a while to the illusion of a summit. As much as he cherished it he knew it was only a substitute, a replacement, and that he couldn't come too often or the fantasy would fade.

A few dozen yards from where the slope leveled off a long, low boulder, twisted and mauled by ancient ice, lay next to the path and offered places to rest. When they came to it he stopped and sat down and patted the surface next to him. Jennie chose a spot about a yard away and sat with her hands on the rock behind her, her head tilted back.

"I really would be pleased to do it," he said, "although I can't promise I'll have anything useful to say. Or anything at all." In truth his own generosity surprised him and had from the moment he'd felt it; as a general rule the last thing he wanted to do was read someone else's material, never mind comment on it. He had far too much to handle as it was.

She was gazing rather dreamily, he thought, at the trees across the way from them. Again he was overwhelmed by her beauty, her appeal, and felt a powerful interest—call it lust, he told himself, don't try to escape it—in her body as it stretched out nearby. He had a sudden vision of the two of them lying together on the path, a blunt and erotic picture of a clarity and even purity that made him want to leap to his feet and start moving again. This is unfair, he thought, staying put. She doesn't deserve this from you.

"What are you working on now?" she asked. Then she looked at him and reddened; she knew she'd gone too far. Her misery was apparent and he forced himself, for her sake and his own, to break the resentful silence that threatened to freeze him over.

"I don't usually talk about my work while I'm doing it," he said without affect. He expected apology or at least acknowledgment but instead heard only the faint sound of a breeze. She was still leaning back on her hands, still studying the trees on the other side of the path. His feelings were mixed; on the one hand he felt she surely should have known better but on the other hand he wondered if this was just his own narrowness, an inability to see things as a normal person might. And he wanted to soften his response because he liked her.

"What I'm working on is very . . . personal," he said.

"Isn't it all?"

"Yes."

She sat forward. "Then I don't understand."

To his amazement his resistance began to ease and he found himself willing to go on. "I don't talk very much because it's bad for the work," he told her, trying hard to be precise. "That's an empirical observation I think most serious writers would agree with, and I'd advise you to take it to heart. My guess would be that it's a violation of privacy; I don't know why it's so tempting except that we're contrary by nature. But whatever the reason the danger is real, and it's a pretty firm rule with me. You'll know you're getting somewhere when you're able to follow it yourself." He looked at the sky, "What I meant, I think, when I said this work is more personal is that I have another, different reason for keeping quiet about it. It's very close to my heart."

"Closer than usual?"

"I think so."

They sat quietly together. He spotted a hawk of some kind, circling, circling in the endless blue sky.

"Please forgive me for asking," she said. "I'm clumsy and I'm sorry." He heard a rustling of cloth and turned to see her shift her body, facing farther away from him and more toward the path up which they'd come.

"Jennie," he said, "this is something I've been trying to get at for over twenty years." The shock he felt when he'd closed his mouth was so vigorous and so hard that he had to brace himself to stand it. How could you have told her that? he asked. How could you?

She turned and her eyes were on his face. He felt both examined and judged, though he wasn't sure by whom. Then she got to her feet and reached out to him. "Come on," she said. He didn't want to touch her but it couldn't be avoided so he took her hand and let her pull him to his feet, and they started along the trail. He realized his legs were cold and stiff from the sitting; he looked up for the hawk but before he could find it he stumbled on a root and almost fell.

Just after the path began slanting downhill she spoke again, frustration in her voice. "Phillip—where do these things come from?" she asked.

"Which? The writing itself or the need to write?"

"Both. Either. You can't separate them, can you?"

"No," he admitted. "I don't think you can."

They walked a few more steps. "Don't talk if you don't want to," she said.

"Some people," he told her, "think it has to do with the earliest years. Myself included, I suppose." They were back among the maples and scrub oaks and the leaves shuffled between their feet. "Childhood and what matters on account of it. Greene—you know Graham Greene?"

"The Heart of the Matter."

"Oh my," he said. "What a lovely book. At any rate, Greene apparently felt that writers were made from those who went through some deep loss in childhood. In his own case he had to leave his parents' home and move into a dormitory at the school his father ran. I'm told he had a saying: 'In the boyhood of Judas was Jesus betrayed.'" He looked at her. "Does that help?"

Jennie's hands were in her coat pockets. She nodded but wouldn't speak. As they circled around an old hemlock tree the same crow (or a different one) called out to them again, and got no answer.

"What you look for now," he said, "is what was lost then."

She stared ahead of him. Their pace had greatly lessened. They were passing across the middle of a small clearing, covered evenly with dead leaves—he often wondered why nothing large ever grew there—and had wandered a lit-tle way off the path.

"I always thought you looked for what you'd had," she said.

"Had, lost. Is there any distinction?"

"Yes. There is. Between happy and unhappy." She stopped, her back to him, facing the falling sun. "Nothing was ever taken from me. I had a happy childhood." She glanced at him and turned away. "I don't feel any sense of loss."

He waited but she was silent and still, her hands deep in her pockets.

"Maybe it's a question of discovering it," he said, em-barrassed by his own fatuity. He wondered if she'd even heard.

"If you were unhappy I'd think you'd want to let go of the past," she said. "Not hold on to it."

"You've got it backwards, Jennie. It's happy people who let go. They move on to something else. When you're fearful or in mourning it isn't so easy."

She turned to him. "I believe I was happy," she said.

Again he waited.

"What will I look for, then?"

She took his coat sleeves in her hands, then broke and ran away.

Somehow—there is so much she doesn't understand about her condition—she knows they'll soon be back. It isn't a question of hearing or smelling them, or of any kind of warn-ing, but she knows before it happens. At first she wants to hide among the trees but she remembers she doesn't have to. It isn't fair, she thinks, they can't see me, and then: if

you keep to yourself you may get awfully lonely. It could be
a long time. It might be just today but if it's years and years
you'll have to find someone to be with, someone to watch.
These two, these here, they're connected to you. They're
yours. There's no way for you to harm them.

And this is your house. It was always your house. They
stay in it now but you were born here, it's the only place you
ever lived, it's part of you. You don't give a thing like that
up when you die.

She rises from the step and walks around to where she
started. The sun is getting low. She folds her arms to wait.

"Let me read you something. Maybe this will make it
clearer."

She looked up from the fire she'd made. "Is it yours?"
she asked, drawing her legs up onto the couch.

He shook his head and held up the worn and faded paperback. "I wish it were."

She stared at the fire.

" 'It was a confusing proposition,' " he read, " 'to want
a girl you'd already had and couldn't get because you had;
a situation common in his life, of having first and then wanting what he had had, as if he hadn't had it but just heard
about it, and it had, in the hearing, aroused his appetite. He
even wished he had not had her that night, and wondered—
say he hadn't—whether he would be in the least interested
in her today.' "

The flames filled the fireplace.

"What do you make of that?" he asked.

"I don't know," she told him. "Give me the book and
I'll see."

chapter

7

Sutherland knows he will be one of the dead. There is nothing to require this or even to suggest it; so far he has been both lucky and smart. But he is certain nonetheless and is resigned, or at least informed, which brings him an unexpected ease, a gentleness. There are thousands of dead men and eventually there will be one more. If not in battle then by sickness, or through quarrel or some pointless mishap, or from his body wearing out. A shame but no less true for it.

Nothing about the war and the way his life has unfolded—the series of accidents that brought him to the army in the first place, that made him fit to serve on the line, that have carried him within sound and range of musket and cannon fire again and again and again—seems fair or even sensible, and try as he might he cannot abandon his frustration, cannot become less puzzled or less angry. Nothing compels him to admire his fate. But his vision still is clear (it is the only thing left him) and he is immune to wishful thinking. About his future there are no doubts.

That, Phillip told himself as he sorted his pages to take into town for copying and storage in the safe deposit box, is a problem solved. Solved by doing nothing, really. Wait long enough and these things always fade; wait longer still and they pass away entirely. He hadn't acted on his impulses, hadn't even betrayed them, and as a result (as so many times before) they'd given up and gone off searching for more fruitful pastures. What you do is what you are, he had learned, and what you don't do you can write about. It was all just leavings anyway, the work had to come first, so why not be good-natured about passing along what he chose not to live? Why not cooperate? Maybe in return he would be allowed, if he saw a chance that made more sense, to act without too great a cost. And meanwhile he could be near her and still be at peace.

But after he'd called goodbye (no answer) and started the car and guided it carefully down the drive, flanked by the low white walls left by Sarah and her plow in the wake of the winter's first real storm, he was forced to admit—the thought came uncalled-for between the Solomon's red mailbox and the Seybolds' snow-covered barn—that it wasn't just inaction that had spared him, or changed his mind. He couldn't dodge that easily. The truth was more complicated and considerably less pleasant: he'd deliberately diminished her by saying too much, he knew, and agreeing to look at her work, by invading his own privacy, a dishonorable trick he had played on them both. One he'd used in the past but beneath him all the same. He'd waited for his opportunity and when it came he'd lectured her (that was certainly the term) about art and life and told her the sad story of his wealth for good measure and then had made her, over time, into a student, a disciple, another audience, a different sort of creature (not lesser, just different), the object of his words and not of his heart and therefore quite safe. It was pathetic to have to chalk this up to the sharing of secrets but it was accurate. Only the deaf and solitary need apply. That's what secrets have become for you, he thought as he rounded the curve and saw the beauty of the valley before him, shining snowy white everywhere and bathed in weak December sun, the creatures of your beastly books; when the writer is done and all that's left is crinkled husks the man living underneath (or what's become of him, anyway) gathers them up for medicine and voodoo charms. Primitive magic that makes him feel safe. Just be glad she doesn't know.

If they told me to get a life, he thought, I could honestly say: no thanks, I don't need one.

But it was too late to change his spots, he assured himself as he drove past the old mill, drab and lonely in the sunlight; however he had done it he had done it, which was what mattered. He was no longer tempted to seduce his first cousin. This was a fine thing in itself, youth being what it was and his self-respect being what *it* was, and more important—as he'd suspected would happen—the passion he'd felt for her had made its way into his study instead. His interest and enthusiasm, deep enough already, had been renewed to the point at which he had to force himself to leave his desk on occasion. This worried him for other reasons but on the whole he was glad of it because he knew the going would get rough sooner or later. He fully expected his courage to fail. So whatever he had gained by getting past his infatuation was more than useful, it was essential; in the end, he hoped, it would see him, like the trickle of water in an almost-dry stream, over and around the rocks and logs and sandy patches that were scattered in his path.

It was hard not to worry. He didn't want to, because he knew she wouldn't like it and it seemed improper and went against one of the few important things he'd learned for sure—that when something big was needed of you, you knew it without question instead of bouncing back and forth—but at times, as he watched her, he was very concerned. She was talking less and less, for one thing, and for another she'd stopped telling him what to do. Not really, not entirely, because it was still her orchard and her house and they both knew it, but she seemed to have lost her interest in directing and advising him, in hurrying him along. She'd quit bossing him around. She was happy enough, if she thought he had the general idea (which he usually had by now, he'd been at it thirty years), to let him do the work himself. This was very unlike her and surprised him no end. He would have been glad if it had come from respect—if he thought she'd finally accepted his growing up, becoming a man and not just a kid brother—but he knew that wasn't why. It was broader than that. It was a change in her feelings about the orchard and the business and the town and her whole life, not only her brother, and every time this came to him it made him very uneasy, almost more than he could stand.

Something had gone out of her, he realized one day as he watched her sell preserves and a wreath (he'd been right, it wasn't too early to stock them) to the Shaws, who showed up five times a year and looked now as if they'd been seventy forever, some kind of energy or drive. Something had gone out of her as if a stopper in her foot had been pulled for the first time, letting her insides drain away. She was the same person with the same dislikes and likes and the same strong opinions but the way she acted was very different; the force that had moved her to *do things* was missing. Or at least there was less of it. When the Shaws got done gossiping and turned to go she just stood behind the register as they walked to their car, her hands spread out flat on the counter in front of her despite the chill. And then, when Peggy Shaw turned around to wave, Janie waved once in return and *brought her hand back to the counter*. And stood there watching as they went. He had never seen her do anything like that before. Normally she would have been started on something new even before they'd reached their dented green Chevy—she would have hustled away from the register to restock the refrigerator case or rearrange the apple display or write something in the books, or to find him and tell him to clean out the cider press instead of uncrating pears as he was doing—but even if she hadn't, even if she'd stood there, she would never have been so silent and still. She would have called out to them or kept waving until their doors had closed, at the very least, and her single weak gesture and return to immobility disturbed him very deeply. Her mainspring's wound down or her gas tank is empty, he thought as he pried off another slat. Her A for effort is all gone. This was a terribly sad thought and he quickly straightened and walked away around the corner of the shed, hiding from her in case she did turn and come after him, which she wasn't going to do. Although it wasn't as if she had never seen him cry.

In bed at night he wondered what she suffered from. It came to him more than once that they bore the same burden—a pair of country spinsters whose only family was each other—but while he had his women friends in Keene and Brat, his arrangements as he liked to think of them, he knew she had nothing similar. She was a woman and even if he supposed that some few women might do as a man did (what on earth did you do if you were a woman with normal needs like him but too decent to take money and gifts like Marty and Claire?) he was sure his sister wouldn't. Wouldn't be able to but wouldn't want to anyway. There had always been long droughts, for her, between trips to the well, years at a stretch without a man, and he knew she could deal with that. But had she wanted a new name? And children? Had she ever wanted to make her own home, away from him and the orchard, or for him to leave and live somewhere else so her babies, her Tommy and her Cindy, could run and play among the trees? Was there not enough reason for her to try anymore? He belabored himself with questions, unceasing, asking how he might help.

And each time he asked—in bed at night, on the tractor hauling customers' kids around in the wagon, pruning dead limbs, driving to Concord or Manchester for parts—he came up with the same old half-assed answer, disappointing and frustrating though it was. He tried to bear it with good grace, which was his only real option, but still he was discouraged. When there's something you can do for Jane, he told himself, hopelessly, when there's something you can do you'll know.

At Phillip's age, and with his years of experience, to try something new—new to the man, that is, not to the art, an approach used by others but never by him—should not have been as daunting or as thrilling as it was. But that was precisely in the nature of the man, he knew, and the art as well; for some it would have been routine but not for Phillip. What a critic might call distance he had always called creation, transcendence, making it up, and it had been his intention to keep himself entirely out of it. After the fact he could see what was personal but before he started writing there was never any of that. One day he would have an idea, an urgent idea with no connection to him, an idea he was forced to pursue partly *because* it had nothing to do with him and he was curious on account of that, and the next he'd have a novel growing. Then came research and spotty inspiration and random detail descending in the middle of the night, then a world sharply separate from his own that he examined and spied on and described in his study—with charts and maps and diagrams penciled on a sheaf of clean white paper, as well as with plain words—and then at last a story told. A story in which he'd exhausted his interest. His books were discontinuous phenomena, external observable events, not truly in the most basic sense—he knew it all came from his mind, of course, from his heart and his life—but enough so to treat them that way. They came to him and bent him to their purposes and when it was over he had in hand another manuscript. They had beginnings and endings and their own precise understandings of time.

He didn't know who was in charge, the worker or the work, but he wasn't sure it mattered. He got where he was going either way. The point was, as he'd tried to explain only once in his memory, that he led his own life and his novels led theirs and the goal in each case was to be left alone. For a given time this became impossible and the process that resulted had its dark, peculiar agonies but after it was over both writer and written, grateful and overwrought, could return to their previous isolated states of benign and satisfied neglect.

But this one was different. And not by accident—as

everything had always been, or seemed to be—but by a version of design. At least a product of his will.

One morning in September he had entered his study and felt utter disgust (he was between projects then) at the prospect of another book about more people he didn't know, another concern that wasn't his, another setting to be read up on and understood and tamed. He'd gone to the bathroom mirror and looked himself in the face and thought: it's getting awfully old, Phillip. They're all starting to run together. You've reached the end of the string. For that day and most of three more he'd been in growing and finally desperate distress, feeling the loss of something irretrievable, trying to assure himself that this bad stretch (like so many before) would pass but at the same time thinking, over and over: I don't know any other method. It's the only way I can. He'd paced the house, walked the forest, cut firewood, gone to town, even driven down to Boston for a morning in a museum (which had scared him out of his wits, like a rabbit on the interstate) without finding any relief. But on the way back to New Hampshire, sitting and eating chicken in a small but pleasant diner outside of Winchendon, Mass, he'd managed to find the trick of serenity and patience that had brought it all clear. It wasn't the making it up that was bothering him, he'd seen, it was the distance, and contrary to firm belief of more than a decade of his craft and art both could be subject to revision—or expansion—on account of his increasing wisdom, itself the boon of age. Even hidden away in his rural retreat, communicating only with his keyboard and his housekeeper and a dozen acquaintances and friends, he'd grown enough (if not from his life's work then simply from the passing of the days, the months and seasons, the thousands of beats of his heart) to require a change in the way he went about things. It's time, he told himself, lingering over the last few bites of breast meat and potatoes because they were so miraculously good, to come clean. Or at least a little cleaner. It's time to take a certain risk.

He had thought of a man, A man from his own home ground, yes, the first such he'd made—but the former home, the vanished one, a place Phillip saw every day and mourned in the seeing, a place he yearned for and could never have. The man had walked roads and highways Phillip longed to walk, talked to people whose voices had rung, almost, in Phillip's ears, been threatened by dangers that Phillip had feared and would never have to face. Above all he was a victim of war, of the war that of all wars (Phillip could not get away from wars) was most fascinating, most horrifying, most dear to the one who was writing him. Who faithfully sought its monuments—the first things he looked for on his infrequent travels, and even the familiar ones he visited when he could—and had once spoken, greatly moved, of sacrifice and loss to the town of New Chatham on Memorial Day (they'd applauded him loudly and he'd blushed a bright red). Who saw in the conflict something just beyond his grasp, a token, a testament or critical clue about to be left behind forever. Who found himself wishing—utter nonsense though it was—that he'd been there and knew what it was like.

That this character existed at all, in Phillip's mind and on paper, was frightening and exhilarating, but most notable was that he'd been born of conscious choice. Against every rule he'd ever worked by Phillip had looked before leaping; he was writing about what was visible in his own person, at least to him, plainly precious to his soul. He was *giving himself away*. And why? Who knew why? Who wanted to know? He could guess at his reasons for singing such a radically different tune, he could rationalize to beat the band, but the truth was he didn't know and didn't care. He could deal with that later. For the moment it was working, and so was he, and therefore happy.

Coming out of the copy shop and turning right toward the bank, his manuscript under one arm and its warm copy under the other, he remembered—with a start—the incident of the stickers. He was impressed by the swiftness of its apparition. A war story, for sure; he had given to his father the tableau he'd pasted up of the federals on one side and rebels on the other, BLUE AGAINST GRAY in golden letters at the top and RIGHT AGAINST WRONG along the bottom, and his father (with a manner as kind as always but at unusual length) had carefully explained that people of good will always thought they were right and so did many who were bad, that rightness and wrongness were hard to decide and in fact difficult even to define, that the soldiers in gray had been convinced of their own rectitude and of the error of the others. In doing so the tall Connecticut doctor—who didn't speak to young Phillie in such broad terms, as a rule—had deprived him of something valuable, grown Phillip had always felt, something vital: the freedom to take sides. Of all his memories of childhood it was one that came most often. It had always stood on its own before, apart from anything, or at most served as one more explanation (not that he needed it, there were plenty of others) for his lifelong passivity, but on Oak Street's snowy sidewalk he was forced to ask: was what he carried with him now some kind of effort to retrieve it? Was the war his father's gift? Was a novel just another set of stickers?

That you can put a stop to, he told himself firmly as he walked into the overheated bank lobby. Stop it this instant. New approach or no, if you actually think too much about why you're writing this it will go dead in your hands, like an old unpleasant fish. You've got your reasons; leave it at that. Instead of crying over one story and writing about a second you've brought the two together. Let them worry about each other.

He searched the bank for familiar faces. There was no one he recognized and he felt slightly let down. The woman who handled the deposit boxes looked quite a bit like Miriam, and whenever he arrived with a bundle (by the time he'd finished a book the box was filled, but once he'd mailed it to his publisher he could take the copy out and clear the space for another) he ended up thinking of her. He didn't really mind the enforced reminisce; the woman, Bernice, was friendly and chatty, and the structure of the chance juxtaposition—remembering the woman he'd almost married as he dropped the product of the toils she'd so misunderstood into a locked metal box, never in all likelihood to be referred to there again—was comforting, if pat. On this day Bernice was not in evidence but as the stiff young man with the long hair helped him instead he thought of Miriam anyway. He wondered briefly if it would be fun to paste a photograph of her inside the box's lid, then was revolted as he imagined opening it to find her there. What a morbid joke, he told himself. And it was provocative and disturbing to realize that while he thought there was a picture of her somewhere in the house he wasn't certain he would be able to find it if he tried.

"Miriam," he said aloud as he stood on the sidewalk outside the bank, looking at the snow on the roof of the Ben Franklin across the street, half his burden gone, "it's true that I miss you." They'd had to part for the sake of his work and her sanity—or put another way, before he resented her so much and she enjoyed him so little that neither had anything left to cherish and weep over as they went their separate ways—but he surely missed her still, after more than a dozen years. Each November on her birthday he thought to send a card, though he didn't (and didn't even know where she was). The fighting about his habits and the way he lived his life he missed not at all but her bright eyes, her humor and quick intellect, her smooth, firm body (and the laying of her hands on him) had left holes in his person he had never managed to fill. Not that he would have chosen to; they produced the kind of dull ache he'd always had an affinity for. But that they were hollow he knew beyond doubt.

He imagined her naked as he walked to his car. She'd been lovely, particularly her breasts. He imagined rubbing again with his palm the warm skin of her back and her buttocks. He could not (and did not want to) evade or deny the fact that he missed her in his bed, yes, particularly, still, which he suspected was demeaning to them both but accepted with good grace as a signifier, at the very least, of their value to each other. From his own experiences and those he'd heard described he suspected that true sexual compatibility was a rare thing, that millions went through life without knowing it at all, and having let it get away for the sake of his work—a wise choice, if difficult even in retrospect—he found nothing wrong with pining for it from time to time. He would rather have it than pine but not everything was possible in life.

She could appear right here beside me, he thought as he unlocked his car and got in, transported from wherever she's ended up, and on the way home I could explain to her everything I've been working on, everything I've discovered, and she would stare at me in annoyed incomprehension just as she did before. She's forty-seven now instead of thirty-three but she'd look exactly the same, gray hair and wrinkles or no, and I would be exactly as upset. Then we'd go upstairs and fuck ourselves into exhaustion just to forget the whole painful experience. The way we always did. It made him weary to imagine it but he lingered in imagining all the same.

Clouds were beginning to hide the sun. He stopped at the stop sign next to Willie's gas station and went right at the fork and the giant IGA sign loomed darkly above him. Now you're thinking about sex, he reminded himself as he pulled into the supermarket parking lot, suddenly enraged and going too fast. Imagine my surprise. The penis always rises. Miriam is only an excuse; you spend all morning congratulating yourself about having brushed Jennie off and the wonderful genesis of your wonderful new novel and sex is still at the bottom of it, isn't it? He was amazed by his own bitterness, and by the breadth of his turmoil. Sex means companionship, he thought, that's all. companionship and loneliness, and so does the damn book. You're a lonely bastard is what it comes down to. Same as your character. Same as you always were. An unending succession of sendings-away: Andrea, Gina, Miriam, Marjorie, that woman from the college whose name you haven't even bothered to remember, then Jane—she really liked you and she was pretty good in the sack too, wasn't she?—and now you're getting ready to give Jennie the boot. He stared into the window at the meager white-clad shoulders of a boy bagging groceries for a frail old woman in a worn fur hat. The point is not, he told himself, whether you commit the crime of sleeping with her but the violence you do yourself in pretending you can simply wish the urge away. Do you *want* to be a man who finds nothing so difficult about the daily presence of an attractive young woman who admires him? Has your self-correction—your self-amputation—gone that far? And why did you arrange it in the first place, then, if this is what you prefer? Why didn't you just say no to Carla when she called? To import this kind of trouble in order to mortify your own flesh by proving how far beyond it you are is pretty twisted, my friend. Pretty twisted for an artist. And an abuse of her valuable time.

He stared gloomily at the window. Pork roast one eighty-nine, he thought. It's a deal. The boy—in a clean new apron and bow tie—turned around to put the last bag in the old woman's cart, and looked at Phillip with empty eyes.

Sutherland tries to make plans but he can't. Feeling his perspective, his attachments, his solemn claim to everything he had when he made this horrible mistake slipping away, he forces himself to consider the future: what he'll do *after* the war, *after* the misery, *after* his escape. But even when he manages to conjure up some cheap, impossible image of a Sutherland living and breathing—greeting his wife and his neighbors, inspecting the house for decay, buying tobacco, looking in the tin box under the cupboard to see what might be left—it doesn't last. Not for more than a second. Like a man trying to climb a dune or an icy slope he finds himself sliding back, always, into what lies behind him, into what he had before. What he'll still have when they kill him. He visits this world if he wants to or no so most of the time he freely gives himself up, tries to lose himself in it. It's a chance to get away, after all. Maybe he can go so far he won't be able to come back. Maybe he'll wake up one morning insane. Sometimes, under the right conditions, he manages to find his past, the genuine past—to see it, hear it, taste it, believe it—for a moment or two, and then he sighs and gives way.

One chilly evening he sits in a crowd outside the quartermaster's tent, in the center of the huge encampment. Some of the others are talking about fishing. They speak in the distant and even tone that all the men use now when they talk about pleasure—about the pleasures they want and can't have, as opposed to the foul substitutes available to them, that they partake of to pass the time—and the words come steady and slow.

The discussion crawls on. They talk about their favorite places. Brag about their catches. Argue about bait. Another excuse, Sutherland knows, to abuse themselves with the lust for home. He rises to go but then sits down again, to his own great surprise.

"I heard stories," says a man from the other Massachusetts regiment. He is tall and very thin and his long ragged beard is beginning to turn gray. He comes from south of Plymouth and his way of talking is even odder than Sutherland's as far as the rest are concerned. One thing they have in this army is accents but some of the soldiers snicker when the thin and dusty man speaks, as if they'd never known anyone like him before.

"I been told," he says, "that two hunnert years ago you could put out to the Georges bank and lower a pail o'er the side and pull it up all full o' fish."

Someone laughs but in the firelight there's no way of telling who. The silence, though disrespectful, is otherwise unbroken.

"I been told," the man goes on, "they dug up quahogs by the cartload. I heard they took five-foot lobsters out of the Long Island sound."

Several of the man laughed openly now. Sutherland stands, abruptly, can't imagine why, stands and looks around. The windy spaces of the night rise above him. He is glaring, he knows, though he can't see himself. The Old Colony man is as startled as anyone; he doesn't mind being laughed at, has never minded. Sutherland doesn't know why he objects to it himself but he does. It's still a very long war, so he tempers his distress.

"Ain't none of you," he asks with all his mildness, all his grace, staring across the fire, spreading and warming his scarred and dirty hands, "heard of history before?"

Having fed him his dinner Jane watched over her father. Sleep eased his face and erased all his struggles, allowing her to love him again. Why is *old*, she asked, such a sad thing? Why is it so difficult for the young? Sleep Father, she thought, Father Tom please sleep. Sleep in your chair. Rest because you've earned it. Though she didn't want to wake him she reached slowly for his hand and took it into hers, lifting as softly as she could.

You're tired, she told herself. You really are. You've worked hard too.

After sitting for a time she heard faint noises from outside. Looking again at the old man, whose gentle breathing was steady, she carefully pulled her hand from under his and went to the window. It was two weeks short of winter and already dark. She pushed aside the curtain and cupped her hands around her eyes, like goggles, pressing their edges against the glass to block out the lamp's shine. There, in the orchard, in the glow from the windows of the house and of the waxing moon, in the fog that seemed to linger in the air though the night was too cold—was that her brother? Was that her Bill she saw, and Pippin? She watched them move between the trees. They bewitched her, like spirits, their feet near-strangers to the ground. She watched them running in the mist.

He knows he has no freedom. Therefore Sutherland waits.

December 15

Dearest Mother,

It's been much longer since I wrote you than I meant it to be. You may find this notable or you may not; I don't know what to make of it myself. Sometimes when I look at my writing paper I miss you terribly, and hate the paper because it isn't you. But then I see right through it to you and Daddy, safe and sound, watching TV in the downstairs den. Either way I don't end up writing—I just think of you instead. Which serves very well. But none of that gets you any news from New Hampshire, or helps you bear missing me (do you? I hope you do) so here's a letter at last. I

wouldn't want you worrying. Don't say I haven't
made an effort.

We've settled into a routine here, or rather
I've settled into Phillip's, and it feels like it could
go on forever. In some ways it feels like it already
has. I'm still surprised by how deeply order and
habit have penetrated his life. By order I don't
mean fussy neatness, though he is in some respects a fussy person; I mean the way in which
priorities are well understood and life is arranged
to satisfy them. At this point I don't think Phillip
could disrupt his own work even if he wanted to,
and any disruptions that come from outside are
absorbed, almost, into the system (the way a pond
absorbs the splash of a stone) and soon things are
back to where they were before. I suppose this is
what's happened to me as far as he's concerned.
Devotion is a useful word in describing Phillip's
life; he is devoted to his work, and to everything
it represents to him, and everything it needs to be
successful, and so in the end to himself.

Not that it comes without cost. As lot gets
crowded out. Phillip is the most isolated person
I've ever met, possibly the most lonely, and this
has made an impression on me. I feel bad about
it at times but I find I've been watching him,
studying him, trying to figure out what's essential
and what isn't. Whether every sacrifice he makes
for art is necessary, or only some of them, or just
the idea of sacrifice, in which case maybe it's all
an elaborate ruse he uses to coax himself into
working as hard as he does: having given up a
normal life—and I'm sure I don't know the half of

what he's given up—he has no choice but to come up with something that justifies the loss. The question, of course, is whether he could get the work done without so much deprivation. My guess is that he could. I'll tell you freely, though I wouldn't tell him, that the hard work is something I aspire to but the self-denial isn't; it's a pretty bare existence, and often sad. At any rate the way he goes about it is admirable, even inspiring. I wouldn't have missed it for the world.

I'm also glad to say that I seem to be helping. That is, it seems to please him to share the house with me (he must have expected this, at some level, why else would he have agreed to it?) and I'm sure it hasn't interfered with his work. Maybe I've even reminded him of some of what he's been missing; maybe when I'm gone he'll spend a little more time in the company of others. I may even suggest it, though that would be out of place.

I'm taking advantage of his system, Mother, to try to establish one of my own, or at least the beginnings of one. I'm getting a lot done too. I have very little to tell you—to tell myself even— about what I'm accomplishing, but I know it's important. It's more than important; you may not like my saying so but I feel it could save my life. I've had so much to learn, so much I was never forced to learn, and something about the situation here has got me started on my lessons, or perhaps opened my eyes to those I've had in the past that didn't take. The important thing is that I can feel it, building up inside me, the substance I'm accumulating here; I feel more substantial every day, more real, and I suspect I am finally growing up.

I fall in love with the quiet hours. That's what I've wanted to tell you for weeks. That's what I really mean. I fall in love with them every day. I fall in love, love, love with the time going endlessly out ahead with no interruptions, no hurry, no show to be run nor any show running me. I adore it. I feel sure I was born to live this way, and I'm almost afraid—not quite but almost—that it's wrong to get so used to it. I know I'll never have all this again. Where could I go to find so much space, so much beauty and time? I never thought of you and Dad as grubbing for bread, of our pretty neighborhood as an ornate box, but that's becoming the view from here. I can see I'm getting spoiled.

This is almost the Garden of Eden, Mother. Nature serves us in our innocence. I feel I can do no wrong.

There have been three snowfalls already, including two big storms, and the layer of white only adds to my joy. The snow in the cities gets filthy, crusty, horrible, but here it stays clean. Unlike Amy and Emmy I've never lived with snow and that in itself is a treat. To wake early and look out on the smooth white skin outside my bedroom window is an astonishing miracle, day after day. Sometimes I wish I were thirty feet tall so I could lie down behind the house and make the biggest snow angel there ever was, just for Phillip and me to see. Sometimes I wish all the people would disappear and all the houses, even our house, even

Phillip, and I would be left alone in all this purity, this peace. To sit in the snow and wait.

I fall in love. I fall in love with them. Silence, solitude, wonder, time. That's what I wanted to write to you about, Mother, my infatuation and its objects, my new devotion. That's really all I have to say.

Your daughter
J.

The house came to Phillip at a time filled with sadness. Two years after the end of his engagement, a year after the failure of his second published book—some might not have called it failure but it had failed to do what he'd expected of it, which was to build on the success of the first and bring him the admiration and fame he still hoped for then—he reached the depths of a period of seemingly endless loss, of a steady falling away: first Miriam, then his excited ambitions, then old friends, a valued job, the apartment in which he'd lived for a third of his life. He knew as it was happening that most of his distress was from having said goodbye to the first and only woman he'd loved and the prospect he'd had of their life together; without that the rest might not have mattered so much. He knew that her going colored everything. But there was more to it than that, more than he could easily see, and the sense of waking each morning to find, in the aching pit of his stomach, the knowledge that another thing he cared for had been taken and not replaced was both painfully familiar and impossible to name.

In the face of this suggestive confusion he was helpless. For months he slept badly, ate poorly, walked endlessly around both his neighborhoods, new and old. Strangers and associates found him odd. It wasn't until he started writing down his dreams—he felt silly but could not remember them for more than three minutes after waking unless he made notes right away, if he so much as got up and took a shower they were gone—that he began to understand; in reviewing his lists, connecting the dots almost, he saw how preoccupied he'd become with his mother and acknowledged that being bereft, this state of emotional destitution, was not exactly new in his life. It wasn't just the many dreams that referred to her, nor the string of parallels between her and his former fiancée that struck him from one week to the next, but other more subtle clues as well. Once he'd thought of his mother he understood, for example, why he was convinced that with Miriam had gone his only chance to have a son, and what made the sight of his ancient kitchen table (he'd brought it up in a trailer at the age of twenty-three) so difficult to bear.

This realization, when he came to it, only deepened his depression, making it ever less likely that he'd find his own way out. There was everything to be lost in understanding how it all revolved around that happy shadowy figure, he discovered, and nothing to be gained. It wasn't a matter of simple recapitulation, of unresolved or even unconfronted grief; he'd long before accepted the inevitability of mourning her through the rest of his life, and not only that but the half-formed, frustrated nature of the mourning that came from his being only five when she died. He knew there were questions he'd been asking since that time (what was cancer? who was Mommy? why had his father never found them another, choosing instead to keep them lonely for so long?) that still represented, for him, all the unanswered questions, that spoke to all the wonderings he might ever have had about his sufferings and pains, no matter how unconnected. So finding her in the very fabric of his troubles was not helpful but instead discouraging, in the most essential possible way; he couldn't just weep for her and go on. He couldn't "get over it" as some had suggested. He was a boy who'd lost his mother, he would never be anything else, and while he tried to show good grace it enraged him all the same to realize that nothing—not his work, not his love life, not the fire downstairs that forced him out of his bright sixth-floor apartment into a dumpy little bungalow he didn't like nearly as much—would ever be separate from that single damning fact.

There was hope in one thing only, the sole saving grace (aside from being a writer, which was her doing too) of his desperate predicament: he had stumbled into it through no fault of his own and could therefore look forward to climbing out the same way. If he'd been randomly victimized as a child, he believed, he could expect to be favored, as an adult, in equally arbitrary fashion. Irrational as this was he clung to it. So when the news about Bertha, and the house and the land, descended as if from heaven to rescue him— he used that word more than once to himself, as a person will shake her head in shamed gratitude on having escaped, through plain good luck, the consequence of some careless act—it gave him great satisfaction as well as relief. He'd had no plan, he reflected, no preference, no opportunity, only the vaguest sense that something was sooner or later going to emerge and give him an idea of what to do. He'd kept on writing because he had to (three novels finished, no one cares, what can you do but begin on another?) but everything else had become ephemeral, slipping beneath his notice. As he'd waited he'd grown afraid, almost to the point of seeking help, that the world outside his bedroom and study would fade away beyond retrieval, but that he was waiting for something—not just playing out his time—he'd never had any doubt.

A month before the letter from the lawyer arrived he went to New Mexico to visit Probyn and they drove as far from the city as they could manage, looking for a desert they had never seen before. They found nothing beyond the reach and grandeur of the land and the wry and kindly fifteen-year-old girl who tried, not quite directly but transparently, to interest them in her flesh late at night in a motel parking lot, but still he knew their expedition as a jumping-off place, a punctuation, the last episode before the start of another kind of life. Imminent change was written all over it. So it didn't surprise him, in any genuine way, when he opened the long envelope a few weeks later and read, with excitement, of the gift he'd received. Astounded him, yes, that such a clumsy thing had happened, that Bertha and her family had existed in the first place, but that it had happened to *him*—not at all. He'd been expecting it. He accepted his good fortune without rancor or dismay.

With time (with very little of it) in the safety of his new home, in his splendid isolation, his worst memories of those years lost their hardnesses, their danger, and then fled altogether. He was left with a gap in his history that he was willing to accept, to defend if necessary, because the changes it had made in him were of such enduring value that it wouldn't pay to ask questions. He was mostly the same but some important parts were different and he was able to sur-

vive now, he felt, another hundred years if necessary, as orphan Phillie if he had to but to survive no matter what. He
wasn't sure how it had happened but he remembered the
main outlines and that was good enough.

The dreams, though—a few of the most disturbing
ones—were not so easily lost. More and more his turning
point was defined by them (or by what remained). More and
more they carried his past. One in particular stayed with
him throughout the seasons, becoming as much a part of his
second life as it was of his first; he waited in strained anxiety
to have it again, which he never did, though memory served
just as well. In it he'd gone to a convalescent home on a
warm summer day to visit an old teacher and had found instead on the flagstoned patio his mother, sitting calmly in
the sun in a cast-iron chair. She'd been happy to see him in
a limited way, hardly matching his joy that she was not really dead but had been living in the country for the last thirty
years, freed entirely from that awful evil presence in her
breast; seated next to her had been a man her own age, small
and glum, whom he'd taken for her companion. They'd chat-
ted for a while, aging parent and child—Phillip working
very hard to suppress his eagerness, knowing he had all the
time in the world—until she'd excused herself and gone inside. He'd waited and waited, sitting silently with the man,
but she had never come back. He'd waited long beyond the
point of despair. Wanting to know when she'd return—wanting to know why she wouldn't, wouldn't ever again—he'd
made an effort to converse in an amiable way, remarking
that they must have been good company over the years. The
man had looked him in the eye for the first time, scowling,
and with fatigue and distaste had said, "Leave me alone."

On waking Phillip had broken every dish in the
kitchen, howling in his undiluted rage.

Standing on a chair with his back to the door, Phillip had to
stop himself from turning in quick embarrassment when he
heard Jennie on the stairs. If he had he might have fallen.
He felt foolish adjusting the ornaments again and he knew
she found it amusing but he couldn't help himself. He hadn't
had a Christmas tree since leaving Bradley. He couldn't say
why but he hadn't. Jennie's suggestion had given him an
edgy feeling at first, a nagging need to escape, but he'd
brushed it aside—more out of a desire to please her than
from impatience with himself—and agreed at once, and was
very glad he had. The tree, which they'd cut themselves and
pulled home on a sled, was over six feet tall, simply and
beautifully trimmed; it gave him great pleasure when he entered the room.

"Festive," he said, stepping carefully down after pushing the red and black Mexican clay bird an inch farther back on its bough, turning to find her more solemn than he'd expected. "That's the word I've been searching for. This tree is so festive." She smiled slightly but said nothing as he returned the chair to its place by the wall. "I guess I don't have a very festive life," he said.

"It's almost Christmas, Uncle Phil," she told him, standing with her hands behind her, palms resting on her hips and fingers tucked into the waistband of her jeans, examining the tree. "You'll have to stop fooling around with it soon."

"Is that the law? No changes after midnight?"

"That's right."

He laughed and wished he hadn't. "I don't think we ever had that rule."

"Some families are more rigorous than others," she said.

Then she stepped closer. "Look," she exclaimed, almost like a child, turning and gesturing with a sweep of her hand to the tree and the wrapped gifts arranged beneath its branches. She smiled more freely, showing at last a different mood, her hand poised at the end of its motion with fingers extended in a graceful curve, like a game-show hostess displaying a prize.

"Wonderful," he said.

She frowned, briefly, producing in him an odd panic. "I'm sorry there aren't more," she said. "It looks a little sparse."

"Oh, no, this is just right," he said. "It couldn't possibly be better." There were two presents from her to him and one from him to her and one for each of them from her parents, along with gifts for Jennie from her sisters and a few things Phillip had received in the mail as he did every year and could identify without opening: chocolate mints from his great-aunt in Chicago, the latest tape of his college roommate's band, Magyar Christmas candies and a calendar from his friends in Budapest. Plus the jelly from Judith Haas. It had been so long (back to a very different time) since he'd had anything like a heap of presents in his home—usually he opened things as soon as they came, unwilling to wait even twenty-four hours for Christmas or his birthday, the chocolates always at least a third gone by the end of the day they'd arrived—that he felt some regret at the thought of disturbing them. It was a trite and profoundly uninteresting scene, he knew, too banal even for him (the monk of New Chatham) to feel quite as excited about as he wanted to, but it supplied a new and satisfying element nonetheless, one he'd be sorry to lose.

"Should we open them after dinner?" she asked. Rather than in the morning, I mean. That's what we do at my house."

"Yes," he said, carefully watching her, "that would be fine. But what does it leave for tomorrow?"

She folded her arms. "Jennie's deluxe Christmas breakfast," she said. "Church if you want to, I double-checked the times. A long walk—the weather's going to be very nice—and then dinner with Judith and her family, remember?"

Feeling chilly, he glanced at the window and started toward the thermostat, then went instead to the fireplace and the fire he'd laid earlier. "It sounds lovely," he told her, reaching for the matches. "But it doesn't seem fair that I should have your attention for the whole day. I don't deserve it."

"Oh, Phil," she said, with affection and—he couldn't help noticing—considerable pleasure. "Of course you do."

He lit the newspaper with a long match and stood back. They waited together as the flames grew from small yellow petals perched on the edges of the crumpled sheets to multicolored blossoms marching slowly up the sides of the pile of twigs and logs, then merged into a single wavering creature sitting around and among the tangled sticks of wood, bathing and consuming them, beaming light and sound to every part of the room.

"You'll want to call your parents tomorrow, and Emily and Amy," he said.

"Tonight," she told him, distracted. "Another tradition."

They watched the fire burn for a few seconds more. Then she stirred. "I've got to get back to the kitchen," she said. "But dinner's almost ready. You might want to go and wash your hands." She looked him over. "And maybe put on a sweater," she added. "It's not quite as warm at the table as in here."

She was almost gone when he spoke. "Jennie," he said, and she stopped and turned. "I can't tell you how much I appreciate all this. All your work and preparation." She waited, so he went on: "You're giving me what I haven't had."

In an instant she was solemn again. "I know," she said, "I felt bad for you," gesturing toward the tree and then pulling her hand back, as if caught in the wrong. "Though it isn't my place. To be honest I probably felt worse for myself." She paused. "I wanted you to be . . . happy," she said. "Us. I wanted us to be." She looked him in the eye—the fire brightened suddenly and between its light and the lamp's her face was briefly but fully revealed to him, which caused a certain pain—and breathed deep and held her hands apart, palms up, conceding a necessity or asking for relief.

"I'm more confused than I ought to be but it doesn't matter now," she said, and then the smile was back, or at least the cheer. "It's just something that should happen. I'm glad you're enjoying it too."

She began to hum a carol as she turned to the kitchen and for a moment, watching her leave him, he wanted her in his house forever.

The dishes were stacked in the sink, though not clean—that could wait, she knew, until later in the evening and if necessary beyond, they had enough for six or seven meals before she had to start washing—and the table wiped down, and the salt and pepper and napkin holder put away in the china closet. Her cake and coffee sat before her; in front of her father, with his left hand wrapped around it, was a glass of Irish whiskey. It was the only thing he drank of his own free will (it was a struggle to get him to take even water or juice) and he refused any vessel but a tumbler of glass. This one, his favorite, had probably come from Myra's lunchroom in town. To her profound gratitude he never took more than three drinks in an evening, or at the very most four, and once she'd poured one for him he always sat quietly and sipped slowly, looking for all the world as if he were intact, the man he'd been five years before. Those evenings on which he refused his liquor were very difficult for her, sometimes hellish. The doctor had suggested more than once that she wean him off it, for the sake of his health, but the fact was—to her deep and continuing shame—that she had no idea how she'd manage without the whiskey and hadn't the faintest intention of trying.

She stared down at her coffee, watching the slow movement of a patch of oil across its surface. It was very quiet, except for her father's breathing and the ticking of the big dining room clock, and she knew she would soon need to break up the silence and her own hopeless solitude with a record or the radio, music and then perhaps later the Dickens reading that was on each year at nine. But for the moment it soothed her and she sat very still, trying as hard as she could to hear it, to be open to it, imagining the sounds that might intrude and stand out against its background, so very attentive to the one that finally did—a big truck going by out on Route 29—that she couldn't possibly say when it faded at last and left the quiet to fend for itself again. As carefully as she listened it still echoed, however faintly, in her ear.

"Where's the boy?" asked Tom, startling her. She looked up to find him watchful and alert.

"With his friends," she answered. "With Mikey and Con. They go out for a while every Christmas Eve." His eyes had come wide open and fixed themselves on her face, clear and expressive, a thing that happened rarely and always preceded a genuine exchange between them, a true conversation however short. The kind they'd had nearly every day before he'd started to change. This time, however, he said nothing but simply went on looking at her. Bizarre though it was she believed she saw pity in his gaze.

"You remember Mikey," she said. "He and Bill played ball together. And Con is Ralph and Estelle's son; he used to help us in the fall. He sells us our feed now. Both very nice. Mikey has two kids and Connie has three. Friends with Bill for thirty years." She was chattering, she knew, a peculiar thing but she didn't think she could stand to have him look at her that way, as if he could really see her for once, and never say a word. "Would you like to hear Aunt Pink's letter now? Or maybe have a piece of cake? Bill won't come back for hours yet, you'll be in bed when he does, but tomorrow we'll all get up together and go to Christmas service. You'll enjoy that."

This last so mortified her that she forced herself to stop talking, despite her fears, and found that it was possible after all to sit silently with him watching her. Difficult, surely, but easier than going on and on without reply. She gathered her courage and met his eyes. There *was* concern in them, she was certain of it, and again she was filled with apprehension and sorrow; the idea that he was once more a caring father, if only for a few minutes and perhaps for the last time ever in his life, made her so wildly miserable that it was all she could do to sit and sip her coffee and avoid his face. Go, she insisted, go away, please go, that's over and done with now. But she knew without looking that he was sitting and studying her—*worrying* about her—the same as before. She heard the sound of the glass against his teeth, of his swallow, and of the tumbler coming down on the table again, and then for some time there was only the ticking of the clock.

"I miss Phillip, Father," she said, her voice unsteady.

"I know you do," he said.

She looked at him. "How could you?" she asked.

"I remember," he said. He coughed, twice, and closed his eyes. "I remember him. I remember you talking about him." He raised the whiskey glass again and took another sip. "I remember how much you liked him. Liked him myself."

She was astonished. "Did he visit with you?"

"He did," said Tom, "at least twice. Good listener. Talked his head off." He laughed, for the first time in months. "You were out in the yard, or on the phone or something. Man asked about the war so I gave him an earful." He laughed again, a strange harsh sound that alarmed as much as pleased her.

She shook her head. "He never told me," she said.

"It happened," said her father. "I'm not lying."

"I believe you. I'm just surprised."

"Lots of folks get along with me."

"I know they do, Father. That's not it. I'm just surprised he never told me."

"Some men," said Tom, "keep a lot to themselves."

She drank from her mug and cut her cake with her fork. Though it was much too early she began to hope she would hear Bill coming in. Maybe he would bring Con and Mikey home to visit, like he had once before. She'd worked so hard to accept her father as he was, as he'd become, she'd accepted so much, that the unreality of talking this way with him now was keenly distressing; it felt something like betrayal. One way or another, she thought, one way or the other, I can't cross the line again.

"What happened?" he asked. "Did you give him the boot?"

"Not really," she said. "Truth is I hoped he'd stick around."

"Too bad," he said.

She pictured the two of them sitting at this table or in the armchairs in the living room, Tom going on about 1943 and Phillip listening silently and observing her father with that look of his, the look of devouring the speech of another, almost, of being fed, and a bitter jealousy rose up in her and made her want to stand and curse. Jealous of Phillip, of Tom, of herself? She didn't know. It didn't matter. She could see Phillip handling the old photos, examining the Purple Heart in its long leather box, and suddenly long-disregarded anger filled her soul—as if he'd stolen the medal or replaced it with a fake, as if it were he who'd fired the shot in the first place. She heard her father giving away all his secrets, like the locations of his scars or the story of her birth, telling how she'd come the day the Germans had surrendered at Stalingrad and he'd celebrated both events at once, drinking with his tank crew on Algerian sands. "On the outside I cheered the Russians but on the inside I cheered you," he'd always told her. She hoped he hadn't revealed that to Phillip but she thought he probably had.

The sound of his glass overturning made her look up. The tumbler was on its side, whiskey spreading over the table and dripping into his lap. His hand was shaking badly and there were tears in his eyes. He was enormously old.

"Janie, Janie, I'm sorry," he said.

She rose to her feet. "Oh Dad," she told him, moving to give comfort, "please don't worry. Don't worry now."

The air in the living room was warm and still thick with the smells of dinner, of coffee and dessert; the night outside the windows was moonless and very dark. They sat on the rug in front of the fire, quietly watching, surrounded by torn paper and the things they'd unwrapped. In Phillip's hand was his present from Jennie, so thrilling he couldn't believe it was real. Her first gift, the larger one, had been a new flannel shirt, much to his taste, and he'd been touched and a little dismayed. You have no one to buy you clothes, he'd thought, but she does; she wouldn't understand how this makes you feel. He'd turned his back to try the shirt on, pleased that it fit so well, but when he'd faced her again and started to thank her she'd thrust at him the second package, small but oddly heavy. He'd opened it to find an antique silver letter opener with a long, narrow, rounded blade that came to a very sharp point, a finely detailed stag's head sitting proudly atop the two levels of hilt at the handle end. It was a lovely old object but more than that it was genuine; it had substance and character, a presence of its own. And it was exactly what he wanted. Exactly. She was so young— how could she have known? It seemed a miracle. As soon as he'd held it in his hand he'd imagined it sitting on his desk, anchoring pages as he worked. As much as he'd wanted to tell her what it meant he'd had the sense not to try.

Now as they sat drinking brandy by the fire he still clutched it tightly, its weight in his hand. More than once he'd put it on the rug beside him but each time he'd found himself taking it up again. He was afraid to let it go. Jennie was to his left and beyond her was the Turner reproduction he'd given her—he'd bought it on a London trip seven years before but had never found the spot—and also her sisters' gifts (slippers from Amy and tapes from Em). On the couch behind them were the books from Carla and Bob, Emerson for Jennie and a history for him, and the other things that had come in the mail. Besides the firelight there was only the dim glow of a small lamp in the corner and the one they'd left on in the kitchen; besides the hissing and crackling of the wood and the whisper of the flames there was no sound at all.

"Let's have a chocolate," said Jennie.

"I thought you couldn't eat another bite."

"I can't, but I've got to try them." She rose, carefully, and went to the couch, returning with the box from Chicago and with one of the Hungarian Christmas candies. Her new place on the rug was a little closer to him and she had to lean to her left to reach her brandy glass.

"We shouldn't do it," she said, holding the candy up

in front of her. It was wrapped in gilt paper. "We should save them for the stockings."

"We don't have stockings."

She giggled. "That's right," she said, uncovering it. She broke it in half and put one piece in her mouth, then handed the other to him. Reaching first to his right to put the letter opener on a bookcase, he picked up the wrapper from where she'd dropped it and threw it over the screen into the fireplace.

"Good," she said, before she'd finished chewing. "A little old but good."

"They always mail too early," he said. "They're afraid it won't get here on time." He ate his half and the familiar taste—sweet chocolate with an orange-flavored center—struggled briefly with the brandy before giving in.

"Do all the children there get these?" she asked.

"They hang them on their trees, as ornaments."

"We should have done that!"

"I'm sorry," he said. "I forgot. Next year."

They watched the fire together.

"What do you send them?"

"Different things. Note cards, mostly. Games and puzzles for the girls. I try to stock up when I go down to Boston."

"They sound nice. I wish I could meet them."

"They're very nice, but it's unlikely unless you visit Budapest. I've given up trying to get them over here."

"OK," she said. "Now the mints." Taking the cover from the box she giggled again. "So small and so many," she said. "And all the same."

He picked one out, hesitated, then held it to her lips. She opened her mouth and took a bite. "I actually like these slightly chilled," he told her. "But it doesn't matter."

She chewed more slowly this time, her eyes closed, and

he examined her face. He was very close to her, so close that he would have moved away but for fear of calling her attention to it. He realized, considering each feature in turn, that she was one of the lucky ones—one of the blessed ones—with no minor uglinesses, no small imperfections. Even the handsomest women and men had those but not Jennie. He knew it was part of why he found her so beautiful; her face (and surely the rest of her as well) was simple and unmarred. He had always been attached to those qualities. She was, he thought, like a rounded Welsh hill, or a piece of polished granite, or the sky on a lovely early June day: you could see and enjoy and not be disappointed, but stay always at peace.

She opened her eyes and looked into his. "Wonderful," she said. Then she leaned forward and took the rest of the chocolate, gently, from his fingertips.

After a moment he got to his feet and she put her hand out to stop him. "Just getting the brandy," he said. He took it from the end table and bent over her, refilling her glass and then his own. There was only an inch or so left when he was done. She picked up her glass and looked down into it, almost modestly, as he put the bottle on the mantel and stood staring at the fire.

"I shouldn't drink any more," she said.

"Why not?" he asked. "There's nowhere to go."

"You haven't had a mint."

"I don't need one. I enjoyed yours as much as you did."

She glanced at him—perhaps waiting for more—and then dropped her head again.

"Jennie, you must be lonely here," he said.

"Phillip," she said, not looking at him. "Please. Sit down."

He laughed and sat, a little farther than before.

"You must be," he said.

She shook her head. "Only very occasionally."

"You're young."

Time passed before she looked up and smiled. "I've had enough of that to last a while," she said.

"I know you go off by yourself."

"Only to the movies or the library." She sipped her brandy and watched the fire. "I'm almost always alone."

He took a swallow from his own glass, then another. "Never to that bar down the highway? Where the kids hang out?"

For a second or more she studied his face. "Just once," she said. "It was . . . unpleasant. I won't do it again."

After that they were silent. The light from the fireplace was so deep and so warm that he couldn't sort it out from the heat of the flames, or from the smell of the food they'd eaten or the feel of the rug or the taste of the brandy and chocolate. He wondered if an observer—say someone peeking through the window from outside—would see the scene as through a golden filter, or some other special effect. He felt desire for her but it wasn't a sexual desire, not really; he wanted only to feel her cheek on his own, to put his face in her hair or press it into her neck and let go of the rest. Very far away, calling out from a high place, was an almost frantic warning, but for most of him the change that had come (after all his effort, all his work, to put her firmly in her place) was a welcome one, or if not welcome at least entirely sound. It was real in every way, he knew, it was what had to happen next, and he had lost all sense of any other possibility. The question of what to do about it would wait for another day.

"I think I'm drunk," she said. He thought briefly of touching her but nodded instead.

"When I was thirteen this was everything I dreamed of," she said. "Sitting with brandy in front of a fire. I'm not like that anymore but this is very, very nice. It's nicer than almost anything I could think of."

He was quiet as she stared into the glow.

"I'm so happy here," she said.

They sat together, looking at each other, and he was surprised to find himself neither embarrassed nor anxious, nor even excited. He could tell he was prepared to accept the situation—one that was, after all, of his own making—and she seemed as relaxed as he. Two months, he thought, can be close to forever; I no longer live alone. Just then the big log in the middle of the fire crashed down through the pieces of burned-up kindling, showering the hearth with sparks.

"Time for bed," said Jennie.

"You never called your family."

"I know. I was having too good a time. I'll call them tomorrow. They won't mind."

"They must miss you," he said, but she waved it away. Then she rose, unsteadily, and opened wide to him. "Good night," she said.

He got to his feet and stepped into her arms, which closed around him. For a few seconds they held each other. He dreaded the moment of letting go but when it came it was not as painful as he'd feared; they didn't move entirely apart but stayed near to one another, her hands on his arms, his on her hips. With the tips of her fingers she stroked his new shirt. "So smooth," she said. Together—he couldn't decide which of them had started it, or whether they'd chosen to do it at all—they drew a few inches closer. She paused for a moment with her hands on his waist and her head on his shoulder before stepping away and turning from him, walking across the room and wobbling up the stairs, looking back just once in silence before passing from his sight.

With Phillip away and the days and nights so cold Jennie felt a little frightened. She had never been much bothered by the weather before—low temperatures were one thing on a skiing vacation, quite another when they went on and on outside the house in which you lived with no sign of letting up—and it reminded her of all her vulnerabilities. Here she was out in the country, alone. She tried not to but she found it odd that Phillip, who by his own admission slept other than in his own bed no more than once a year as a rule, had suddenly decided to spend the week in Boston. He'd said he had research to do and she believed him, but why now? Why with so little warning? For a moment, as he'd told her, she'd even thought him cruel. It was unfair but at times she suspected him of testing her by going, as if he questioned all the joy she was finding in living in New Chatham, living in his house, or thought it might be cheap or shallow. Let's see how she likes it when the wind blows, she heard him saying, when I'm not there to talk to and it's down to ten below.

It was true that he'd asked her to come along with him, asked more than once, but she'd known he hadn't meant it. Even he, she thought, had been fully aware of the relief on his face when she'd refused. He'd had several other suggestions, including surprising her parents with a visit (not practical even if she'd wanted to, with so little notice the fares were much too high) or staying in some nearby town she thought she might enjoy, but the truth was she'd been looking forward to it—to his total and thorough absence, to being able to pretend for six days that she owned the house completely, that it was hers—until the moment he'd gone. She'd felt her first small doubts driving back from the bus station, and after walking through the simply unbelievable cold from the driveway to the house and thinking for a terrifying moment that she'd locked her keys in the Volvo she'd been ready to change her mind. But by then it had been too late. It *was* her house at that point, she'd known, and she its guardian; she'd accepted this charge until he returned.

He'd also done a lot to prepare her for the week: he'd given her lists of numbers and names, he'd made sure she had enough food and warm clothing—what an embarrassment that she'd come without a real winter coat, he'd insisted in December that she buy herself one—and the car had been checked and serviced at Williams Auto in town. He hadn't acted like a man purposefully abandoning someone, in fact he'd seemed to be doing it with regret, or apprehension. After thinking this over it occurred to her that his departure might, after all, have had more to do with his own needs than with any effect it would have on her. When she realized this she felt foolish and ashamed. His life doesn't revolve around you, she reminded herself; at times he hardly knows you're here. He went to Boston on account of his book, that's all, not you. The timing wasn't his choice.

If I were in there too I'd keep her company, she thinks. She wouldn't know it but I'd be there just the same. She'd be less worried then. She would feel so much better without knowing anything different. Without even knowing why. How could it be wrong for me to do her that favor?

And I so want to be inside.

Instead, held back, she stands for hours at a time in the strange unfelt unfeeling cold, hands on the sill, looking in through the glass, wondering about everything. My house? she asks again and again, my house? She comes to understand that she can no longer be bored, that her eyes don't dry out from the staring, that her feet and legs refuse to grow tired. My house? My house? Moving her fingers along the clapboard she touches but doesn't touch; when a bird cries overhead she hears it, but can't say for sure if it reaches her ears. I'm something different, she thinks, not the same as I've been. I'm not a woman—not really. I'm something different, something new.

I wonder, what's her name?

On the fourth day the cold broke and the thermometer climbed to thirty-seven. After all the strain of living with a new kind of winter it seemed like summer to Jennie. And her good cheer was bolstered when she turned on the kitchen radio—she'd had, she discovered as she twisted the knob, some vague notion of finding music to dance to—and heard a woman talking about near-record lows and all the trouble people were having with frozen pipes and cars that wouldn't start. So it wasn't just me, she told herself, standing in a patch of bright sunlight on the vinyl floor, it really was horrendously cold. She felt enormously relieved. And lucky that she hadn't had any problems of her own, with the heat or the car or anything else. Then she reminded herself that it wasn't just luck but also Phillip's preparation. She was grateful to him and sorry as well; she imagined him checking the daily weather in New Hampshire—standing shirtless in his hotel room, his smallish, pleasingly muscular frame bent over the newspaper, his skin pale and smooth and his black hair unbrushed, his dark eyes quickly searching the temperature columns—and worrying about her. She hoped he hadn't.

Because it was so much warmer and she so much happier—she was astonished by the depth of her response to the change—she felt she had to get out of the house. She didn't want to go far (it might turn cold again or worse yet start snowing) but she needed an adventure, and after a while remembered something she'd been saving: a visit to the attic over the garage. You wouldn't do it if he were here, she thought at once, you'll just be spying, but there seemed no particular harm in it. It wasn't as if he had ever told her no.

She put on her boots and jacket (her old jacket, not the huge new coat she'd been shuffling around in) and went outside. The sky was thin clouds in a penetrating blue and it was even more pleasant than she'd expected. She considered walking in the woods instead but after a turn and a half around the house, examining the bushes and trees and rabbit tracks in the snow and enjoying the feel of the sun on her face, she went to the garage. Its steady peaceful gloom gave her pause for a moment as she slipped through the door; it wasn't new to her at all, she'd come in dozens of times to get the shovels and other tools, but it had a different aspect on account of her purpose. It was almost like a church. The brilliance of the light coming through the tiny holes in the sides just emphasized the difference between what was inside and what was out: a whole house and yard and sixty-seven forest acres at her disposal and the one place, she suspected, that she really shouldn't be. Then the humor of that image of Jennie in a fairy tale—"Don't go in the attic," said the troll as he departed, but the princess couldn't help it—overcame her hesitation. The fact was that Phillip hadn't ever told her not to and there was no reason at all to think he would mind; he'd even taken her there himself. There was nothing magic, nothing sacred, not even secret. The owners were dead. She wanted to meet them, that was all. Still she used a special caution as she pulled the ladder down.

She has no more heart but she feels it beating faster. She has no more arms but she folds them very tightly as she paces the lawn. I don't want her there, she thinks. The house is hers but that is mine. Ours. Mine. Those things belong to me. She hasn't yet been to the attic herself but she knows, somehow, what it holds; she doesn't understand why those objects still exist at all, what use they are to anyone, but is sure they should not be disturbed. She is almost in a panic from her desire to protect them. She would weep if she could.

Out!, she shouts silently, standing in the snow between the house and the garage. Get out! Get out! As she raises her hands to the sky she is aware—suddenly, drastically, completely—of her current capabilities. It makes her horribly afraid and she lowers them again. Papa, she calls out, Papa, do something. Her voice is so weak. Papa, where are you? Come out from those trees. But her Papa doesn't come and that girl is still up there and though her anger is great she doesn't want to cause harm. She can only mutter and pace. Come out, come out, she begs in a whisper. Before it goes further. Oh, please do come out!

For long minutes after climbing to the attic she stood under the beam, just looking, taking note of what was there. Then she began to go through the boxes and barrels and crates. She was brisk and industrious, almost like a clerk; each container, each treasure got only brief examination (whose things am I handling? she asked more than once) before she put it away and moved on to the next. It was a fascinating treasure: the toys and games of a hundred years before, the many books, the old clothing, the watercolors, even oil lamps and a leather harness. At first she thought it astounding that Phillip—of all people!— had been ignoring these things for over ten years, but as she slowly became aware of her own agitation, her unease at being where she was and doing what she was doing, her empathy increased. She simply couldn't stop herself although part of her hoped she would. What is it, she wondered, the curse of the mummy? That's even sillier than the troll. But this time it wasn't amusing. She wished there were an electric bulb on the ceiling, as below, or that she'd brought a flash along. There was adequate light coming through the small windows at either end of the attic but a glow of a different kind—the kind that she could switch on and off, as she chose—would have been more reassuring. It was colder in the attic than outside, much colder, but she'd dressed warmly by a habit of several days' standing and though aware of the chill she didn't mind.

When she got to the boxes of postcards she stopped. They were the remedy, somehow, to her growing distress; they were a balm, a fitting instrument. Some of the fronts were attractive, even beautiful—especially those whose dyes had faded through the years, leaving delicate pinks and blues of a shy, haunting quality—some interesting or informative, some dull, some banal, some so murky as to be almost blank. But the backs claimed her attention. Long-dead words, she thought, but the words weren't dead, it was their authors who were; the words still had their vigor. They might have been written the day before. These people, some born a century ago, might have been her own friends, dropping a line from the beach or the mountains or a cousin's in Topeka. Their greetings were familiar and showed no differences of culture, revealed nothing of their age.

She crouched and held them in her hands. They were talismans, she knew. It was as if she were so overwhelmed by the larger discovery, by the fabulous hoard that had been waiting silently for her for so many weeks, that after exultation faded she needed refuge and relief. Who kept these? she wondered as she looked at them. And why? It was hard to shuffle through them with her gloves on her hands but after a while she got the knack.

Whoever had put the cards into the boxes had carefully divided them into sets, Jennie found, by recipient or sometimes by subject, and then arranged them by date. The sets didn't seem to have much in common except location; every card she looked at had been mailed from New England or to New England or both, and scenes of the region were far the most common, though there were many of Florida and the far west as well. One series showed rural and small-town

New Hampshire (she supposed there was no other at the time they were made) and she was amazed and pleased to find a picture of New Chatham, around 1916 according to the postmark, looking not very different from what she'd seen since she'd arrived.

But most of the sets contained cards to one person. The names, male and female, were unfamiliar to Jennie. One of the larger collections had been received by a Miss Ludivine (or Lulu, or Ludy, or Lu) Gauthier, who had worked for the *Worcester Telegram* and lived in Worcester, except when vacationing at a cottage in Rhode Island, between 1906 and 1915. Perhaps she'd come first from Quebec—among her correspondents was a Michelle Durand, a few of the cards were in French, and one had been mailed to a Mrs. Gaspard Gauthier "c/o J. C. Boucher, Boucherville, near Montreal, Canada." Several referred to an unrequited passion on the part of an unidentified admirer; Jennie was most moved by one that read, "Home, sweet home. But oh! so quiet and I don't need a rest," and by another that insisted, "Please reciprocate." She could almost, but not quite, picture Ludivine as she read, and badly wished (eight decades late!) for a portrait of some kind, or for a message in the Gauthier hand to go with those from her friends.

And then there was A. R. Henderson, of Salem, who'd received these words in July of 1912:

all right Art
don't hurry
Ed

and Miss Delia Walsh, whose souvenir of an insurance company's New York headquarters carried the inscription: "Will you please get me insured my health is poor I can't

afford to pay what I can't have the pleasure of spending";
and William Craven, whose Emma had sent him in 1909 a
card of a couple embracing in the moonlight, with the cap-
tion "You are the only girl I ever loved," and had written on
the back: "Is it true? That's what he said last night."

But by far the largest group—it took up half a box—
was Irene Wentworth's post office collection. Wentworth,
postmistress of Center Durham, New Hampshire, had been
sent dozens of cards of post offices from all around the country by family, friends, and neighbors over more than twenty
years until 1956. Some were intimate, some chatty, some
formulaic; others bore requests such as "Here for three
weeks forward what you have" and "Expect to be home Monday so please send my mail." Reading through them was
like reading a biography, Jennie thought, or even living a
life. Despite the steady pleasure it must have given Wentworth the extended repetition of a simple theme depressed
her, in a way; it reminded her of the habits of an old friend
of hers, a childhood companion who returned every year to
their hometown to renew the same meaningless relationships and then went away again. Names and phrases caught
at her, stayed with her as she read: "The Coutimores," "Sure
I got dirty but I'll make out OK," "Will write later a letter."
Chilly though she was she went through all of them twice,
from beginning to end, comparing signatures and handwrit-
ing to puzzle out the relationships, terribly saddened when
she came to the last one for the second time ("Another P.O.,
always think of you when I see any") and there weren't any
more. Nineteen fifty-six was close to forty years gone but she
felt, unreasonably, that it wasn't the end, that Irene was still
alive and waiting somewhere, perhaps nearby, though in
that case her cards would probably not be resting gently in
an attic in New Chatham.

Holding one of the post offices—Hinesville, Georgia—
in her left hand, she moved to the window at the north end
of the attic. She knelt by the glass and looked out. The
clouds were thicker than they had been, the light a little
fainter, and she was reminded of the need to get back inside
the house, of the subtle fatigue that was joining with the cold
to weaken her muscles and drain her of energy, to urge her
to the floor. If you go to sleep now you may die here, she
thought without alarm, and peered through the glass at the
bare trunks and limbs. The wind was picking up. Not far
away she saw a white garbage bag—or maybe it was cloth,
a piece of someone's skirt or sweater—flying from a branch,
like a flag of surrender.

She returned to the cards and looked around to make
sure they were all in their boxes, then carefully fitted the
covers on. You're going to take them back to your room, she
told herself. Aren't you? You are. You know you shouldn't
but you are. And you'll hide them there, you won't tell Phillip; you'll keep them to yourself. It's wrong but it's what
you're going to do.

Crouching in the shadowed attic, fingers resting on a
shoebox, she stared at the ladder before finding her way
down.

She can't say what it is but something—an instant's flash
of sunlight off the top of Cobb's hill, snow falling from the
branches of a big pine behind her, the memory of her sisters'
smiles—gives her patience and calm. She returns to the
house with a new determination. She eyes the door. Very
well, she thinks, very well, I'm agreeable. What's mine is
yours; what's yours is mine. I may be all alone—I *am*
alone—but in your own way you are too.

The girl is in the attic but can't stay there forever. She sits in the snow to wait.

January 6

Dearest Mother,
  I begin to understand.

Yours always,
J.

chapter

12

Following a gory and anguished encounter he is called before the colonel. The two men have served in the regiment together from the day it was formed. They were boys less than half a mile apart. They watch each other with pity; the candle's light moves back and forth across the canvas walls and ceiling; in the endless dark outside, an orderly curses at a cook.

The commander looks bad but not as bad as his soldier. Sutherland's head is bandaged (a minor wound, he waves away the questions) and his uniform covered with blood. After a relentless and unforgiving day of wading through dead and dying bodies he feels like a loathsome butcher; he knows that every bit of the disgust that has accumulated in him over more than two years is now visible in his face. A vague sense of duty suggests that this is neither manly nor appropriate but he is certain he doesn't care. No reason to care: the other is as weary as he, and they're alone. No need to pretend.

"I'm making you a sergeant, Jack," says the colonel. He speaks slowly and a little imprecisely, as if he has been drinking, or feels pain in his lips or his tongue. "They'll have to approve it but I've no doubt they will. In the meantime let's assume it's been done."

Sutherland watches the officer's face. He is tired enough to drop. There is a camp stool nearby but having refused its offer when he first came in he is reluctant to change his mind.

"There's more pay in it for you," says the colonel. He waits, relaxed and still. "You know you deserve it," he says. "It's long overdue."

Tempted though he is, the exhausted, filthy man doesn't speak.

"Have you nothing to say?" asks the colonel.

Sutherland licks his lips. "What I want is something different," he answers in a low, gentle, even voice, almost a whisper, thin from fatigue but from other things as well. It sounds like the words to a song. For reasons unclear to him he looks at the ground.

"I can't," says the colonel. "I can't do it. I'm stuck here and I need you. So you'll stay too."

"God bless you, sir," says Sutherland.

The colonel watches him. "I know I'm a rotten bastard, Jack," he says. "You don't need to tell me."

"We could both go," says Sutherland. "We could be back there in a week."

The commander rests his forehead on his hand. Night sounds find their way into the tent—cricket, owl, wind in trees. Sutherland notices a smell he can't identify and looks around him; nothing catches his eye except a photograph of a pretty young woman in an elegant dress, propped up on the crate next to the cot.

"We could," says the seated man. "We could at that. I see it plainly."

"They'd cheer us."

"They would."

"We'd eat real food again."

"Yes."

"We could walk up and down the avenue til we bust."

"It's true," says the officer to his knee. "We could."

Sutherland leans forward. "Your wife," he says. "You'd see your wife." He glances again at the picture. "She must miss you awful bad."

The colonel raises his head from his hand, smiles briefly, and stands. "Sergeant Sutherland," he says, "you'll stay here for the time being. That's my order."

Sutherland's own eyes, though he can't see them, remind him of nothing so much as a crippled dog waiting to be shot.

"You can go," says his colonel.

As a girl, Jane knew, she'd been eager to please. Her parents, her teachers, Mr. Perlman at the store—nothing had mattered more than their good graces. She'd worked long and hard to secure their smiles. As early as five or six she'd been aware sometimes of trying too hard, and worse yet of annoying some adults on account of it, but her need had been so deep and so strong, she recognized decades later, that she could never have stopped.

As a way of being Jane it had had its ups and downs. She'd suffered badly from a sense of being misunderstood— by those who thought it was the praise she was after, or that she was weak and dependent, or even vain—but had always been certain that her only true desire was to make her elders happy. To make sure they didn't want her to be different, better, behaving in some other way. (Or to be elsewhere, worst of all.) And she'd seen nothing wrong with this, nothing selfish or mean; her concern had been for others and not for herself. She just hadn't been able to live with the tension of wondering if they still liked her, that was all. It was very straightforward. As much as forty years later it didn't cause her any doubts.

The day she'd come running home from the Carbonneaus, her mouth full of the liverwurst she'd been afraid to swallow, her mother—her own mother, who should have understood at once—had welcomed her with astonishment. Even after spitting it out she'd gotten questions instead of comfort. "Why didn't you just say, 'No, thank you?' " asked her mother. "Why didn't you just tell him your sister was allergic?" Looking deep into her mother's puzzled blue eyes, longing for water, remembering the whole incident in horrible detail—big, hairy Mr. Carbonneau going to the counter and cutting off a hideous piece, holding it out to her, talking all the while about how good it was as if good meant the same thing to a shambling white-haired truck driver and a chubby little girl—she'd known that her mother would never accept it, would never see why she'd had no choice at all but to open her mouth despite her terror and let the awful substance in, and had felt for the first and last time the frantic, aching pain of a child who is thoroughly and irrevocably alone. Unable to speak, unable even to cry, she'd thrown herself in desperation at the familiar blue dress and found survival, if not relief, in the surprised, enfolding arms.

In the end it hadn't hurt her, her need for approval; as she'd outgrown her chubbiness and her play sets and the swing behind the house it too had amazingly fallen away, leaving behind a young woman with breasts and hips and a self-possessed manner who could stand to be complained to, or scolded, or even disliked if need be, though she rarely gave reason. It was almost, she'd thought more than once through the course of getting older, as if she'd had enough worrying in her first ten years, enough concern for people's thoughts and feelings, to last her the rest of her life. Maybe other children were somehow less aware, less attuned to their own reliance on the moods and whims of others, and felt its full force only when old enough to begin to understand how fragile their family and friends really were. Maybe she had been born, somehow, with an empathy lacking in most, a precocious sense of the nearness of grown-ups to the brink and the utility of helping them regain firmer ground. In any case after a certain age it had become second nature to her, this maintenance of good terms, something she accomplished almost reflexively by reaching into the reservoir of solicitude she'd stored up and doling out enough to keep everybody calm. By the time she reached eighteen she'd been truly independent, not that she hadn't before but in a better, new way, a way that allowed her to stop trying to influence others altogether and instead just concentrate on being herself, which seemed to do the trick as if by magic. She could honestly say that in the last thirty years no one had really thought ill of her, no one who'd known her even slightly; a few strangers had been rude but by and large five minutes of conversation had always been enough, without her even thinking about it, to get a person on her side.

Thirty years was thirty years, but a lifetime it wasn't; sleeping with Phillip had brought everything back. Once again she'd been eager, determined to please, and once again she'd lived from day to day with the still-familiar anxiety, the ongoing concern over everything she might have done wrong. She'd never told him, of course, that she felt so much the child. It hadn't been just sex, though their beds had seen the worst of it, her need to do well by him (she'd had so little practice) at times fighting and even drowning the intense, racing pleasure he gave her. It had started with that but leaked all over their friendship. Things had eventually reached the point at which Jane, while concentrating hard on continuing the motion that showed signs of being just right, had at the same time pictured (with a critical eye) the dinner she'd cooked on Friday, wondering if she'd made enough, or had sat in Phillip's living room reading the paper and feeling bad about both the sculpture she'd bought him at the show in Northampton and the fatigue that had kept her, two nights before, from driving over to see him as planned.

From the start she'd brought him apples. "You've never had one of these before," she'd say on a bright summer evening, placing a perfect, handpicked specimen on the counter in his kitchen, stepping back to admire it and also to watch his face, biting her lip to keep from telling him that no more than a few hundred people in history, probably, had ever had the privilege of eating so round, so unblemished, so lovely an example of that particular variety. "This one won't keep. Eat it right away," she'd tell him briskly at sunrise, having walked back from her car after finding the fruit she'd left in it at half-past ten in her urgent need to rush inside and kiss him, hating the strange expression that was always on his face in the morning after that first open-eyed look of affection in the bathroom or the bed. For weeks he'd reveled in her gifts, in the tastes and colors and shapes and especially the names—Gravenstein, Esopus Spitzenburg, Smokehouse, Rhode Island Greening—which had delighted and intrigued him, prompting questions for which she hadn't always had answers. One story that she had known, that of the Greening (first grown around 1700 at a tavern at Green's End, near Newport, behind which innkeeper Green had raised apple trees from seed), had pleased him so enormously that he'd taken her right there in his yard, on her knees, the moon just rising over the forest, hanging weightless for her to watch as he caressed her and the warm breeze played on her skin. But in time he'd seemed to grow bored by the offerings, or at least unmoved, and that, though his respect for her passion for the orchard and her search for its beauty remained strong, had been the very first hint she had been given of the end.

She had reflected more than once, speeding down the asphalt on the way to Phillip's house or waiting, nervously, for him to arrive at her own, that the apples in their many forms were a lot like Jane, the Jane that wanted badly to win his favor; they worked so hard, each in its own way, to be exactly what you were looking for at a given moment, for a given purpose. One was perfect for that first bite in the afternoon, too early for dinner but with covert hunger prodding; one was brilliant—flamboyant—but somehow soothing to the eye; one sat uncomplaining on the shelf where you'd left it and was still firm, still crisp when you discovered it two weeks later, long after any other would have turned to tasteless mush. One was good for pies, another for sauces, one was huge and another could be slipped into a pocket without stretching the fabric. Maybe that was why she felt such attachment to them, such sympathy; the way they'd been bred, over so many generations, to satisfy, simply to please, and then left in their maturity to stand alone (or even disappear) was not entirely out of her experience. It was testament to the pointlessness, ultimately, of trying so hard to be loved. In fact, she'd understood one wet afternoon, in a sort of epiphany out in the muddy gap between the Spies and the Macs, that the apple tree itself, the very genus *Malus*, was the monarch of that realm, the all-time great survivor of affection gained and then relinquished; not only was it prone, for no reason at all, to turn out new varieties at random, varieties that might fill any need or pique any whim, but it would do so even when neglected, rejected, abandoned entirely. Especially when neglected, to her deep admiration—she knew of famous apples first discovered in the woods, or in forgotten pastures and fields, away from orchards altogether.

And when Phillip's interest in her had begun to disappear Jane had wondered, inevitably, if she'd grown, like a dog, to resemble her master. Had she in some way acquired the sad quality of those fruits that had been left to fade away? Was it now the bitter end of her day in the sun? If people could stop eating the Northern Spy, she'd supposed, for all its flavor, then Phillip could stop wanting her, but this thought had brought neither comfort nor insight; she'd remained as puzzled by one as by the other, as hurt by Phillip's diminishing desire as by the drive-ups who asked for the abominable Delicious, or Cortland, and contemned her for having neither. Most confusing and painful of all had been the thinning and eventual dissolution of his lust, a new and precious phenomenon in this late stage of her life that she would have cut out of him and kept for herself had she known how to do so. She was attractive to him, she'd been certain (though not without sporadic doubt), she'd learned all the things he liked, he was a healthy normal man with an appetite for women, so what had been the problem? Who ever had said it had to pick up and go, just like that, like a traveling salesman who'd sold the whole town? But gone it had, for all her efforts, and a year and more later she was still sunk in grief.

Eventually his reluctance had been too much for her pride. There'd been no doubt at all about who was leaving whom but it had been left to Jane, not Phillip, to make the final break. She'd had the feeling that he might have gone on seeing her forever—taking walks with her, listening to her problems with tree borers and her father, attending to her physical needs—as long as she'd agreed not to demand of him enthusiasm, or passion, or any interest at all in anything beyond his own obsessive work. But the idea of such an arrangement had been completely repugnant to her, and even in her panicky distress over his withdrawal she'd had the sense not to hold on. She'd told him briefly of her bewilderment and sorrow—and even, very bravely, that it was his loss more than hers—and then had taken herself away.

At a party not long after their last night together (when Lynn and Hugh had called she'd gone all the way to Middlebury with them, against her better judgement, in the foolish hope of finding some distraction from her need) she'd overheard, by a freak of acoustics, something not meant for her ears. As she'd stood at one end of the loft in the converted barn, examining a large and sloppy canvas by the host, she'd spotted Hugh and another man watching her from the corner. Turning quickly so they wouldn't see she'd nonetheless understood the strange man's words, barely but clearly audible above the noise of the gathering, matching the look she had noticed in his eyes. "My god, she's got a magnificent body," Hugh's careless friend had said. "What is she, pushing fifty? It's amazing. Just look at her."

In her already weakened state this had thoroughly shocked her. Was it true? She'd never known it. She had somehow come all that way—sailing blithely through the years in which it really might have mattered—without being aware. Maybe she'd been told and not wanted to hear it, or maybe she'd never been told; she'd known as she stood there that she was going to forget all about it again as soon as she possibly could. But Phillip: had he felt that way too? Had he thought the word *magnificent*? Then why had he never said so? And why, oh why, had it not been enough?

She knew of all her own faults—she knew them vanishingly well—but still he had been wrong to give up on her, to let it get away. He had been very, very wrong. Like an absentminded thief he had stolen from them both and she hoped, devoutly and desperately, to discover how never to forgive him again.

chapter

14

"In a certain year in the seventeenth century, a candela-
brum in a church in a small town in Scotland is knocked
over during a Christmas service, starting a fire that kills
twenty-seven people."

"I was thinking about a woman who makes a man ride
his bicycle up a huge hill every day to reach her. She won't
let him walk or drive his car. After he showers they have
sex. If he doesn't ride all the way up without stopping—she
can watch him through her window—she won't sleep with
him that day."

"A women gets a note from another woman she knows
whose brother was killed in a robbery. The note is about a
basketball game but the paper is a quarter-sheet of photo-
copy waste, and when she turns it over she sees the heading:

III. Victims of situational crisis; 1. emotional responses to crisis; a. expressions of pain."

"You shouldn't tell me so much."

"It's OK. I'm drunk. I doubt I'll even remember."

"You're not that drunk."

"I guess I'm not."

"The coast of Tasmania is gloomy and wild because the ocean comes halfway around the world. There's no land at all between that shore and Argentina and the waves gather power the whole way. When we get there we stand on a dune looking west and can't see any blue. The water's white to the horizon."

"You aren't alone?"

"I'm with Charlie."

"I don't know him."

"You don't want to."

(A sort of wind moves through the room.)

"I was also thinking about an older man in a library, sneaking looks at a young woman. He finds her lovely but doesn't want to embarrass her. He feels badly—he's ashamed—but he can't help himself. She seems so uncorrupted. He's very curious, and wonders if he knows her somehow; she reminds him of his youth. Just then she comes over to his table and says, 'If you don't stop looking at me I'm going to knock your teeth out.'

"I'll bet that's happened."

"Haven't they all?"

"Yes. Depending on how you mean that."

"You know how I mean it."

"Then yes."

"There are so many of them."

"Stories?"

"Yes."

"It depends."

"On the moment?"

"More or less."

"More or less?"

"It isn't so much the stories as the telling. Without the telling the stories don't matter. Without the need to tell them, unhealthy creatures that we are."

"For telling stories?"

"For loving them more than our lives."

"Isn't that what art is?"

"That doesn't make it healthy."

"So where the need is there are stories?"

"Now you're catching on."

"A woman I know once said, 'He made me feel I was a project he endured for the sake of art.' "

"I know her too."

"Do you?"

"I'm sure I do."

(They are not alone.)

Jennie never spoke of her disastrous year with Charlie. Her family had some idea, and one or two close friends, but there were things they'd never know if she could possibly help it. It was important that no one ever find out he'd hit her. Not because she still cared, on and off, what they thought of him—oddly, she sometimes felt an impulse to protect him, although he didn't deserve it—but because the only way for her to gain control of it, to be able to live with the fact of it, was to cut it out of her life altogether and send it far away. She couldn't help but remember the moment (most often in the middle of the night) but that was going to be the whole of it, she was determined; it was not going to have any presence in her life. No one was ever going to refer to it again. So far she'd been successful and except for one short exchange with Charlie himself, no one ever had.

She knew she should have seen it coming. She should have been warned away. There had been pushes and shoves over the months, objects grabbed and furniture broken, lots of ways in which he'd used his greater strength to bully her, wear her out, overcome those emotions of hers that he didn't like with the physical expression of the passions that ruled him. But he had hit her just the once. In her dorm room (the biggest on the floor, in the building, maybe even at the college) he'd punched her hard in the face, surprisingly not in a fit of rage but in a measured, almost tranquil way, and knocked her down against the wall. They'd paused together—he standing motionless in the center of the room, she leaning against the pitted plaster next to the bookcase, her hand on her cheek, waiting for the pain—while they tried to accept the truth of what he'd done. (She remembered much later her astonishment at the grief that had passed over his features, very briefly, as if he'd known for just an instant that he'd crippled his life.) Before long they'd heard a knock on the door.

"Jennie? Are you all right?" Nikki had asked. "Jennie? Charlie?" Silently and with great speed, Charlie had laid the mostly empty bookcase on its side and scattered the books on the floor. "Pushed the bookcase over," he'd called as he did so and Jennie rose to her knees, her back to the door, and started stacking the books. Without seeing Nikki's face as Charlie let her in Jennie had known what was on it: a sour, skeptical expression that would have been there no matter what.

"Need any help?" she'd asked.

"No thanks," Jennie had said, amazed at the rational sound of her voice. "There aren't really very many." She'd

133

paused and rested her hands on her thighs. "To tell the truth, Nikki, we were having a fight."

"So I gathered," Nikki had said. "Try to keep it down, OK? I'm studying. And stop throwing things around, it isn't safe." Then she'd gone.

The two had stayed apart for five days after that, by far the longest such separation in their history, five blank days for Jennie that she still couldn't remember, like the time she'd had viral pneumonia and a fever of a hundred and three. On the sixth they'd met by chance on the path outside Geitner and walked together to a low wall nearby. As he'd sat down beside her he'd stared at the bruise on her face and reached out, eyes grave, to touch it.

"Forget it," she'd said. He'd pulled his hand back and looked away from her, at the chapel and the fountain and the dying elms between. Aware of others passing by they'd waited quietly in the sun.

"How do you feel?" he'd asked when they were alone.

"It hurts, Charlie. My face still hurts. I can't sleep."

"It won't happen again," he'd said softly.

"It already happened," she'd told him. "Once is enough."

"Yes. Yes, it is."

Several times in the period that followed she'd thought, if only he'd hit me again. If only he'd hit me and leave it at that. I could walk away then without a second glance, I could call the police, I could start going with dumb Frank— he's got fifty pounds on Charlie—just for protection. My ass for a bodyguard, that would be fine. Anything other than life as a cliche, the woman who gets hit ands stays. Anything other than this, this destruction, this slow humiliation of a thing I once adored.

She had admired her own honesty but could suddenly tell him nothing. She had cherished his strong feelings but now found them ugly, even foul. Their days had become false and hopeless and both knew it and for all the troubles they'd always had before—the arguments, the hurt feelings, the problems in bed, the acquaintances one or the other had objected to—each false day had taken something worthy from the treasure they'd been storing up together, hour by hour and minute by minute, until he'd made his fist and swung. She'd seen the bitter recognition on his face and felt it on her own and yet, to her almost total mystification, they had gone on throwing bad money after good and reducing each other to sloppy burdens, to bad memories, when they could have chosen to walk away with something precious and intact.

In all their time together between his violence and the end—she'd simply started, one day, to hang up the phone when he called, to not open the door when he knocked, to walk silently past him when they met, though where she'd found the strength for these things she had never been able to say—the only thing she'd enjoyed had been the stories of Giovanni. She'd known him as her boyfriend's aging father, a burly gray immigrant with a sweet voice and accent who'd watched basketball on TV, worked long hours in the garden, and spoken to her four times during the weekend she'd spent at his house. But in the misery of their failing affection they had blundered, by accident, into his adventures of thirty and forty years before, when he'd come to America after the war and tried to make his fortune as a short, dark alien whose English wasn't very good. As if he had become their last remaining common friend.

"He worked in a candy factory," Charlie had told her. "Didn't I ever mention that? They had lots of them in Boston. He made a certain kind of taffy. There were cooks who mixed the hot molasses, there were guys who spilled it onto cooling tables with water running underneath, there were winders, and then there was my dad. He was a candy spinner."

"I thought he was a welder," Jennie had said.

"That was later," he'd told her. "First he made candy. He'd cut a piece off the spool, flatten it, and put peanut butter on. Then he'd roll it up and stretch the roll out long and thin, and cut it into pieces. Someone else did the wrapping."

"Did he eat it himself?"

"I don't think I ever saw him. He once refused to take one from me. But that was much later, when I was six. After he'd gone to the phone company."

"The phone company?"

He'd sighed and shaken his head. "My oldest brother worked at the factory too," he'd said. "He ran errands. One day a forty-year-old machine broke down and they couldn't get any parts. They didn't know what to do. My brother, he was fifteen, he took one look at it and said, 'Hey, my old man can fix that.' They laughed but he insisted so they let him find Giovanni. My dad—he was an expert in Milano—he borrowed some equipment and got the machine up and running and was hired as a welder on the spot. He never went back to making candy again."

"He must have been grateful to your brother," she'd said.

"He beat Johnny black and blue," Charlie had answered, turning pale at the words but pressing on nonetheless. "I wasn't there but I heard about it later. He kicked the crap out of him. He kept yelling, 'What if I'd fucked up, you stupid kid?' "

Even after she'd started speaking to Charlie again, then stopped, then started, then stopped, all because she still cared for him but couldn't stand the fury that her attachment seemed to draw from his heart, like oil or the sap of a tree, she'd pictured Giovanni at work in his factory. Not with a torch but with the taffy in his hands. Not behind a mask but with a smile. In her dreams he'd worn an apron and a stiff white hat, with a dusting—nonsensical, she knew—of white powder on his shoulders, and his sleeves rolled up high on his dark and hairy arms. He'd worked all day on the candy line, the same motions over and over, without ever seeing the final product of his effort, almost too tired at the end to walk back across the city to his family, stopping at the whistle to fill a bag with unwrapped candies for his children. Sometimes he'd eaten one or two himself, on the way, if it wasn't too cold. But after his son, blinded by an odd devotion, had secured for him his future—forcing upon him once and for all his many cares and obligations—he'd sworn an oath never to taste them again. And over the years he never had.

chapter
16

With Jane's birthday on the way Bill tried to think of something special. He knew if he did she would look at him in wonder—it wasn't the sort of thing he usually gave much attention to—but he was ready for that, ready to wave away her questions and let the act speak for itself. He wasn't yet too old to change. She had always worried more about him than he had about her, at least as far as his happiness was concerned, and he was beginning to recognize, with an erratic sense of shame, how one-sided it had been. Hadn't she gotten him just the things he wanted for Christmas, year after year? Hadn't she helped and advised him for days before his big date with Meg Flowers in his senior year of high school, hadn't she ironed his shirt and talked at length about kissing and even lent him her car? (He knew he and pretty

Meg might easily have married as a result of that date and the ones that had followed, though he wasn't sure what exactly had gone wrong—had he tried too hard to make her that night, or not hard enough?—and he often wondered what it would have meant to Janie if they had.) And be honest, Bill, he told himself, it's not just long ago: isn't she protecting you now from what's happening to Dad? Because she knows how much it hurts you to see him that way?

It felt good to be more thoughtful about her, he realized, it felt right, and he made sure he kept on top of it and didn't get distracted. There was something to be learned if he could follow it to the end. On most days he liked to think that his newfound concern was due both to his maturity and to the troubles that seemed to have fallen on his sister—she had never really needed him before, that was all, and now she did—but the fact was, he occasionally acknowledged in a half-hidden, frightened way, that he had somehow reached the point at which he could imagine a time without her. He understood very clearly, which he hadn't before, that he might someday lose her and find himself alone.

So what would she like? he asked himself six times a day. What would she enjoy? Some music? A painting? How the hell would he find that? Nothing to do with the orchard, that was certain; if anything at all she should get far away. Maybe a trip? That idea had a certain consistent appeal but every time he pursued it he ended up imagining her wandering lonely in some beautiful place, wishing only for companionship, and though he doubted this would really be the case—she's been alone for all these years, he thought, she certainly knows how to do it by now—it made it so difficult and distressing for him to think about the details that he could never make any progress.

It's that Phillip she'd want, he thought one evening,

reading an old *Baseball Weekly* and smoking a joint in his room. It's him she'd be missing. Not just any friend, any man, but that one for sure. That ass. That fancy nothing. It made him very angry and he had to put the paper down, and the joint, and beat his hands on the wall. That faker, he thought, that big can of shit. What the fuck is his problem? How much better does he think he's going to do? It tore a big hole in the pit of his stomach but he couldn't help seeing at that moment exactly what had been bothering his sister, what had been making her so sad. That was her last chance, he thought. It was her last chance and she knows it. Holy mother of Christ. He was briefly so angry that it shocked him—the term "seeing red" came to mind—and he pounded the wall with his fists once again and spit the words "Damn! Shit his goddamn stinking ass!" in order to get past it and gain some sort of control.

A rapid knocking interrupted. "Bill? What on earth is going on? Are you all right?" He got up and went to the door and opened it, smiling at Jane as she peered into his room, looking just as she did when she examined the new leaves for wooly aphids, or the apples for worms.

"Sorry, hon," he said. "I was upset about something and I beat the wall a little. I won't do it anymore."

To his surprise she didn't look at him but kept on scanning his room, the bed and the bureau top and the floor and the corners, as if something she'd expected to find there was missing. "What's the matter?" she asked, her eyes moving back and forth.

"Nothing," he told her. "Nothing important." He turned to briefly survey the room himself, as if she had a reason to be searching so intently. "Is Dad asleep?"

"I hope so," she said. She sighed and stopped looking

past him and almost smiled. "I wish you wouldn't smoke dope, Bill. I know it's silly but I wish you wouldn't."

"It isn't very much," he said.

"I know it isn't, but even so."

"What difference can it make to anyone, Janie?" he asked, a little sharply. "What the hell else have I got to do?"

He understood right away that his anger at the writer (it still boiled in him somewhere) had informed his words and tone—and his anger at her, if he were honest, for getting herself into that mess in the first place—but he was unprepared for her reaction, for the lowered head and slumping shoulders, for the sob, as if he'd scolded her terribly or called her a name. Now he was furious at himself as well, at all three of them, and stoned too, and he fought desperately to get calm and to do something helpful instead of making things worse. He reached out and took her into his arms and to his amazement she clung to him, rather than pulling away, and laid her head on his shoulder. She was in tears.

"Darling, I'm sorry," he said. "I shouldn't talk to you that way. I really hate to see you cry."

She laughed a little through her sobs. "When have you ever seen me cry before, Billy?"

Although he didn't feel much like it he forced himself to laugh too as he reached to stroke her hair.

"Never, I guess. So there's all the more reason to hate it."

She gripped the cloth of his shirt tightly in each hand and sniffed twice, then sobbed once more. The sound pained him like a burn. She shuddered and seemed after that to relax, and though his shoulder was getting wetter he sensed the worst of it was over. His impulse was to release her but instead (through some wisdom he hadn't really known he had) he only tightened his embrace, spreading his feet very slightly so he could stand as steadily as she needed him to. She opened her hands and moved them up nearer his shoulder blades, the palms flat on his back.

"It's OK," she said. "It's not so bad for me to cry." She laughed again in a weeping sort of way, a strange sound from a woman whose laugh was usually open, big and easy. "In fact I'm kind of enjoying it."

"I'll cut down on the dope," he told her.

"Oh Bill," she said, "that doesn't matter. That's not it."

"I'll help more with Dad," he said. "I know I've left it up to you. It makes me wild to even go near him but it must bother you too and it's selfish of me to stay away like I have. It isn't fair."

She was silent and unmoving for a second or more, still clinging to him, her hair pushed up against his jaw and chin.

"I appreciate that," she said carefully. "It would mean a lot to me. But I don't want you to do anything you can't stand doing." She paused. "And that isn't why I'm crying."

"I can stand it as well as you," he said.

"I don't know if that's true," she told him. "If it is I'll be glad, but I honestly don't mind looking after him if I have to. It's awful but it really might be much worse for you."

"OK," he said. "We'll see if we can at least get you some relief now and then."

"That would be lovely," she said.

They stood for a time in his doorway, the air gradually clearing (his joint had gone out) and the radiator quietly hissing in the corner, holding each other as if the soft dancing music were about to commence. There's a fabulous woman in my arms, he thought. A beautiful woman. She's really special. So how did this happen? To someone like her? How can it possibly have come out this way, that she has no one but me? Who on earth is there to blame?

"Aren't you going to ask me why I am crying, then?"

"No," he said, with enormous restraint. "Cry away, anytime. We have ways of making you talk but we aren't ever going to use them."

He could feel her warmth through the thin cotton under his hands. She tightened her hold on him for a moment or two, pressing so firmly against him that it made him uneasy. Then she let go and stepped back, looking at him with a face that did indeed seem relieved and even happier. She reached out and took his collar in her fingers.

"You're a sweet man, brother," she said with an affection that made him want to start crying himself.

"I'm a fool," he told her.

"Maybe you are," she said, "but so am I. I wouldn't let it keep you up nights." She stepped closer and kissed him very gently on the cheek before turning to walk away. He half expected her to thank him—he found he wasn't ready for their exchange to end so soon, there were still things he had to tell her, he realized, so much he needed to say—but she went down the corridor to the stairs and then was gone.

Through the night Sutherland wonders if they'll ever move forward. If the drums will ever roll. He knows, Jenkins knows, everybody knows what the situation is; the forced march, the deployment of their regiment and the others over the hill, the orders overheard all make clear that when the time comes they'll be charging. Just as they have before. Charging a fixed line and dying. He understands as a matter of course that the forced march wasn't fast enough, the deployment not skillful enough, the orders not farsighted enough to save them from this duty. Maybe this time he'll be in the first wave, he'll be freed from the sordid pretense in the very first moment. Maybe this time he'll end up watching Shepperd die, or Vose. He isn't sure what he prefers, in fact doesn't know if he is capable of preference anymore, at least not with the choices he is given; he would prefer to be back on the bluff at Captain's island, jumping into the river with Jeremy and Nathan and Nathan's bridle bulldog Tim, but that gets him exactly nothing. He is simply a soldier, waiting for word. He will do what they ask.

Maybe I should leave, thought Jennie one evening, washing dishes in the kitchen, wondering where he was. This has all come on so fast. Or maybe we should talk. I can't stand the thought of missing him but I don't know how long I can go on this way.

It's been years, Phillip told himself, pacing his study from window to door. It's been years but I remember. To think, at my age, that I could sit with all that tension, sleepy from the strain of avoiding what's impossible to miss. I can't believe how much I want her. If it weren't for who she is—who *I* am—I would have kissed her long ago. At that I don't know what stops me. We're adults. We should be together. Who am I, who are we, to waste a blue moon like this?

She wasn't sure if it was true desire, mature desire, but it was something she'd never felt before. Not for Charlie or anybody. She'd had fun with her body and knew all about lust but this was different. How can it be real, she asked, when he doesn't feel the same? How could it have anything to do with a man who sees in you the daughter he maybe could have had? Sees the student, the fumbling apprentice? It can't be him so it must be Jennie; it must be this moment in your hard-to-figure life. He's Phillip the artist, Phillip of your mother's heart, even Phillip of the Yarrington house of New Chatham, New Hampshire, but he isn't your lover. He doesn't want to be. He hasn't the time.

Would she scream? he wondered. Would she cry? Is

she expecting me to touch her? Have I the faintest of ideas how she feels about me? It was as if an epic saga—the struggles of boy Phillie, exile journey and return—had come back to him as vengeance, a text he'd once known line-for-line but had frantically tried, with some success, to wipe clean away.

How could I have gone without for so long? he asked himself. This kind of love is in me too.

They kept their distance on the first floor and on the second closed their doors. They made cocoa and green tea. The last big blizzard of the season—though they didn't know it was—covered the house and the grounds once again with a blanket of endless and unforgiving white.

At night he comforted himself. He needed little beyond her presence. This too brought something back but instead of shame he felt sadness, instead of anxious he felt foolish, wiping gently with his tissue, his warm flesh cooling in the air.

Going by his bedroom very late on a Tuesday (looking for the book she might have left in the hall) she thought she heard him groan and at that moment she knew—she *knew*, like a hunter standing firm amidst the echoes of the shot—that she was more or less to blame.

She is comfortable inside, although so very much has changed. To her surprise it doesn't matter that she sees their every moment, their every act, whenever she chooses. After all it's my house too, she tells herself, but is sure that's not the reason for her lack of embarrassment. The way she is now, she knows, she isn't capable of minding. Her lost modesty causes no grief. It's just part of the package, is what her Papa would have said.

As she remembers that she wonders about Papa and her

sisters. Are they're somewhere like she's somewhere? I suppose I'd know it if they were, she thinks, and then, but maybe not. The idea of the three of them waiting together—in a house or in heaven or somewhere else, it doesn't matter—makes her jealous and desperate, eager to finish and move on. The possibility that there is no end to this existence, that she'll just live without living in her own house forever, is too horrible to worry about and so she doesn't. You lasted eighty-six years with no problems before, she reassures herself, you can pass the time now. You really don't know and you'll just have to wait. Nothing even to stop you from heading into town, if you want to, or to Fitchburg or beyond.

The man's body is a marvel. Of course she's seen a man before—in a whole life you couldn't avoid a few minor accidents of that kind—but never for long and never at such close range, in such excellent light. She wonders if her Papa was something like that (he was about the same size) and is particularly curious about whether he ever resembled the way the man looks as he waits by the toilet for half a minute or more after rising, trying to relax so he can empty his bladder. Of course he did, she tells herself, those are the mechanics. How do you think you were born? But it seems so large as the man stands there with his hands on his hips, so large and misshapen. And even now she's slightly shocked to think of Papa that way. And the mechanics have always been just a vague whisper anyway, like the mercy of Christ, nothing flesh and blood like that, that you could hold in your hand; she never really understood.

She senses that soon she will know even more.

Early one morning she watches the girl. So that's how its done, she thinks, feeling what once were her eyes grow very wide. I can hardly believe it. If I were still alive and kicking she wouldn't know I was here.

*　　*　　*

"Does it bother you," she asked, "that I'm the one who brought it up?"

"No," he said. He drew a shaky breath. "Does it bother you as much as it's bothering me that we're talking instead of doing?"

"Let's not then," she said, starting to rise to her feet, to open her arms.

"Jennie," he said. He found his own hand held in front of him. "You must remember I'm responsible."

"So am I," she told him, sitting again.

"You know what I'm saying. Your parents sent you here."

She smiled a smile that struck him as cold, remarkably so considering what she'd ventured not a minute before. "You should know better," she said. "They most certainly did not. And in any case they're aware that I fuck."

"Fucking college boys is not the same as fucking Uncle Phillip."

She shook her head, slowly, her expression unchanging. "Don't you want to?" she asked, with a pleading overtone that made his throat and chest ache.

His own strained smile was more bitter than cold. "My god, of course I do," he told her. "You haven't any idea. Didn't you hear what I just said? The last thing I want is to talk."

"But here we are talking."

"That's what happens sometimes."

Her proposal—"Let's go to bed now," a simpler and more irreducible suggestion than any he'd ever been party to before, that he could remember—still drove the beating of his heart. No woman had ever said that to him, not in words, maybe with hands or eyes or gestures or some roundabout way of coming to the point but not like that. He'd longed for it always without really knowing and now the center of his longing—the woman, if he were passionately honest, of his dreams—had come out with it that way. If she'd tried some other tactic (like Miriam that first time, gradually raising the bottom of her T-shirt as they lay on the bed playing Scrabble until he'd finally gotten the message, or longhaired Anne in high school sitting gently in his lap) they would probably be embracing right now. But her approach had been so open, so carefully direct, that he could not mislead himself. He was thoroughly aware of everything that was at stake.

"Look," she said. "I don't want to marry you. And I won't get pregnant." She stared at him and was suddenly self-conscious, for the first time, self-conscious and annoyed. "And no one will ever know, Phil. You do understand that, right? No one but you and me."

"We should think about it," he said. Weak as it was, it was all he had.

She sighed and leaned her chair against the wall. "I knew some people named Clark," she said. "They weren't married but they were both named Clark, it turned out. The odd thing was that with such a common name they could have claimed it was coincidence or something distant but they didn't. They spoke about it very freely. Their fathers were brothers only two years apart."

He watched her, struck dumb.

"Even in public he would stroke her thighs."

He started to reply but she'd brought the chair legs down and this time she did stand, to display herself before him. "I know you want me," she said, "I knew it before you said so. You make up your mind and we'll take it from there. In the meantime I can't do this anymore, so I'll see you later on."

"We should think about it, that's all," he repeated, with the smallest degree of conviction, but she had already left the room.

"Happy birthday, hon," said Bill. The blown-out candles gave their smoke to the still air of the dining room. Looking past the cake and the table she noticed the flower he'd laid down in front of the photograph on the sideboard, the one of her mother and her arm in arm, in the fine silver frame. The cake itself was done all in flowers, roses, overdone if anything; she recognized Esther's enthusiastic hand. They were pink and if she squinted she could almost pretend they were apple blossoms. Esther wouldn't have thought of that and Bill wouldn't know it mattered but it gave comfort to Jane that she could find them there. In the center HAPPY BIRTHDAY JANIE was perfectly nice but WE LOVE YOU was almost more than she could bear; she wanted to pick up a fork and scratch I KNOW into the icing below it. Your affection is the least of my worries, she said in silence, and turned to her father to see how he was.

He looked much as he always did. "Happy birthday, girlie," he grumbled when she caught his eye, his old grin barely shaping his lips before his gaze wandered off around the room. They looked together for a moment at the curtained window, beyond which she pictured the heavily falling snow.

"Do you want to have some cake now?" asked Bill.

"I'll cut it," she said, and reached for the slicer.

"Dad and I had such a nice time yesterday," he told her, "walking down to Schmidt's mailbox. I was thinking we could do it again soon, if you wanted. When the weather eases up."

She laughed and lifted a big piece onto a plate. "He

won't go with me," she said. "He only wants to go with you." A thumping caught her ear and she turned in her chair to see Pippin lying blissful with her snout tucked under the radiator, her tail striking the floor. The fur of her head and shoulders, Jane knew, would be too hot to touch.

"Maybe he'll like it if we all go together," said Bill. "Did you make a wish, darlin'?"

"I forgot."

He slapped the table. "Second chance, then," he said. "I was talking and distracted you. Do it on this one, it's only fair."

The second slice broke as she raised it from the platter but she made a wish anyway as she transferred it, piecemeal, to the plate, a fond wish for a setting—call it rather a reward—that she'd been dreaming of more and more often these days: the Garden of Eden simply filled with apple trees, not just the one (who needed knowledge?) but the many, the thousands, and the animals too in their innocent prime, lion cuddling the lamb, hawk preening the sparrow, and also Jane at the center before her corruption, Jane naked and peaceful, Jane naked and contented, Jane naked and alone.

Maybe they know I'm here, she tells herself, a little frightened. Maybe I disturb them or distract them, ever so, when I come in or go out, when I get too near. Am I somehow in the way? Maybe that's a problem, the one that's keeping them apart.

No matter, she thinks. In the end it won't matter. Nothing could hold it off for very long. Soon I won't have to choose between them. Soon we can all be together in the night.

*   *   *

Going to her room he found her sleeping and did not wake
her. It was easy to change his mind. Standing in the doorway
he embraced her youthful beauty and watched her lie there
and sleep, lie there and breathe, washed from top to bottom
in his affection and his need but still content to stand and
wait. She was naked despite the cold. Her breast was cradled in her hand.

Sutherland rises to a fiery dawn and thinks, this is the day.

Waking in the gentlest possible fashion, resting in the pale winter light, looking up at the blank space high on the wall that she has cherished, entreated, shyly worshipped all these months, that she has turned to for relief, she feels a weight and a softness in the center of her belly that she has never known before. If not hushed by the hour and the quiet of the house she would be silenced by pity and by awe. She has arrived somewhere new, she understands; the meter of her life has been altered, forever, and its season has been changed.

She hears him beside her. Without turning to look she settles back into sleep.

Part

II

The major sin is the sin of
being born.

—SAMUEL BECKETT

Sutherland dreams of the colonies.

As a boy he often wandered; now he dreams. Dreams that find him always, find him sleeping and awake, dreams of what he never had. For young Jackie the views were wide enough, the water clear enough, the marshes empty enough, but most of that has vanished and the soldier needs more. The dreams are what he feeds on. A hard and desperate situation.

He is never long alone now. He follows in his dreams a boy and a dog, no dog he's ever seen and no boy either but he knows them very well. As they run by the river and push through the reeds he chases after them with envy, with something close to ill will; he is their forebear, they his; he weeps to think they'll never meet. Their world is near, very near. He calls out to them and they turn but won't answer; he reaches for them but they quickly run away. He can watch if he is silent and accepts his condition, and their own and the land's, can stay if he respects his place and theirs, but this is far from easy for him. His dreams are like the brittle piece of pink South Seas coral he once held in his hands; he wants to hurl them to the ground, break them into a million pieces, but the fear of God prevents him. The dreams are his no more than the coral. At least this much he understands.

The boy comes to the palisade. Across the road there is a gate. Once it was guarded day and night but the natives are dying or sick or gone and those few that come to trade are almost always well behaved. The animals (most feared were the wolves and the bears) have been driven west and north. And there are so many more important things to be done. The boy has orders from his father to stay inside the palisade but he ignores them when he pleases. He spends far too much time away from his chores and knows a reckoning will come—the reverend's barbed eye is upon him—but cannot change his sinful habits. He is lucky: the teacher likes him. He is clever and learns well and when trouble comes the teacher intervenes.

He opens the gate and the dog pushes through. As it passes he thumps its flank and its tail wags with affection. But it does not speak; it is mostly silent now because he trained it to be. There are many who think very poorly of the dog—of any animal that eats without earning its keep, as his father would say—but as long as it leaves the chickens alone and the fish bones in the corn, and is quiet when it should be, no one bothers to complain.

Outside the fence there are several houses more and

he moves quickly past them, to avoid being noticed. It is the end of June. Walking out on Braintree street as he has so many times, moving down the rutted way, he squints at the sky, a vast plain of blue and white. He has a long way to go. When the weather is good they all compare it to England, as if that were the Lord's perfect country and the colony a spoiled copy, but in the winter they are grim; they behave as if the cold and the snow were invented just for them. Tired as he is of their talk of sweet England—go on back, he wants to tell them, you should never have come—he much prefers the warmer months. He would rather hear them pining for the fields of Lincolnshire than see them stride around all full of their resentment and forbearance. To him it is as if they are condemning his home. You chose to suffer this new world, he thinks, you chose to, and I sometimes wonder why.

He passes the little neck road on his right and Butler's hill on his left and then reaches the great neck. Often he follows it down to the river, to the oyster banks or the Indian camp, but this time he continues across. The dog rushes back and forth, chasing mice and butterflies. When it's hotter he'll go to the Dutch captain's bluff and swim the river and back, just for fun, but today he doesn't want to. Something stirs him to find a larger image of his world and he knows where he should be.

The tide is almost out and the swamp track close to dry. He crosses quickly to the island. He climbs its rise—not as high as many others but so much nearer what he's seeking—and stands with the dog looking off to the east. It is warmer than he thought, he is perspiring from his walk, and he strips off his shirt and feels the soft air cool his skin.

The trimount stands noble and tall across the water, no more than two miles away, its green-clad shoulders strong

as it shelters its town. He cherishes the sight while the dog
pants at his feet. Turning he sees the gentle rise behind him
and pictures the neat brown village (that he's so happy to be
free of) lying on the other side. To the south the mudflats,
cut by the river's channel, are spread dark and wide, and
across them he sees the southern creek wind the marshes to
meet the wider waterway, gleaming in the sun, backed by
the slopes of Roxbury. To the northeast the mound of Graves
landing is full-lit, its house and barns just showing through
the trees, and beyond it are the north creek and then the
broad Charlestown hills, standing back to either side the
way his sisters often stand behind his mother. Directly north
the land is rougher and he doesn't know it well. He has
never been there. He has never been to Charlestown either,
or to Graves, but his father took him once on a visit to Boston
so he knows the winding road and the narrow neck and the
town itself. He searches for the road but can't make it out,
which disappoints him. He wishes he could go to Boston
again, that he remembered it more clearly

This is his favorite place. The trimount and the people's common pasture beside it. In the channel between rising Barton's point and the Charlestown dock he sees the
ocean ships and their tall brittle masts, and feels the breeze
that fills their sails.

Why England? he asks. Who would want to be there?
He knows well when they first landed there was almost nothing for them but more is added every summer, they are working very fast. In the few years since they started they have
changed the town's name. They have opened the school.
There is talk of a bridge across the river, instead of the ferry,
and they will soon build larger wharves. And there are always more houses, longer roads, bigger flocks. They are raising this new England, he thinks, a fresh country of their own;

what failing makes them miss the old one? What error drives them to complain? He kicks the dog gently and the dog laughs back at him. This is my home, he thinks. My England. Perhaps I'll go elsewhere some day.

Out in the river he spies a small boat. In the back bay, by the neck, he thinks he sees another. He envies them fiercely. Out there, he asks the dog, how would you like to be out there? But the dog has only questions. I can't tell you, says the boy, I only know I want to go. We'll find a boat somewhere, you'll see.

He squints at the sun. Time to start walking back. His parents will be angry; he prepares himself to lie to them, a thing he hates to do. Kicking the dog until it rises to its feet he moves a thing down the path, never turning, never looking at his island, his outpost, his lonely glory. He knows he'll come another day.

What a beautiful place, Sutherland thinks as they leave him. What a lovely place it was.

As a boy the solider wandered. Now he marches. And dreams.

chapter

20

Willie Williams made tracks for the coffee machine. He knew he shouldn't think of it—if he followed doctor's orders he'd never have another cup—but on a day as long as this one there was room for an exception. He still had plenty of work to do. He hadn't slept well so he'd been tired to begin with and had been bent over or flat on his back, jammed under greasy metal, for hours and hours, and one little cup of coffee couldn't hurt. Or it couldn't hurt much. Better than nodding off over a running engine and packing it in right then and there. At least he didn't smoke anymore.

The dark green Volvo was almost ready. Soon he'd move it out and pull the Subaru in. A lot of his friends, particularly the older ones, asked if he minded working on so many imports, as if all the time he'd spent learning Chevies

and Fords in his youth had been some kind of religious experience. Hell no, he told them, I'm just glad of the chance
to take the customer's money. Someone shows up with a
Piper Cub I'll try to fix that too. It wasn't that he didn't care
for cars, or couldn't tell one from another; he cared as much
as he did about anything and he noticed every difference.
He wished he could go to a mechanic's convention and
spend three or four days talking nothing but detail. (There
was no one in New Chatham with the first idea about engi-
neering, not any real idea.) But the way he looked at it the
customers paid him because they liked their cars; if they
couldn't find cars they liked they might not buy any and if
he couldn't fix the cars they bought they'd go on to someone
else. Either way he'd be shit out of luck. He was just grateful, in the end, for the feeling of starting one after he'd
worked on it, that had been towed in stone dead, and hearing
it catch and roar. It didn't much matter whether the roar was
American, German, or Japanese. It made him happy just
the same.

He took a hot, delicious sip and heard a second-story
window open, first the sash and then the storm, in his gabled
house next door. His wife's gray head poked out. He held
the coffee where she couldn't see.

"Can you go get Tip at Emma's after you close tonight?" called Susan in her too-loud outdoor voice. She was
wearing that black sweatshirt, the one that made her look
like *Mission Impossible*, and something very private tightened his lips and held them together. He nodded without
speaking, knowing she'd understand, and she drew herself
in and pulled the storm window down.

He shook his head, thinking of Tiffany. No one ever
used her right name these days. "Tiffany Rose," he said
aloud. After three healthy boys he'd badly wanted a girl and

he'd got his wish okay, but try as he might he hadn't been able to get her to act like one. She was pretty and shapely enough—in fact he was starting to get a little bothered about the boys who kept calling—and pleasant in a womanly way, and she wore skirts and dresses now and then instead of jeans, but there was something about her. She had never been girlish and now she just wasn't feminine. Not as he saw it anyway. She was so sure of herself, so ready to go any-where or do anything, so independent. At least she's capa-ble, he thought, don't have to worry about her, and then: I guess I taught her that. Maybe it's part my fault. She sure doesn't sit and wait for help like the ones I always knew, which has to be a good thing. Still he felt bad, as he often did, remembering the shy little girl who'd needed her daddy about a dozen times a day and been almost afraid to ask, the one who'd lasted for a year or two somewhere between babyhood and the first grade.

But back to the Volvo—he was wasting working time. All he had to do was get the new belt on and set the specs. He balanced the coffee on the fender as he reached in. Be sure to ask Phil, he reminded himself, what the hell hap-pened. Who'd been driving it? The damn thing had been in just after the new year and here it was back already, needing another tune and various niggling adjustments. It sure wasn't Willie's fault. Someone must have screwed it up. Cer-tainly Phil wouldn't blame him, he knew that, they'd always had a good relationship. His job was to make the car right. It was way overdue for the junk heap already—one hundred and forty-seven thousand miles—and he'd keep it moving another hundred if asked to. The man had the money to buy a new Volvo from that crook Sammy Krisch and his crew of goons but he liked the one he had, Willie could see that with one eye closed, and would spend to keep it going.

When he went to start the engine his elbow caught the coffee cup and knocked it to the floor. "God damn," he told the radiator. He looked over at the pot and saw just enough left for another cup. If you go and get it now, he thought, you'll beat Davey to it. He's due back any minute. But he found he would rather keep working on the car. Maybe later, he told himself, maybe in a little while.

It was a very good relationship. He considered Phil a friend, not just a client. That morning around half-past nine they'd had a long talk. Willie had a greeting after turning around in his old swivel chair to see the battered Volvo coming. "Hey, Phil," he'd called a second time, realizing he wouldn't have been heard the first, jumping up to hold the door open though the cold came rushing in. "I haven't seen your sad butt in weeks."

"Not so sad, Willie," Phil had said.

"That's nice. Anything I should know?"

Phil had smiled. "I doubt it," he'd said. Then, "Did I ever tell you you're the only one who calls me Phil?"

"Is that right? What do the rest of them call you?"

"Phillip, every one. And I had nicknames as a child."

"What do the women call you?"

"Hey you."

They'd laughed together.

"Names matter more than you think," Willie had said, returning to his chair. "Take mine."

A personal favorite."

He'd laughed again. "I know," he'd said. "Willie Williams out of Williamstown, Mass. What a joke, huh? No one can believe it. But what's the big deal really? My folks named me before we moved there, and there's lots of Williamses, and William sure is a common name. And it sounds fine when you say it. Bill Williams would be a whole lot sillier, it seems to me."

"As I say, I like your name," the other had told him, settling down on the edge of the desk, which wasn't like him. He usually stayed just a minute or three.

"Say, you probably know about this. Isn't there a writer named William Williams?"

"I imagine there've been several. But yes, there was one well-known one."

"Is he dead? What'd he write?"

"He died about thirty years ago. He wrote wonderful poetry, also stories and essays. He was a doctor, too."

"Pretty good namesake then."

"Yes."

They'd stared at each other, or rather at each other's middles, almost out of things to say.

"This one time," Willie had begun, breaking the silence and warming up quickly, "I went over to Bennington with this buddy of mine to see a girl he knew there, Lord knows how he met her. He was sure he was going to get lucky and why I went too I don't know—nothing worse than riding home in a car with a guy that's just had some and you're about ready to bust it's been so long—but maybe I had hopes of finding action myself. As it happens I didn't. Not that time." He'd paused, remembering the girl he'd met on their next trip, the one with the sweet hips and long hair and modern ideas, and then brought himself out of it to find his customer neither impatient nor annoyed but looking instead like the cat that ate the canary.

"Anyway," he'd gone on, a bit confused by that strange and happy grin, "you had to sign in at this dinky little gatehouse to get into the place. I gave my own name and address—why not?—and then my buddy put down 'Jose

Valdivielso, Washington, D.C.' Valdivielso played short for the Senators at the time; believe Stephen had an autographed Senators ball for some reason, maybe an uncle there. I guess he was afraid to give his real name in case he and the girl got in trouble. So we left the guardhouse and went walking down the drive, and before I knew it this cranky old geezer was coming after us and shouting 'All right, which one of you clowns signed in as Willie Williams from Williamstown?' "

Phil had loved the story, laughing loud and long. Maybe longer than he should have. It was a good story and Willie had been glad to tell it but when they'd finished he'd felt a little antsy and looked up at the clock.

"Speaking of ballplayers and your name, how about Billy Williams?"

"That's right. Cubs man. I think there was another one too, I checked it at the library once."

After that they'd sat without words until Willie had risen to his feet. "So what's wrong with old Ingrid, Phil?" he'd asked. And they'd talked about the car.

It isn't just the long day of hard work, he thought seven and a half hours later, as he finished with the Volvo—deciding also to say something about the wear on the clutch—and dropped the dented hood down. It's that damn talk we had. There was something about it. Something peculiar. People are always calling him peculiar but I never agreed; now I see it maybe a little. Oh hell, what the hell, there's a first time for everything but whatever they say he's a pretty nice guy. And pays cash the same day.

He stood back from the bumper, hands on his hips, looking at the faded green paint and listening to the sound of Davey's rattletrap coming into the lot, and then his son's voice and Tip's above the slamming of the doors. He must have gone and picked her up on the way back from Loveman's, he thought, how did he know to do it? Maybe they planned it that way last night, to save their parents trouble. They were both so grown-up now. Willie was sorry he wouldn't get to go himself, later on, and see her coming down the Corbetts' footlit walk in the dark. He nodded. "God I love that girl," he said.

What becomes of the orchards? she asked herself. What becomes of them without me? Helen Rosenfeld was speaking
but it was hard to pay attention. Fortunately Helen rarely
noticed when your thoughts wandered, she just went on talking. She was telling about some battle over money at Keeler
State College, where she taught, not knowing how preoccupied her audience was. Tom had spent Saturday night in the
hospital, Bill had fallen and badly sprained his ankle the
day before yesterday—just missing, by not much more than
a foot, getting his head crushed by a tractor wheel—and this
morning Jane herself had felt exhausted and depleted despite nine hours of sleep, almost unable to get out of bed for
the first time in years. All the thoughts she'd been having
for the past few months about age and mortality, about the

dead ends she felt their lives had slowly come to, were rushing back now with greater energy, doing their best to prevent
her from attending to anything else.

To her comfort the distress wasn't wholly unrelieved.
There was much she had learned to accept, she found,
though not with good grace. Her disappointment for her
brother—that he'd accomplished so little—was constant
and deep but fairly easy to contain, to keep quiet inside,
because it wasn't her worry in the end and she knew it. He
loved her and helped her and he owed her nothing else. And
while it made her sad every day that there were no other
grandchildren, that of the three of them only Betty had managed a family, she also knew that Betty's were enough. That
important task was taken care of. But what disturbed her
much more than anything else was the thought of all the
apple trees, alone and friendless, after she was gone. Subdi-
vided for new houses, cut down for cabinet wood. They're
not babies, she told herself, or even lost kittens, they're only
fruit trees, and when you die they won't feel pain. But still
she felt a certain horror.

"Something wrong, Jane?" asked Helen.

"A little," Jane lied. "I'm slightly envious, that's all.
Wondering where I'd be now if I'd gone into teaching."

Helen laughed. "You might be at Keeler State, honey,
so please do count your blessings."

"It isn't all bad."

"Of course not." Helen shook her head. "I've had a
wonderful career. And we came to New Hampshire to get
away from the city so I can't blame old Keeler for giving me
a job, no matter how feeble it is. But the point is that I'm the
one who envies you."

Jane felt herself smiling, though it wasn't sincere. "I do
love my work," she said.

"We all see that," said Helen. "I don't know anyone who doesn't want to be in your shoes at times."

"It's a burden, too," Jane told her, looking around the bright modern kitchen with its European devices, so different from the one her own mother had made, and feeling herself threaten to drift away entirely. "It's the mission of my life."

"I had the strangest kind of dream last night," he said. "So much clearer than most."

She laid her head on his chest.

"You don't dream much, do you?" she asked.

"I used to," he told her. "A long time ago. But for the last twenty years it's every few months at best."

"You dream on paper."

He sighed. "I often wonder if that's so."

They lay in silence for a while and she listened to his heart and to his breathing with one ear and to the morning with the other. She felt, lying with him in these very early hours, like the guardian of the world's most wondrous treasure. He would never understand it, how great a gift he gave. She knew she should let him go to his work, that she would have him again tomorrow, but her greed overwhelmed her and she held him more tightly, trying to become a part of him and of the bed, willing him to stay forever.

"I dreamed of a mountain. Of a high three-peaked hill. On the shore of a broad but very calm reach of water. It was so still as I watched it, Jennie, so clear and so real. I swear I smelled the mud, even, and heard the birds cry."

"Was it China?" she asked.

He shook his head no. "Somewhere closer to home."

*   *   *

She pauses by her father's blue armchair. After so many trips around the house, searching, more than she can count, she thinks she knows of every single thing her cousin kept. It surprises her how well he chose; what's in the house she's glad to have them use and what she doesn't want them touching is either vanished or up over the garage, out of reach. He seemed to know which was which. Thinking this makes her fearful for a moment, that he in some way saw her coming—that he knows she's there now!—but she quickly gets beyond it. Give him credit, she reflects, he's just decent and respectful. Rugs and tables are one thing, books and paintings are another. He's just sensible, that's all.

Looking at the chair brings many memories that please her. Papa reading his novels; Margaret entertaining Harry Munsett, around the time he first proposed to her; Alice playing happily with her dolls underneath, peering out with that lovely sunny smile. But the brightest, the most nourishing image is also the most recent: Kate sitting quiet with the cat in her lap, knitting or looking through a magazine or just thinking, enjoying the afternoon sun. Kate who was so good to her. Who asked so little, who did so much that was unpleasant. Even now (without a body, freed forever from such ugliness) she is embarrassed to think of what she put her helper through. She always felt ashamed of what wasn't her fault, of all that came with being old, but Kate reassured her. "I love you," she would say. "I don't mind this one bit." And later, after she'd put Bertha into a fresh flower-print dress and everything was nice again: "There's nothing to be done except be sorry you have to go through this. It's just what happens at your age, it's not a failing on your part. You took care of your family all your life, now I'm taking care of you, and I'm very glad to do it." For all her devotion to her Papa, for all her closeness to her sisters— she knew at times she'd been unsure if they were one woman or three—Bertha had never cared for anyone so much as she did for Kate at those moments, never adored anyone so fiercely. Lying in bed later on in the evening, trying to fall asleep, she often shuddered to think of what her old age might have been without the fortune of the girl.

Kate left her just a week before she died. She is miserable recalling this and would cry if it were possible. No one knew she was as sick as she was, as close to the end, not even the doctor, and Kate's mother needed help. There was nothing to be done.

"I hate to go," said Kate.

"Don't be silly," Bertha told her. "Don't be absurd, young woman. You belong with your mother."

"Only until she's better. Then I'll come right back to you."

But she did know, thinks Bertha, she knew it all without knowing. She must have known, must have; why else would she take that photograph? She said she wanted it by her bed so she could say good night to me, she said Look at this wall! when she lifted the picture off and saw the clean square behind it, I'll have to scrub it when I get back, but I didn't believe a word of it. Now that I think it through I knew for sure it was goodbye. She took that picture because she understood perfectly well that I'd be gone before she got back, that she would never see me again. And she wanted my permission. I remember I nodded—she held it up and I nodded, didn't say a word. I loved that picture dearly, it broke my heart to see it go, but I wanted her to have it. I wanted her to know how much more I loved her. More than anything in my life.

She waits by the chair and remembers the photograph, her Papa's proud expression and his arms spread wide around them, sitting pretty for the camera as he stood so strong behind.

For a moment as she sees it she can also see Kate, with her curly yellow hair, cross-legged and laughing at their feet. She bears the hard weight of knowing that it was the only thing her young companion took, that everything else went to those who came after, that wherever she is now Kate was robbed of the pleasure of having all she should rightfully have owned. She hopes again (foolish though it aeems) that she's wrong, that she's mistaken, that if she looks just one more time she'll find hidden somewhere in the house a picture of Kate, an object that she owned or a lock of her hair, she'll have revealed to her what has become of her friend. She knows these things won't happen but keeps on hoping anyway.

"I don't suppose you're back in touch with that man," said Helen. "From the summer before last."

Jane flinched, though she tried not to. "No," she said.

"I'm sorry to bring it up. I know I really shouldn't have. I've always wanted him to come to his senses, that's all, and wishful thinking makes me ask. Forgive me for intruding."

Jane reached out to touch the other's hand. "It's all right, I don't mind," she said. "I really don't. I think you're sweet to care. But you should know, he did come to his senses. That's exactly the problem."

"I don't understand."

"I'm not for him," said Jane, taking up the pot to pour another cup of coffee. "I don't think anyone is."

"Can I ask about a book?"

"What do you mean?"

"Excuse me. About one of your books?"

While she waited she sat on the edge of the bed and

almost reached for this thigh, then crawled onto the mattress and lay beside him, not touching him at all.

"You can ask," he said at last.

"You won't mind?"

"I won't mind."

"In *Paradise*," she asked, "when Rachel meets the broker on the street—what is she talking about?"

"Infatuation, as I recall it. Love and marriage. And also sex."

"I know that. I just reread it last month. But isn't it sort of unfocused? What is she actually saying? What's her point?"

He sat up and confronted her, his hands on the bed behind him, then turned away. "I have some advice," he said. "When you're in the park, and you come up on someone painting? Be sure to look at what she's chosen to paint, rather than her execution."

She was silent until he faced her.

"The eye is all," he said.

With that he got up and went to the closet for his robe. She sat up herself then and crossed her legs, watching him as he tied the sash and searched for his slippers, the cool air raising goose bumps on her naked flesh. On his way out the door he stopped and looked at her again; his hand was on the doorframe and a faint beard darkened his cheeks and his chin.

"What really brought you here?" he asked.

It was her turn to look away.

"I'm not sure," she said. "Everything has changed so much."

He watched her, unspeaking.

"Doesn't it happen to you?" she asked. "You work things through, you consider every motive, you're as certain as could be and you start on your way. But then something happens. It fades—it fades with time. You get confused. Days pass, weeks pass, and it's all gone somehow. Gone away."

He watched for moments more. "I don't think so," he said.

As her hands went out toward him she felt the blush but didn't care. There was only the very little that mattered to her, really, but it mattered very much.

"Don't leave," she told him. "Stay here with me now. Please don't leave."

And then tried hard to read his smile.

It is a difficult position. There must be many others like her who are in it, maybe hundreds, maybe thousands, spread out across the globe, all with their own burdens, their own complications, but just as unprepared as she. She has no help at all, she's on her own as never before, but she senses that her quandary is also part of her purpose. If it weren't a puzzle she wouldn't be there. There is a test for her to pass. Somehow her decision—her final decision, to which she can hardly dream of coming—is very important, is everything. Someone wants you, she thinks from time to time, to render judgment on these people. That's what this thing is all about.

But at other times she doubts it. Not that the problem they present is all tied up with her presence—this she's come to accept—but that she is required, in the end, to absolve or to condemn them. She was never the sort of person who arrived at firm conclusions about other people's business and she hasn't become that now. If that's what they want they should have chosen someone else, she thinks. Even my Alice would be better than me.

What they are doing is wrong but still she loves them. She can't help it. They fill her with affection. There is much she doesn't like, doesn't approve of, but she feels that they are hers in some way, peculiar as that is, that they belong to her, members of her family, foundlings in her charge. She came to them but in the larger sense they came to her, to be watched over, to be—if she dares think it—protected by her, and she has full responsibility. I was never a mother, she thinks, never even came close, but they could be my own children. That's just exactly how I feel.

What they are doing is wrong but the unseen woman loves them. She finds she loves them just the same.

As she moved down Helen's driveway—turning to wave and smile and see the other smile in return, appreciation rising as she remembered how kind her friend had always been—she thought again of her orchards. The talk of Phillip had distracted her but it was now appropriate, she urged herself, to consider what really mattered. Tom probably hadn't very much time left, Bill could have been killed the other day, and who knew what might happen to her. Who knew, even, if she might wake and change her mind one morning, give it all up, sell off half a dozen heirlooms and start out for California or Australia or France. If she had no descendants she had a legacy, the trees, and it was time to make arrangements so that she could be free. For them to disappear once she wasn't there to tend them would be loss beyond loss; for them to go on living, bearing fruit while she slumbered, would be the meaning of her effort, the destination of her journey. If nothing else.

Jane hurried quickly to her car and started it at once, the sooner to see them again, and to begin making plans.

She rose and fell and rose with a rhythm all her own, to which he was a grateful party. She breathed steadily and deep. She pinned his arms to the bed.

The Wound-Dresser

Bearing the bandages, water and sponge,
Straight and swift to my wounded I go,
Where they lie on the ground after the battle brought in.
Where their priceless blood reddens the grass the ground,
Or to the rows of the hospital tent, or under the roof'd
      hospital,
To the long rows of cots up and down each side I return,
To each and all one after another I draw near, not one do
      I miss
An attendant follows holding a tray, he carries a refuse pail,
Soon to be fill'd with clotted rags and blood, emptied, and
      fill'd again.

I onward go, I stop,
With hinged knees and steady hands to dress wounds,
I am firm with each, the pangs are sharp yet unavoidable,
One turns to me with appealing eyes—poor boy! I never
    knew you,
Yet I think I could not refuse this moment to die for you, if
    that would save you.

On, on I go, (open doors of time! open hospital doors!)
The crush'd head I dress, (poor crazed hand tear not the
    bandage away,)
The neck of the cavalry-man with the bullet through and
    through I examine,
Hard the breathing rattles, quite glazed already the eye, yet
    life struggles hard,
(Come sweet death! be persuaded O beautiful death!
In Mercy come quickly.)

From the stump of the arm, the amputated hand,
I undo the clotted lint, remove the slough, wash off the mat-
    ter and blood,
Back on his pillow the soldier bends with curv'd neck and
    side falling head,
His eyes are closed, his face is pale, he dares not look on
    the bloody stump,
And had not yet look'd on it.

I dress a wound in the side, deep, deep,
But a day or two more, for see the frame all wasted and
    sinking,
And the yellow-blue countenance see.

I dress the perforated shoulder, the foot with the bullet-
    wound,
Cleanse the one with a gnawing and putrid gangrene, so
    sickening, so offensive,
While the attendant stands behind aside me holding the tray
    and pail.

I am faithful, I do not give out,
The fractur'd thigh, the knee, the wound in the abdomen,
These and more I dress with impassive hand, (yet deep in
    my breast a fire, a burning flame.)

Thus in silence in dreams' projections,
Returning, resuming, I thread my way through the hospitals,
The hurt and wounded I pacify with soothing hand,
I sit by the restless all the dark night, some are so young,
Some suffer so much, I recall the experience sweet and sad,
(Many a soldier's loving arms about this neck have cross'd
    and rested,
Many a solider's kiss dwells on these bearded lips.)

—Walt Whitman

He wakes, his mind clears (he sees his condition, he thinks of Jennie), he sobs in desperation.

Now he's ready to decide.

chapter

24

"Come on, Dad," he coaxed. "Don't want to let me get ahead." The stiffness in his ankle slowed him up just a bit but not as much as he'd feared. So long as they kept to the center of the drive, between the ruts, where the ground was hard and level, he could move along just fine. He knew this was also much better for his father, who was easily distracted or held up by small obstructions, and he found it made the walk a little more like a trip somewhere, an outing with a purpose, although of course it had none beyond being something to do.

His father stopped and looked at him. It was a look he was getting to know very well. At first he'd felt demanded by it, or scolded—it had a lot in common with the way the man had always stared at him, before, when he'd done something

wrong—but he'd come to understand it as a request or even
a plea from someone who'd always been too proud to ask for
help and was now, in any case, mostly beyond words. Tom
wanted him to go back and stay close and he was happy to
oblige. He hurried up the slope, swinging the bad leg a little
more quickly than he should have and bringing it down a
little too hard, feeling some small pain but ignoring it as best
he could, smiling all the while to carry reassurance with
him.

"Here I come, Dad," he said. "Here comes ol' Stumpy.
You hold on half a sec or two." He reached the motionless
figure and took his arm and they started down the drive
again together, a bit more slowly than they might have but
at least, thought Bill, we're moving steadily on, which is the
most important thing.

By God this is fun, he exclaimed to himself, though he
wanted to say it out loud. What had he been thinking all that
time? He should have done more and he would have done
more if he'd had any idea of what was in it. Janie believed I
couldn't take it, he remembered—*I* believed I couldn't take
it—and look at me today: I'm doing so great I'm like the
perfect loving son. His father went outside nearly every day
now, which he rarely had before, and was usually relaxed
and contented around the house, sitting at ease in one chair
or another, even drinking less whiskey (Jane had reluctantly
admitted) although he still needed a glass most evenings.
They were both of them greatly changed.

And it wasn't just a matter of trying harder, that
seemed clear. Bill knew he'd learned a lot in the last month,
about being strong and generous, about facing your fears; it
was fair enough to say he'd done some serious growing up.
His duty, or his responsibility—call it what you want, he'd
not seen any alternatives—had been so plain after that

strange conversation with his sister, the one in which she'd broken down, so huge and unavoidable, that he couldn't have shirked it any longer if he'd tried. But the simple truth was that the joy he'd discovered in taking care of his dad, the thrill it gave him, came not just from doing the right thing but from the pleasure it brought Tom. Who would have imagined that after a lifetime of independence, of stern distance, it would mean so much to the man to have his only son looking after him now, in his old age and his weakness? Not Bill, that was for sure. Never in a million years.

Even hurting his ankle had increased his understanding. For one thing, the close call with the tractor—"Sweetheart, you could have been *killed*," Jane had said, her voice gone all wavy, holding him as Danny ran back to see if he was okay, the untended machine perched dangerously on the lip of the hollow behind the shed, coughing smoke from its exhaust—had put everything in a different light; it was obvious but she was right, he could have, and more to the point who knew how long his father had left? No use in pining after Dad later on, when he'd passed—this was his chance right now to show his love, to put his effort in. And for another, his disablement and forced inactivity had clued him in to what the old man was going through. Watching Janie give directions to the hands as they stood in a circle, some regulars and a couple of extras she'd put on to get by, he'd felt at first very angry and then very surprised. So this was what his father had to suffer every day! His own place, for God's sake, and now no one would let him touch it, and even if they did he couldn't do a damn thing. That train of thought had been sobering and scary and then filled him with a deep sympathy for his parent, a thorough, mature concern, of a kind he'd had just flashes of when younger and certainly hadn't felt at all since Tom had started acting strange.

Well here we are, he thought, two crips, as they neared the driveway's end and the asphalted road. One looking after the other. I'm temporary, he's permanent, but we're all permanent in the long run aren't we? What if that wheel had gone over my shin? Then maybe he'd be able to walk down this drive and I wouldn't. I'd be sitting up there in the house in one of those damn chairs, with half a leg in my pants.

It was very peculiar to be thinking this way but so much in him was altered that he was well beyond fighting it. And in fact it was an adventure. Nice to know that he could, after all this time, explore fresh territory—who knew what it might lead to? Who knew what he might try? There was a word that people said a lot these days, very popular with longhairs, that he'd always disliked but now felt a certain claim to. *Liberated*, that's what he was. In the past he'd complained about it being used that way—"My dad liberated Italy," he'd explained more than once, "and that's the only thing it means"—but now, as in so many ways, he had different ideas. You're just happy, he told himself. For the first time since forever. And who the hell knows why?

The only bug in the works was his worry for Jane. She'd been right in what she'd said; it wasn't life with the old man that had been making her cry. He'd relieved her of so much and she was crying just the same. Not in his presence (probably wouldn't again) but he knew that she was. He also knew what had begun it (that Philip jerk, of course) but it had widened out from that, taking over her whole life, and he sometimes despaired of ever seeing things improve. Plus he felt guilty about Tom's clear preference for him. No one needs her now, he'd reflected one evening, looking up from his paperback to see her playing another solitaire as their father nodded at the mantel, the dog snoring at his feet. Not Daddy. Not even you. What exactly has she got left?

Although unable to answer he'd found the question thought-provoking. He'd been surprised by his own confusion and his concern had led not, as it usually did, to some attempt to cheer his sister, but to the guess that there was more there—maybe much more—than he would ever really know.

"Let's go, Dad," he said as they pulled up short at the road's crumbled shoulder. "Your choice—which way're we headin'? Left or right? North or south?"

Looking for evidence. Searching for clues. That's what she was doing. She turned the flat rectangles over in her hands, then turned them over again. It wasn't possible that something so special, so different—so separate, so intimate, so old, so common, so engaging, so deliberate, so rare—could be devoid of meaning for her. She had been led to that stale sealed attic (by Philip or herself or by some luck or fate or whisper) for a reason, she suspected. She cared too much for it not to be so. She loved the shoebox fiercely, almost as much as she loved Phillip, and it was full of pictures, full of words, which simply had to form a message. It was there somewhere, she was certain, a prize she was obliged—obligated—to find, and failure hadn't stopped her trying.

She was hypnotized by the postcards, she knew, perhaps even obsessed. At times she wanted to hug them, to kiss them, to bring them to his bed. Almost as if they were a part of his anatomy. But so far she hadn't told him. Beyond the shame she felt over her furtive petty theft (for she knew it was that) she wasn't sure what he would do. He'd lived in chosen ignorance—productive, if not happy—for so long, and the closed and peaceful attic was so important to him as a symbol, an expression even of his tenets; what would he say when he found it disturbed? She sometimes felt like a grave robber. That's what I would be to him, she thought, if he knew, picturing his sad face, eyes dark and skin light. He buried the Yarringtons there.

She looked again for an unwritten card, although she knew she wouldn't find one. She had the most powerful impulse to send a greeting to her sister but she didn't want a fresh one, from outside the box. She wanted one of these. On the other hand, even if there had been a blank, to remove it from the rest and mail it halfway across the country would surely have been an offensive act. Mostly she was glad she didn't have to make the choice. She imagined picking one of them out—the correct one, whichever that might be—and taking it to her sister, silently holding it up, first the front and then the writing, to allow the other to glean whatever sense had been waiting there for sixty or ninety years before tucking it away and returning to New England without a word of her own, content to have transmitted what she'd been asked to convey. It seemed this might be the point after all. But if so she had a problem: how was she to choose it if it wasn't meant for her? If she wasn't, by definition, capable of understanding? She sat and puzzled in frustration, feeling beset and almost foolish, reading and rereading the familiar ancient words

It was wonderful—it was beautiful—to have these hours safe from Phillip. And he safe from her. She didn't want him to see the postcards and she knew he wouldn't, he absolutely wouldn't, if she chose the right moment to spread them out on her bed. He would no more dream of interrupting her time than of setting fire to his forest. And she'd had the good fortune to inherit from him this discipline, by

which he too now benefited, long before they'd become lovers. She hadn't once had the urge to go to him when he was
working, except faintly a few times at the very beginning,
after that first night, because before they'd ever embraced
she'd learned respect for working hours.

She was proud that her solitude wasn't wasted, no more
than their closeness. She could have both and know the difference. She was getting something done, yes, in spite of all
her passion for him, and that was very good, but even better
it made her passion that much deeper. When the working
day was over and she went to seek him out she felt so
strongly about him that she could hardly even see. To know
that you would not, under any circumstances, be touched
until five o'clock—to know that loneliness, desire, curiosity,
fear would have to wait until then, or be addressed not by
contact but by some other means—was a marvelous thing.
It made her tremble as she filled her pages. He was only
yards away but he might have been, or she might have been,
in another state, another country, some odd and far-off astral
plane. To have a thing of great value that was unaffected,
undistorted, by their attachment to each other, that she
could reach for and rely on—that was sweet. That was
lovely. Almost better than his heartbeat. It intensified her
joy.

She stared at a fading picture of a grove in California,
a lush grove of lemon trees heavy with fruit, and thought of
her sister. They had walked in such groves from time to
time. She gathered the cards up into the box and turned
again to her desk.

He glanced at the sky. Time to start walking back. "Getting
cold, Dad?" he asked. He felt the old man's grip tighten on

his arm. Still a lot of strength in that right hand, he thought. It used to be ungodly strong. He smiled at the memory and looked up to see his father smiling too.

March 3

Dearest Mother,

Of course I am! Of course I'm worried about Emmy. How could I not be? But there's so little I can do.

Although you don't actually say it I feel almost accused, by your letter, of being unconcerned. You know that nothing could be further from the truth. Maybe I don't see her problems just the way you do, maybe I understand a little better what it's like to be young—I know, Mother, that's cheap, but in this case it's germane—maybe this man doesn't strike me as quite the threat you and Dad consider him to be. I do give you lots of credit for being fair, open-minded parents, believe me, and the fact that you're worried is more than enough to bother me too. You've met him, I haven't, you've talked to Em, I haven't, and I trust your judgment absolutely. If you weren't upset about the situation—just on account of its basic facts—I'd be worried about *you*. But she's strong, you know. I can't think of anyone stronger. She's fully capable of surviving her own mistakes and is entitled to make them.

And in any case there's no way for me to help. Can you imagine what would happen if I called her up and said, "The folks think Benny's a creep and won't get a divorce, so don't move in

with him?" Do you really think what's needed is
for me to alienate her? If I phoned on any pretext
now she'd know who put me up to it.

From what you say she hasn't really decided
yet. Try to be patient—maybe she won't give up
her apartment right away. And if she does she can
always find another later on, when she gets fed up
with the guy. This isn't marriage, remember; if it
were I would be on a train right this instant. But
people our age move in together all the time. It
doesn't always mean what you and Daddy think
it does.

Maybe he'll even turn out to be okay.

Thanks for asking about Phillip. He's fine
and hard at work. I am too—it's very nice. The
winter shows signs of ending at last and I'm
dreaming of the spring. I'm sure it's going to be
like nothing I ever imagined. I don't know how
long I'll be here but New Chatham owns my heart.
If I can adore it this much in the snow and the ice,
the sun and birds and flowers may be more than I
can stand.

When I was a girl I ran to you with everything right away, Mother; good, bad, thrilling,
frightening, whatever moved me I had to tell you.
Even at college I called you every third day. It
may make you sad not to speak with me now but
you should know that I miss you all the more for
it, that you're a part of every single thing that happens to me. I run to you ever minute, every hour—
just inside of me, that's all.

Don't worry about my sister. I won't say she
knows what she's doing—she doesn't, Amy

doesn't, I certainly don't, nor does Dad, it's only you, Mom—but she can look after herself. Really. She's a star. It will be all right, you'll see.

Kiss me in your dreams. It won't be long before we meet.

Your daughter

J.

chapter

25

They are gathering the corpses. Every so often they find a
live one. Had it rained in the night there might be many
more but thirst has finished the work, mostly, of the shells
and musket balls. Soon he will have to stand up and help.
He wants to stand and help. He has another minor wound
(inflicted by an artillery lieutenant from Bangor, of all people, charging crazily around with his saber in the air) and
on account of both this and his veteran status—he is longest
in the regiment now, he and the colonel—they have left him
to sit with his coffee. But it is important for him to be part
of it. He is so wildly lucky to have survived again, so much
more sensible of his luck than he was yesterday, that he
feels an obligation. To leave a single body (a single blown-
off hand, a single boot, a single kerchief) lying out there in

the mire would be the same as leaving himself. His chest aches as he imagines it. He drains the last of the coffee and then stirs his flesh to rise.

Within his eyes there is a fury. He had thought himself beyond it but on this morning the result is so ludicrously bad that he is unable to comprehend. Even after all he's seen. How could so many experienced men get shot up so badly? So many men who knew better? What on earth made them do as they were told? There is something in you, he has discovered, that wants to have faith, that wants fiercely to trust your leaders; no matter what the evidence you long to believe in them as capable and wise. But that was the last time for Jack Sutherland, he promises himself as he carries a fat bearded soldier, with two others, to the end of a row laid out beside the remnants of a fence. That was the last time. If he hasn't the courage to run far away he can at least protect himself. Martha deserves that much from him. His good fortune so far he tears to tiny pieces and throws to the wind, as a proof of his commitment. Thank You, Lord Jesus, for sparing me, he prays. From this minute on I will take my own care and You can give Your grace to others. I've had more than I deserve. He is not in the habit of talking to the Lord but here he is standing in a field of guts and blood, surrounded by dead men, picturing his wife in their home on Franklin street, and he feels sufficiently moved.

"I count myself afraid," his father had written one midnight long ago, "to make myself known to the Creator, because my imperfections are so great that I doubt any good for me can come from His attentions. But then I recall that this is His concern, not mine."

He is thinking of his wife because she wrote him a letter. He is thinking of his father's diary because in the letter she referred to it. He was fearful or bringing the diary with him, lest it be lost or destroyed and so withheld from his descendants, but has regretted this decision many times (though he knows it by heart) and now regrets it again. He pauses between corpses to touch the letter through his tunic and is comforted by its presence. In some way it describes to him Martha in their bed, and the diary on a shelf above, and the cries of the cart-drivers on Main street and Green street and the Watertown road.

"The whole town *has* changed," she wrote. "As your father always said. With so many of you gone I can see it much more clearly. There are fewer in the neighborhood this moment, perhaps, than were there when we first met; it has an empty and derelict air. And at the same time others are crowded. The factories are working day and night and the air is very smoky and the ground—for example, that by Washington's fort—is badly littered with waste of one kind and another. There are foreigners everywhere, new workers and their families. Though it is uncharitable and unkind I cannot divest myself of the feeling that *they* should be at war now and *you* here with me. Our town will never be the same, I am certain; I had intended to write 'village' but that is an old and meaningless word I retain from my earliest girlhood. There is no more village here. I should hardly use the word 'town.' We are a city, in law and in fact, and we are bound to accept it. I am glad your parents and mine know nothing of it; it would make them very sad."

"The land is taken," his father had written in April of 1838. "It is consumed as by a beast. The swamps, the flats, the pastures. And what is not is made barren, despoiled, because it has no protector. The people seem not to know what they have. Part fault I give to those across the water who so eagerly undo the Lord's work; they believe His hills were created to be pulled down, His ponds to be filled, His oceans to be dammed, and their influence on certain of our citizens here cannot be denied. But even their example is not enough to explain it. The lack of devotion is a terrible mystery. I weep to recall the country of my childhood. I weep to imagine what my children will receive.

"It is less than three years since they tore away the last of their mountain. By God that was a glorious thing. Now it is merely a rounded hill, still comely, grand houses rising everywhere, but by God it was glorious. We all admired it so. Good riddance to fair Pemberton say I, nonetheless, because without its companions it was the grossest reminder of the evil of man. The trimount stands unharmed in my memory, as in others, and that will serve until we perish.

"God save us from this fate. I think not. But I will trust in the Lord."

One of the bodies in the dirt softly moans. He goes down to his knees without a sense of expectation. Sure enough, the man is all but dead; Sutherland detects no motion in his chest, and when he touches the neck cannot sense any pulse. Perhaps it was the last cry to come from those lips. Perhaps what he heard was not a man's voice at all but the sound of a soul flying off, escaping the filth and desolation of the battlefield, going wherever it might go.

"There is hard news of Rebecca." wrote Martha. "It is as hard as it could be. I hesitate to tell you as I know you are weary and burdened enough and need strength and cheer from me, not further sorrow. But when you found my falsehoods out, were I to use them, you would be very angry with me. I know how much you care for her and you must have the truth.

"I will be straight: Thursday week the reverend saw her on a back street by the bridge in Dock square, near the taverns where the drivers and the boat men congregate. She had been drinking but that is the least of it. It appears she is making her living with those men. Of course I would not believe him all at once but he was convinced by their encounter, though he did not want to be, and if he is honest as I credit him I am now convinced as well.

"Jack, she made advances to the reverend himself. I blush this instant as I write the words. At first she did not recognize him and she asked him—that is, she made an invitation. Before he spoke she understood her mistake and her mouth and eyes were large, as he tells it, and she started to flee. But he called to her and she was persuaded to remain. He said not a word of reproach, he insists, but only coaxed her to return with him to the rectory and have a meal and some hot water to wash in, and decent clothing from his wife. But she refused. She managed crudely to thank him but then she ran away.

"He assures me has told no one, most especially Mrs. Hamilton. I suppose I must believe him. If she is brought to rescue quickly must it may be that her reputation can be saved as well, assuming she is removed to some other town or State. I will do my best to find her, Jack. I abhor myself for telling you this, dear husband, but I feel I have no choice. I can in no way begin to write lies to you now. Perhaps you will pray for her. Perhaps that will help."

He looks around him. Impossible as it seems they are making steady progress. They are emptying the field. An odd thought at such a moment but he is relieved to see how many living there are nearby, walking here and there among the dead, and how vastly the one outnumber the other. Relieved and also frightened. That many more of us to be killed yet, he thinks; that many more of us to aim at the enemy. That many more to go on giving lives away. We are well supplied for slaughter and it need never stop.

He stands staring at the long rows of corpses, whole and shattered. He is grateful that his father cannot see them. He thinks briefly of Rebecca and is glad for her too; better for her to endure the pains of that life, he is certain, than of this. Like himself she is degraded but she may one day rise above it. She is not deprived of hope.

Before the end his father wrote of a journey to the north, to Cape Ann and beyond. Of a river brown with sawdust and the runoff from a tannery, a river with dead salmon floating in it. A river he had fished in when employed there as a boy. "Are they so common," he had asked, "that we waste them in this way? Can we doubt there is an end to it? I made my meals from those creatures for the good part of a year and thought myself fortunate, though some complained of tedium. I called them fools. There I was, as were Moses and his tribe, eating dinner from God's hand! As if in some way deserving. And now nothing is left; from Gloucester to Plymouth that blessed gift is all gone.

"I curse myself and my fellows. I mourn what fleetingly passes. Do we so stupidly believe there is no limit to beneficence? Must we destroy His every beauty?"

The field is wholly cleared now. There is only the smell. That was the last time, thinks the soldier, the husband, the fighter, the son. I mean to get back home again.

26

In 1959, when Phillip was twelve, his father's sister Carla stopped coming to the lake house. She'd been up for several stays during the first part of that summer, accompanied twice by the good-looking young man she intended to marry, but at the end of a longer visit in early August—during which she and Phillip's father had a strange and strenuous conversation, their voices continuing late into the night as a worried boy lay on his cot on the upper floor, trying bravely to sleep and to not understand—she left in haste and stayed away for good. Not only for the rest of that season but for all those that followed. Except for a brief meeting at his step-grandmother's funeral, in 1962, Phillip didn't lay eyes on his aunt's face again until he arrived in Massachusetts for college, six years later.

At twelve he was far from old enough to be informed of what had happened, or even to think of all the possibilities himself, but he understood enough to piece together an explanation: his father didn't want Carla to marry Bob and was somehow offended that she was going to anyway. A minor issue in his opinion but clearly serious to them. It was important, he recognized, to distinguish between the problem of Bob and the problem of Carla's recalcitrance; having lost both their parents in childhood, left only with a stepmother (their father's third and final wife) who felt little attachment to them and had few resources of her own, the two were especially close, his father acting as Carla's parent as well as Phillip's. He had urged her, reasoned the boy, to give it more time, and she had refused and had also told him (at great length it appeared) to butt out and stop bossing her, she was twenty-four years old and would make her own decisions. For his father to break with Carla over Bob himself was unimaginable to Phillip, but for him to be dismayed by her rejection of his guardianship—that was all too familiar. Had she handled it better everything would have been fine. Late one evening, sitting on the dock tossing pinecones into the water, Phillip imagined coming home with a B minus or even a B on a project he had never spoken to his father about and cringed as he pictured the consequences. His father was the most responsible person he knew, the most responsible person he could dream of in a million years, and he took his duties very seriously. It was something you had to expect from him if you wanted to get along.

For the rest of that summer Phillip felt oppressed by the shrinking of his already tiny family to the minimum possible enrollment: one parent and one child. Since they'd first come to the lake house Carla had always been there too, and he departure set him thinking about the peculiar nature of his history and what it might mean for the future. Here was his father, deprived of his mother while gaining a sister at the age of nine (as if he were not allowed to have one without losing the other), and of the stepmother he'd briefly adored at the age of ten, and of his father at thirteen and his wife at twenty-six, and now his sister at thirty-three; there was his aunt, robbed by death and divorce of three parents by the time she was four, forced to give up the last of them—her only brother—twenty years later because she'd found a new protector; and his mother, herself an only child and an orphan when she married at nineteen; and here he was, down one parent, four grandparents, one step-grandparent and an aunt before the first hint of hair had appeared on his chest. There were maybe two dozen kids in all of Connecticut, he guessed, maybe five or six hundred in the whole country, who had lost so many forebears by such a young age, and the logical next step—of becoming one of those who had no forebears at all—was too prominent to ignore. All through August he wondered what would happen to him if his father died. He supposed he would go to live with Carla and Bob and was both guilty and amused to feel one afternoon, in passing, the faint, timid wish that it might be so. He knew his father would have very specific plans for any such eventuality and more than once considered asking about it but could never quite bring himself to do so. For one thing he was fearful that his father might deprecate or even dismiss his anxiety and for another he knew it would hurt his father, upset as he must already be about losing half of what little family was left him. That he might simply have restated the pointlessness, under the circumstances, of their separation, and urged his father to make up with Carla—fixing the problem before it became so substantial—didn't begin to occur to Phillip until many years later, when his father had long been dead.

His aunt's absence left a hole in his established routine. His time at the lake had always been divided according to whom he spent it with—his father when he wasn't at the office (which he drove back to five days a week, and in emergencies too, for most of the summer), the babysitters and housekeepers that were hired, neighbor parents and children like Mrs. Zulalian and her sons David and Dan, and most important Carla—and to lose one from the lineup threw Phillip into confusion. There were all sorts of things he had done only with her (he wondered if he would ever play miniature golf again) but beyond that he missed the special quality of their companionship, the frankness of their conversations, her concern for him and her curiosity. She was the only one who was ever tender with him, or gentle. She was the one who asked after his moods, who worried about how he felt. He wasn't always comfortable about a woman doing the asking but he was wise enough to know, and to know that *she* knew, that she was in some ways substituting for his mother, something his father had never successfully managed. Over the years he'd spent very little time wondering what it would be like to have a mother, because it was much too painful, but sometimes when Carla's questions or remarks embarrassed him or made him physically ill at ease he would think *My mom might have said that* or *I guess if I had a mom I'd be old enough now to want her out of my hair*, and then he always felt better. He didn't want her for a mother—he wanted her for what she was to him, his pretty young aunt and his friend—but saw that among her kindnesses were her efforts to let him know a little of what it would be like. He didn't want a mother at all but he was much less lonely to think that if he ever did need one there was somebody who might be willing to try.

Whatever the reasons, the lake house without her was a less appealing place. By then he was spending many hours on his own—the Zulalians had started coming for only a part of each summer, and his habits had become quite solitary in any case—and he wandered around the house and the yard, remembering her, thinking how much more fun he'd be having if she were there. His father, it was clear, was aware of his thoughts but was unable to help or even comment. She stood unspoken between them. Before long Phillip was eager to get back to Bradley, away from all the missing her, away from the burdensome knowledge that his father (who, while more distant than he might be, had never withheld anything important from his son) was depriving him of Carla's company for reasons that just didn't justify the hardship, now matter how he tried to see it from the other's point of view.

Now and then he would find himself overcome by sadness, very suddenly, for no immediate reason, and then horribly confused in trying to straighten out just what he was crying over, and why.

Not long before Labor Day, during his father's two weeks of actual vacation—he'd kept his schedule free and arranged for another physician to cover, so that only in the most extreme situations would he be called back to town—they had a big cookout party for some people around the lake. Most of the guests were adults but there were five other children there, two of them his age. One was a boy he had never liked named Andrew. He was certain as soon as he saw Andrew arrive that they were going to have a fight—he knew he would pick a fight, if it didn't happen naturally and of its own accord—and felt badly for his father but at the same time independent, in an oddly satisfying way. What a jerk, he thought as he watched Andrew walking around the yard. What a dumb jerky guy. He tried to keep his peace while they were eating chips and burgers but when Andrew started to read one of the comic books he'd left lying on the porch (despite his father's pointed request) he went and snatched it away. Soon they were saying nasty things to each other and using dirty names, and when the other tried to escape into the house Phillip caught up to him just inside the door and hit him hard on the arm.

Andrew punched back and shouted and the whole room turned to look. In a moment someone had pulled them apart. Andrew's mother came over to grab her son's elbow and Phillip's father, standing at the other end of the now-silent living room, spoke harshly to him in a very loud voice, so harshly that some of the guests raised their eyebrows. In an instant he'd forgotten about Andrew entirely. He'd forgotten about everything. Shamed and desperate he walked slowly around the corner into the kitchen, which was fortunately empty, and then slipped quietly outside—making sure not to let the screen door slam behind him—and went down to the lake.

He stood on the shore looking up at the sky and out at the water. The sun was just going down, shining orange behind the trees, and the surface was shimmering. He heard footsteps on the stones.

"So this is where you went."

"Aunt Carla," he asked, without turning around, "does everybody hate me?"

"It's OK," she said softly. But he knew she wasn't there.

One day in February of 1960 the phone rang. He was reading on his bed; his father was still at work. "I'm doing a terrible thing," said Carla. "I'm asking you not to tell your father I called. But I so wanted to talk to you." He stood there and nodded, too overwhelmed by her voice on the line to do anything else.

"Phillie?" she asked. "Are you there?"

"Yes."

"Do you want to keep talking or do you want to hang up?"

"Keep talking."

"OK."

There was silence for a while.

"Listen, buddy," she said, "I really miss you, and I wanted you to know I'm thinking of you. I also wanted you to know that I'm not even angry at your dad anymore and I hope he'll get over being angry at me so we can all be together again. Does that sound good to you?"

"Yes."

To Phillip his aunt seemed very sad and self-contained, though he knew she was doing her best to be cheerful and excited for his sake. He wanted to explain that he was much older now and could talk seriously about things but when he tried he found he couldn't get the words said.

"OK, here's the deal," she went on. "First, find a pencil—here's our new address and phone." He wrote down the information as she gave it to him (she spelled the street name for him three times) and wondered where he was going to hide the piece of paper, not that his father would ever search his things but he'd have to choose a place he felt comfortable about. "I know you're not going to call me up," she said, "except in an emergency—which is what I wanted you to have the number for—but I would like you to write to me, if you feel like it." She paused for him to answer but his voice still wouldn't work. "The thing is, do you have a friend who could accept my mail for you? Someone you trust? They would probably have to be honest with their parents, and their parents would have to agree not to tell your dad, so maybe I'm asking too much. Think fast."

He thought fast. "Nathan," he said at last. "Nathan at the model shop. He would do it."

"Phillip," she asked after a pause, "are we talking about a grown-up here?"

"Yes."

"Are you absolutely sure you can trust him?"

"Yes. He's my friend. I already told him about what happened with you and Dad. He feels bad for me. He'd be happy to help."

She was silent for a time. He heard static on the line and pictured a bad storm somewhere between Bradley and Boston, dropping ice on the wire.

"OK," she said. "I suppose the idea of another kid was pretty stupid anyway." It was one of the things he liked best about her, that she could admit it so easily when she was wrong, when he'd had a better idea. "Listen, if any of this makes you nervous—now or ever—you know you don't have to do it. You don't have to write to me if you don't want to. I just wanted to be able to send you birthday cards and so on but if Nathan doesn't work out, or you just don't want me writing to you, you let me know and I'll stop."

"I want it," he said, and hoped she knew what he meant.

After that she asked him about school and his hobbies, then (as always) what he was reading these days, and then casually about his father. He explained that there were problems in the practice—several longtime patients had coincidentally become gravely ill all at once, and his father's valued assistant of seven years had moved to Kansas—and then, venturing onto solid but frightening adult territory, he informed her that his father was greatly upset about the difficulty between them, although of course he wouldn't mention it.

"Oh," she said. "Do you suppose he's still very mad at me?"

"I don't know," Phillip told her. "Maybe not so much."

"Do you suppose he'll get mad all over again if he finds out we got married without telling him?"

They waited through the longest silence yet. "Probably," he said at last.

She sighed. "Well, I'll give it a while," she said. "He doesn't know where I am but he knows how to find out, and you—you can tell him if it ever seems right." He almost laughed at the thought of his suddenly producing Carla's address and confessing to his father that he'd had it all along but had withheld it. She also seemed to understand the weakness of her suggestion.

"Hey," she exclaimed, making an extra effort to be cheery, "what about you Any girlfriends yet?"

"No."

"Can't find anyone as good as me, huh?"

"No."

She laughed. "I've never found anyone like you either but Bob is the next best thing. He really is, honey. He sends his best and that he hopes he'll get to meet you again before long."

Phillip's heart was pounding. "Tell him hello from me," he managed.

"I will," said Carla. "I'm going to go now, this call is costing a fortune." He knew she had to go because she was starting to cry. "Please write to me, OK? Oh wait, where's that model shop? What's it called? What's Nathan's other name?" He didn't know the last but she said the rest would be enough.

"I miss you too, Aunt Carla," he told her.

"Goodbye sweet Phillie," she said, and hung up the phone.

She was everything to him. He understood that as soon as he'd put the receiver down. It was like finding something he'd give up for lost long ago, or getting at last the answer to a frustrating riddle. Wave after wave of relief and joy that she had called and that he knew where she was passed over him, and also deep grief that he could never see her now, could never spend the time they used to spend. Upset as he was, he vaguely suspected that he would feel some of that even had his father approved of her marriage, and as he wept for a longer time than he could remember ever doing (I must have cried like this, he thought, when my mother died) he found room for a small but bitter hatred of Bob as well. That passed, though, in time, diminishing through the minutes and then the following days and weeks, vanishing forever after his single effort to excite himself by imagining them in bed, something he was utterly unable to do although his fantasies in general were very rich by that time, and fully detailed.

To Phillip's astonishment his father never forgave Carla. Not in any way that showed. As they exchanged cards and letters over the years, and then long-distance calls (he'd asked the operator to reverse the charges, or she'd call him at the booth at the gas station near the highway, to which he'd ridden his bike), he waited for something to arrive in the mail from her with his father's name on it, or for the phone to ring and his father to say, "Oh—it's you," or for his father to approach him and admit that he knew they were in contact (it was obvious he did) and would Phillip please inform him of what was happening in Carla's life? But nothing like this occurred. Not even after the funeral, at which he saw their eyes meet. He realized it wasn't all his father's fault; by the time he was fifteen he was more than a little angry at his aunt for not breaking the ice, and not long after that he was able to tell her so directly. But at least with Carla he could speak freely, without restriction. The news of Amy's birth when he was sixteen he could barely contain; he had to run down to Nina's house to lead her outside and tell her all about it, though her parents looked at him oddly for barging in during dinner, because he couldn't tell his father. He was ashamed—he felt disloyal—that he hadn't, and in the following days his resentment of sister and brother both rose to almost unbearable levels. Finally he knocked on his father's study door and though no reply came turned the knob and walked in.

"Dad, Carla has a daughter named Amy," he said, amazed at the steadiness of his own voice. "You have a niece in Massachusetts. I thought you should know."

His father put his pen carefully down on the desk, removed his glasses, turned slightly toward Phillip, and closed his eyes.

"Thank you," he said. "Thank you for telling me." He sighed and dropped his glasses on the desk as well, less gently than was his habit, his eyes still closed. "I really mean that, Phillip. I've wanted to ask so many times."

"Then you should have," said his son.

The older man was silent, his head tilted slightly back, his hands folded in his lap.

"You ought to write to her."

This caused the eyes to slowly open, annoyance visible in them but also something surprised. "Thank you," said Phillip's father, "for the suggestion."

"I have the phone number too. She's home from the hospital now."

The eyes closed again. "That's good," the thin voice said. "Please write everything down for me and leave it in the kitchen. I'll give it some thought."

"She's all you've got except me."

"That is certainly so."

After that there was silence, Phillip standing in the doorway watching his father's tired face, wondering if there was something more he could do but afraid to choose wrong.

Once he'd taken this bold step and his father had wired congratulations—and sent to Boston, Phillip suspected, a considerable sum of money—things were better and at the same time worse. He had tacit permission to speak openly of Carla but this made it far more frustrating that his father still refused to. In the past, embarrassment had served as sufficient explanation for the lack of reference but that excuse was gone now. What could she possibly have done that would deserve this? he wanted to ask. I know you love her. I know she loves you. What's the point, what's the point? He went so far as to arrange for her to call the house one evening when his father would be there, in hopes that he would pick up the phone, but as was often the case he was lying down when it rang and the longer Phillip let it go—by instruction and agreement it was his duty to answer and stop the noise as soon as possible—the more convinced he became that his father would continue to ignore it, which he did.

In Phillip's two years at home after Amy was born his father sent, besides the telegram and the gift, exactly two letters to his sister, receiving four in return. The doctor made no attempt to hide his correspondence, leaving the sealed envelopes out on the hall table with all the other mail for Phillip to drop in the box on the way to school. They might have spoken on the phone but he didn't think they had. At least he was able to stop sneaking around, to stop feeling guilt over his dishonesty; at least they were talking, though it wasn't doing much good. And while his father never thanked him for maintaining the connection with Carla all those years it was clear that he was grateful. It was a relief to at last be reassured that he had done the right thing for all three of them. It made him feel a good deal older.

His decision about college was obvious from the beginning, assuming he got into at least one of the Boston schools he'd applied to. He was accepted everywhere and as it happened his father's preference conveniently matched his own. It occurred to him in passing that his father might also want him near Carla, to help keep track of her, but he soon rejected that notion. It would have been a gross violation of the man's responsibility, at least as he defined it; how would he feel later on if he decided on the basis of his own interests, rather than his son's, and it turned out for the worse? Phillip knew that if his father had truly believed Chicago was right he would have insisted on its selection (after all, he was paying), and it made him very anxious to imagine the battle that would have resulted in that case. It was beyond him to think of any reasonable way out.

As they sat in their usual booth at Schilmeister's eating T-bone steak and fried potatoes, the night before he left home, he tried to find a way to express his gratitude for being sent where he wanted to go, his renewed understanding of his own youth and dependency. The problem was that there was no right way to say it. "Thanks for agreeing with me," "Thanks for trusting me," "Thanks for giving me what I want," "Thanks for being right this time"—none of them quite covered the ground. As his father, in a rare expansive vein, told stories about his own college days, the son understood that to refer to it at all would have injured what dignity the elder had left. His father knew he was going to Boston at least in part because Carla was there; his father could imagine the bitter fight they might have had just as clearly as he, and was equally glad to have avoided it. He was gracefully preparing for the end of eighteen years of overseeing his son's life on a daily basis and deserved full support in what was surely a painful moment. Phillip abandoned all thought of discussing anything troublesome and started in earnest on his meal, tasting from time to time the glass of wine his father had asked the waiter to bring him and laughing at the skillfully told anecdotes and jokes. He had a very good time, to his gratified surprise.

Before they went to California, Phillip had eight happy years with Carla and Bob and their children. His father drove him to college and helped him move into his dorm room and then as soon as he was gone—before he was even on the newly built six-lane highway, surely, on his way back to Connecticut—Phillip used the pay phone to call his aunt and uncle. They couldn't see him that evening, which was crushingly disappointing, but he met some interesting classmates in the dining hall at dinner and the following morning they came and took him out to breakfast, the first of many over time.

Carla, to his amazement, looked very much the same. He could not watch her without being reminded of both of his serious high school girlfriends; the implications were obvious. She acted much like the old Carla as well except that she was a mother now—a mother for real—and what had once come to him, in occasional installments, was entirely committed elsewhere. To compensate he had the widening of her eyes, at times, when she looked him over or heard him speak, and a deference not unpleasing. She quickly got beyond her tendency to talk slightly down to him; she was visibly impressed by this intelligence and maturity. And he *was* older, it was true, almost impossibly so, old enough to see clearly how appealing she was, how appealing she had been to a boy of eleven and twelve, and also honest enough to admit to himself that it made him quite uncomfortable to be alone with her. It seemed to make her uneasy too. But then as Amy got bigger and Emmy was born they were able to relax. The babies seemed to break up what had long been held between them, something Phillip considered both a loss and gain. His mother was not the only thing she wasn't and could never be; let her just be what she was. He was otherwise on the verge of a whole new life, in any case, and she simply didn't need to stand for so much.

Her husband he eventually came to greatly admire but it took him some time. For this he easily forgave himself. Just as he had grown enough to acknowledge fully his attraction to Carla he could appreciate their intimacy, and at times it was more than he could bear. He never let it show but occasionally it bothered him so much that he had to leave their presence. This was not simple jealousy, he recognized after several months of it, sexual, filial, or otherwise; it was more like impatience, or intolerance, or some other need to reject their relationship that he just couldn't see. Late on a Saturday night, after Bob had let him out of their shiny black Rambler a block from his dormitory—he'd been out to their house in the suburbs for dinner with a young woman they knew (he hadn't found her exciting) and then later some bridge—he realized with a powerful shock that it was on account of his father. In rejecting Bob-and-Carla, not Bob himself but the two of them as couple, he was upholding his old man's honor. He found this amusing and saddening both. After that it went almost away.

The children were very attached to him, and he to them. He loved to give them gifts. Playing with Amy and Emmy sometimes made him miserable as well; he suspected it was because they had two parents and each other and Bob's large family and him too—a gross oversupply of affectionate relatives, as far as he was concerned—but even at his worst he was glad to sit with them, to play with them, to take them for ice cream and to the zoo. Aside from their delight in him he was happy to be trusted.

Through all their years together the break between brother and sister was unhealed. He knew they still communicated from time to time—he once saw a letter from his father lying on his aunt's bureau, as he wandered their house waiting for them to come back from the beach so they could go out to dinner—but neither ever shared any content with him. Carla would not talk about her brother in front of her children and when Bob was present he always took over the discussion with his fervent assertions of the importance of family and getting past things. When aunt and nephew were alone she would listen but refuse to be drawn into responding, except at times to nod and smile. Likewise his father on his frequent visits home. As he grew from teenager to young man and from student to working writer his patience diminished, though understanding increased; at times he thought the effort of not talking about it with him would be too much for one or the other, that one of them would crack and begin to babble, but it never happened. A small family but a stubborn one, he often thought. This has gone beyond absurd. All I want is some progress before it's too late. Then he wondered how on earth it had become his place to decide what was progress and what was not.

One day at the swimming pool he heard Carla say "your uncle" to the children and knew she was referring not to him but to his father. For a short time he wondered if she was actively hallucinating, genuinely crazy, seeing his father sitting there with towel and goggles instead of him. One evening as they stood in a spacious living room at a party for her father-in-law's sixtieth birthday, watching Bob and his siblings crowd around their happy parents, he saw her wringing her hands over and over, her face dark and strained, and understood how desperately she wished her brother were there.

But there was no reconciliation. Not until his father was dying in the hospital, another in his line going away much too soon, and not even then really, although he wept to see his sister and she kissed his head and hands. They both wept freely in the end but were unable to discuss what had somehow come between them, to uncover it, and when Phillip tried to leave the room they begged him to stay. That the scene was no interruption of the many years' estrangement but its seamless continuation was painfully obvious by the time it was over. His father's illness had everything to do with their separation, it turned out, and their separation with the imminent threat of her abandonment; it was almost as if his father had come to blame her for all the loved ones he had lost and perhaps even for his own early death, which he'd long foreseen, and she in turn had sent him away before he could leave her by another, more permanent method. For years Phillip had prayed he wouldn't die before his father, who might do something awful if he did, and he felt at the funeral, along with everything else, profound relief—even a sick kind of pride—that he had managed to outlast him. Perhaps, he guessed, Aunt Carla had been living with a burden much the same.

*   *   *

In 1973, two years before the hospital room, three years after Jennifer was born, they moved to San Francisco on account of Bob's career. By then, at the age of twenty-six, this latest loss of family seemed tolerable enough to Phillip, if not easy to accept than at least acceptable. Inevitable in an accommodating way. He saw Carla at the hospital and funeral in 1975 and all of them on visits to the coast two and five years later. But while the children still seemed to care strongly for him—Amy and Emily anyway, Jennie didn't know him well—and Carla and Bob were devoted in their attentions and coaxed him to move west, it wasn't really the same. He was called "Uncle Phillip" but he was just another houseguest; he went with the kids to Santa Cruz but it wasn't as it had been when he'd taken them places he knew.

The distance seemed to grow larger. A visit to Boston in the summer of 1981 was cancelled by them for reasons he never fully understood—they simply didn't take the trouble to explain—which resulted in deep bad feeling on his part. And he in turn never bothered to tell them so. It was the beginning of a change. As the spaces between calls and letters grew wider he saw what was happening and wanted to stop it but couldn't think of a way, or even a good reason. By then all his writing had given him patience and a degree of resignation and he thought: what is, is. If I've got to be my father now that he's dead and gone, I do. Bob and Carla are life; maybe I prefer art. Maybe they aren't happy with what I've become.

And there was satisfaction for him, although he hated to admit it, in living out the other role. He wasn't sure if it had to do specifically with Carla and his father or if it was broader than that. Perhaps I'll have a son, he thought, who'll hide her letters from me. Or maybe he'll hide letters from one of the girls.

The last time he saw Carla and Bob was at Bob's twenty-fifth college reunion, in 1984. They were graduates of the same institution and his own fifteenth was going on but he ignored it—as he had his tenth—and drove down from New Hampshire only because they were there, though he judged it a major mistake. When he saw them enter the restaurant he was gripped by a desire to avoid them, to turn around and walk out before he was noticed; though visibly older they were otherwise the same but he felt so deeply altered that he didn't know if he could even sit at the same table with them. As they spotted him and approached he worked to calm himself. By the time they reached the table he had summoned what warmth was available, he was certain, though it felt like a curse.

The dinner was one of the most awkward he'd had. He blamed himself entirely and was filled with self-loathing. Carla was puzzled and hurt but Bob seemed to understand. The next day they had lunch together, for her sake, but that the bottom had dropped out was clear to them all. "I'm sorry I can't have you up to the house right now," he told them. "It's a difficult time for me. But I hope you'll see it someday."

"It sounds wonderful," said Carla.

"I know you'd like it, I'm sure you would."

"We're so happy for you," she said.

Driving back to New Chatham on a lovely June day he imagined her face—at seven, at fifteen, at eighteen, at twenty-three—floating outside the windows, over the blacktop, against the backing of the trees, and regretted what might have been.

What's this? she asks herself. What's this what's this what's this? I know these don't belong here. Something is wrong.

When the girl is at the market she can enter her bedroom without hesitation (she still has some discretion, although most of it is gone) and that is where she now stands. She felt curious and came exploring. Having looked in the box she found under the desk she doesn't recognize the contents but they have a smell to them, she thinks. Not a smell—odor is something that has become very distant and add, along with taste and temperature and even the time of day—but an air. A certain nature. There is no question that they were taken from the attic, the family things. Taken wrongly and in secret. She feels angry for a moment, so angry that were it the man she might be tempted to do harm, but it passes very quickly and she finds she still feels curious. Even more than before she found them. She sits on the bed to study the matter, the neat and tidy bed that hasn't been slept in for weeks.

After lengthy thought it comes to her: property of Alice. One of her many hobbies during the difficult years. By trying very hard Bertha can remember Allie buying postcards at flea markets and receiving them from friends, sorting them at the dining room table, sitting sleeping in her wheelchair with one grasped in her hand, its face turned upwards to the afternoon sun. It disturbs her that so much effort is required to picture her sister. It disturbs her that as she does so little sweetness comes with it. Alice, she thinks, she tries to say aloud, attempting to kiss the postcards. Alice, Alice, come back. But it isn't Alice who is missing, she reminds herself, though she is here and Alice not; it is she herself who isn't where she ought by rights to be. She doesn't know where Alice is but she is more convinced than ever that she is someplace, that Papa and Margaret are with her. She is barely able to stop herself from putting the shoebox under her arm and setting off down the road to find them—not because there is any obligation to remain but because she hasn't the first idea of where to go—and sits breathless (or what would be if she breathed) on the brightly colored afghan, hoping for an indication, a direction, a sign.

But these are all I have, she thinks. Something brought me here to see these cards, to put me in touch with Alice. I am in danger of forgetting. I'm losing more and more each day. Something made the girl take these out and bring them here where I could find them. I can't go up there but she can and did—I didn't like it but she did—and I have to take advantage. I have to figure out what's being said to me.

She sits there and puzzles in the suppertime darkness, waiting for the greater illumination of spring.

"I thought you should know," he told her.

She turned away from him. "You thought I should be slapped in the face with it, you mean."

"No. Janie. You would've found out sooner or later." He began to pace but stopped himself, holding tight to a low limb for support. The Macs were all covered with big fat buds, not so very far from blossom, and the space in which they stood was filled with a faint but steady hint of the aroma to come. He'd always loved an orchard when everything in it was green; it was like an empty stage. "Look, I'm sorry if I handled it wrong, but I wanted you to hear it from me. Instead of someone else."

"Instead of seeing them together myself."

"Yes, damn it, instead of that," he said. "It damn near dropped me when I did."

She put her arms around a trunk.

"Janie, I'm sorry. If I was mistaken please forgive me."

She stepped back and shook her head. He could see from behind how much gray there was in it. "No mistake, Bill," she said. "It's just that there was no good way for me to find out. It would be bad no matter how. You understand that, right?"

He nodded but she wasn't looking. "Yeah," he said. "I guess I do."

She said nothing.

"Makes me want to fight him," he said.

Jane turned and he thought she would defend the man, or tell him to mind his own business or at least not judge what he knew nothing about, but she had a sharpness in her eye. If he didn't know better he might have said she looked mean.

"How old did you say?"

"Twenty, maybe twenty-two."

"You're kidding."

"No." He shook his head.

"Is she pretty?"

"Janie. C'mon."

"Is she beautiful, you asshole?"

"Yeah." He said it low but he knew it didn't matter; she could have told from the way he was blushing and looking at the ground. "Yeah, I think she is."

His sister turned away again. She walked carefully out into the lane between the rows, almost as if searching for the exact middle distance between them, and adjusted herself until she was standing up as straight as could be, squared to the whole orchard, looking directly down the avenue between the McIntosh trees to the next grove beyond.

"All right," she said. "I'm glad to know it, Billy. And I am glad to hear it from you. But I need to be alone now."

"He'll be sorry," said Bill, backing helplessly away.

"I wouldn't count on it," said Jane.

"You should leave me."

"I should."

"Before you can't anymore."

"Yes."

The wind from Canada blew and carried midnight through the room.

"I'm starting to need you here."

"I know."

There is smallpox in the colony. And with the sickness, fear. The land is much too large already and the people far too few.

I hope you can forgive us, the soldier whispers to the boy.

The dog searches for its master.

She often looked at the apple as she sat at her desk. Paying
bills, writing letters, just resting and thinking, it was there
for her attention because she'd never put it away. Deep red
marble—she wondered where they got it—with black veins,
perfectly shaped and polished to a shine, beautifully simple
in that artful artificial way. Nothing like a living apple but
very like one all the same. Although it was in the form of
a Delicious she admired it. Although it came from bastard
Phillip. She sometimes passed her hand over it the way she
did with her fruits on their trees, in their baskets and boxes,
and while similar in some ways (smoothness, roundness, cir-
cularity) the sensation it gave was very different in others.
There was a coldness and hardness that while solid was also
sad. Like the bones, like a fossil, she'd thought more than

once. Like her relationship with Phillip, what was left of it that was. Unchangeable, static, with no further meaning or use, but she couldn't remove it from her life. Couldn't free herself. It had taken its place forever, never mind all her regrets.

It's maddening, she thought one evening as she felt its weight on her palm, eyes closed to stave off the moment of going upstairs and getting ready for bed. I'm more attached to this apple than he ever was to me. He held me in his hand but was able to let go; I hold his leavings and am not. She pictured herself getting up, going to the sideboard, opening the door and putting the apple inside—easy as anything but she simply couldn't do it. She pictured throwing it away. Just let it go, her sister Betty always said in response to any distress over anything, a clumsy and annoying piece of wisdom (if that) but one she would very gladly have followed if she could, with respect at least to Phillip and for that matter to her whole life. She was choked by unbreakable bonds. You won't give in and turn Daddy over to Bill, she told herself, though it's what they both want. You won't give up the farm. You know you'll never move away from this boring useless place and the man who makes you feel bad. You're stuck, is what it is, under the guise of your *responsibilities* as you like to think of them but aren't they really just traumas? Isn't your life made up mostly of hurts? You're afraid to let them go because there's nothing much beyond them, isn't that the case?

The house was quiet and still. The only sound was Pippin's breath, a steady rasping in the corner. Again she'd stayed up much too late; she'd be exhausted in the morning but instead of sleeping in and letting her brother and the help take care of things she would struggle awake and stagger out to make her near-useless contribution. At least Bill understood somehow, or anyway accepted it. At least he'd stopped asking her what the hell she was doing and telling her to get to bed earlier. She was shamed by the concern she could see in his eyes but it was limited to that; eventually she'd get back on her customary schedule and he'd stop looking that way. She had avoided his pity for forty-five years and would lose it again just as soon as she could. She depended, she'd found, on his respect.

But is it me who fails to understand? she asked, thinking of her brother's quiet worried expression. Am I missing my own point? It was a deadly serious question; more and more she'd had the sense that she was not what she had always assumed herself to be. In some hidden but fundamental way. She was Jane, she knew for sure, child of Tom and Cynthia and sister of Betty and Bill, guardian of the apple genes, but something simple and essential, something prior to the rest, was struggling to make itself known. Or was it? Hard to say. The idea of Jane as changeling, as a limb cut and grafted to an entirely different tree, had a certain persistent appeal—the promise of new clues, perhaps, to a strangely dormant life—but was probably just a dodge. An evasion. Truth or not it was of no real help; it couldn't provide her with a useful path to take, she was forced to admit, or with the energy to take it.

Marble stains, doesn't it? she thought, wrapping her fingers around the apple and squeezing, her eyes still closed. It doesn't come this way; it's dyed. They got some regular white or gray and left it in a bucket of something deep, deep red for a week or more. If I broke it in half I'd find it white in the middle, wouldn't I? If I knew who made it I could go to them and have them tell me what they'd done. She tried to get herself to raise it over her head—to at least play at destroying it, though she knew she never would—but even that was beyond her. She relaxed again and sobbed.

The old furnace clanked in the basement for a few noisy moments, stirring itself into action once more at the end of another long and difficult season. Jane opened her eyes and saw her desk laid out before her: the ledgers, the letters, the checkbook and the bills. The loose papers were arranged in neat and orderly piles but one stack was still unweighted. She lifted the apple and placed it squarely on top of the invoices to be mailed; though the sheaf was almost half an inch thick the marble made a loud hard thump as it hit, nearly falling from her hand. One good thing, she thought, it's too heavy to stray. It stays where you put it. I'll find it there in the morning.

She wonders if they'll marry. Of course she has her own opinions but these are not very strong, confusing as it all seems to be, and they go back and forth. It isn't as it was in my time, she thinks. Not that I knew so much about it. But things have changed and what's more this is an odd situation. If they asked me I wouldn't know what to advise. I don't even know what's allowed! Considering solely from the girl's point of view she tends to feel they shouldn't but when she thinks about the man she's far more open to the idea. This may be his last chance, she tells herself. The way he lives he won't ever get another. She isn't sure this is a bad thing but spinsterhood is not for everyone. Perhaps he really is better off alone but perhaps not. She wonders if he has any true sense of what he wants.

Would she have kept apart from men the way she did without her sisters and her father? Had Papa died young and Margaret married and moved away, would she have then done the same? And Alice too? The thought of the three of them dispersed to separate houses—not that they would have gone very far—is strange and upsetting but intriguing as well. Instead of *our* china there would have been *Margaret's* and *Allie's* and *mine*, she thinks. Instead of dinner every day, Sunday dinner once a week, maybe only once a month, with husbands and children and servants all around. While she kept apart from men they also kept apart from her, she realizes, and mostly also from her sisters; she never pined for a husband but none ever came riding up to the house, either, to carry her away. She knows she wasn't beautiful but neither was she ugly (she starts for the mirror to look at her face but remembers just in time) and her Papa had plenty of money. The three of them were all healthy happy girls. It isn't easy to explain.

Perhaps it was Papa who scared off all the boys. All the men. That is an interesting thought. It seems unlikely—while naturally protective and a bit stern at times he truly loved having guests, and hearing his daughters praised—but there had to be some reason. Lots of the boys showed lively interest in school but after each of them finished that attention was soon gone. As if they were fun to flirt with close at hand but too far away, in their house out in the country, to be worth the trouble. Or as if everyone had been discouraged somehow. They still came into town for church and for socials but it wasn't the same. It is true, she thinks, that Papa was a lot less fond of our going to dances after we got out of high school. Once we got to be twenty. He seemed to take things more seriously then.

Of all the young men in New Chatham and in neighboring villages Harry Munsett was the only one who ever came calling. Calling in a formal way. He was Margaret's suitor for many years, a frequent visitor, a decent-looking man with a promising business. He never seemed very hurt by Margaret's rejections (though who knew what he was feeling inside) and they enjoyed his good nature, his fine manners and grooming. He brought gifts for every one of them, told jokes, talked politics with Papa, savored the food they cooked for him as if he never ate anything but dirt anywhere else. And like a calendar he went down on one knee every so often and made his proposal. They all urged Margaret to marry him—as much for our own sakes as for hers, thinks Bertha, because we wanted him in the family—and she had a dozen chances. Even Papa liked Harry. No matter what they told her, though, no matter how Harry asked, Margaret always refused. "I just can't leave you girls," she said.

But Margaret, thinks Bertha, never did what these are doing. Maybe if she had she would have gone away with him. From the way they act it changes everything. If she had tried it maybe it would have changed her too. Maybe it would have taken her from us, with its magical call.

It seems so powerful, she thinks. I don't know. It frightens me. It seems so violent. I know they wouldn't hurt each other, wouldn't choose to, but it looks as if they are just the same. How can it be good for them to force each other that way? How can it be good for her with all his rough intrusions? And doesn't it hurt? It looks like it might. If he ever used something of metal or wood they'd arrest him and jail him for the rest of his life. But because it's only him it's supposed to be fine. How can she lie there and stroke him so gently after what he does to her? She's just a girl, just a girl. How can she smile?

They must get married now she thinks. They *are* married now, really. Once you've done that together what choice do you have? Once you've seen each other act that way who else could you go to? I never knew, I never knew. I'm not

even real and not even part of it and it almost takes me over
when I watch them. And I can see them getting lost in it; I
see them melt away. I never would have believed it. It's like
they're trying to be born.

Margaret, she calls out, hey Margaret, did you ever?
Did you ever, did you and Harry ever? My darling sister—
where are you? Where are you? Oh dearest Margaret, please
say no.

After trying for hours to close out a chapter Phillip rose from
his desk. It doesn't end there, he thought, the way you
planned it was wrong, so give it a rest and go on to something
else. But the idea of starting fresh—from a brief scribbled
note or a blank screen entirely, those were his choices—was
beyond him, impossible, and he accepted his fate with good
grace. Not much sense in doing damage in the name of getting on.

He paused before leaving his study, to listen. But he
had no real reason. She's not here, he reminded himself as
he opened the door and stepped into the hall. She's gone to
Amherst, to the library. You're free to do as you please.

As he went to the kitchen he found he wasn't very hungry. An apple fished out of the fruit bin (strange to be eating
one of these in late March, he thought, how far did it come
and how old is it now?) was enough to fill him up. Nor did
he want to sleep, nor to read, not even the paper—he hoped
to get back to work and another writer's words would only
interfere—and for once the impulse to put things in order
or make overdue repairs was totally absent. It's Jennie, he
thought as he stood in his living room, bright sunlight touching the furniture, flooding the walls: she gives you so much
peace you don't need that anymore. It was slightly unsettling

to be so content. Between his work and his companion he had no nervous energy for sorting old catalogs or fixing broken window clasps. No little problem to be solved. He almost wished he were more frustrated by the hitch in his chapter; it was very unlike him to be taking it calmly. Hard to believe you're coming so close to normal after all these cranky years, isn't it? he asked himself. But don't worry, you aren't so very far gone; you're standing here being neurotic about not being neurotic, after all. The day you become entirely unselfconscious is most likely the day you die.

As he climbed the stairs to the second floor he intended to lie on his bed for a while and see if insight would come— new attitude or no he still kept a rigid schedule and needed to find a way to turn out at least a few more pages before dinnertime, if humanly possible—but when he reached the landing he found himself turning left instead of right. He didn't know where it had come from but once in his head the idea of looking at Jennie's things would not go. She spends so much time in my room, he thought, and I none in hers. It's as if I'm not in her life though she's far into mine. He was aware that this was reasoning both fatuous and thin—he strongly suspected that his house, their embraces, the work she was doing were her life now, for better or worse, and in any case she would be happy to address any imbalance—but he needed it to keep going. It was a thing he had to do and he might not get another chance for a very long time, another chance that combined her absence and the sort of courage (or bravado) that he was feeling at the moment. There has to be something she's hiding from me here, he told himself as he opened the door and let himself in, there has to. Don't know how I know it but I do. It's a necessary piece.

Very quickly he felt shame and a longing for her presence. As if he'd come to a party and found nobody there. This is silly, he thought, and pointless; it's like reading a cereal box. You're just killing some time until she's back from Massachusetts. He had no interest in her things beyond the fact that they connected her firmly to his house, that she had to return to him at least once more. The sweater hanging on the hook was significant only because it suggested, sweetly and painfully, her soft warm body, and the books and shoes and photographs because they documented a particular past, a personal experience, the history of someone he cared for. He noticed a picture of her parents he'd never seen and stepped closer, to examine it; he wondered if they'd just sent it or if Jennie had brought it with her and either way why she hadn't shown it to him yet. His aunt was disturbingly like the young woman he remembered, her image a troubling complication, but he was amused to see that Bob resembled his own father so much more than he had when they'd last met. If that's the secret she's been hiding it's not a shocking one, he thought. Maybe she's embarrassed to bring the three of you together. It wouldn't come as a surprise.

He turned as if to go—he wanted to be out of her room long before she came up the driveway, although he planned to mention to her that he'd been in it, he would think of some excuse—but was reluctant to follow through. Though he'd avoided her desk, out of respect and superstition, he couldn't leave without approaching it. It was one he'd used for several years in the middle '70s before admitting it was too small. Look, he told himself: there are her pen and her paper. This is where she works. He felt childish and even giddy, spying on this part of her life, which he suspected was partly in acknowledgment of the extremity—the absurdity, even—of his own exaggerated views. So you're looking at

the place where someone writes, he thought, big deal. You
could let her in to see yours too; big deal there as well. You
looked at her sweater, you looked at the picture, now open
the dresser and look at her underwear. It's all a violation of
her privacy, all the same thing, but this is no worse than the
rest of it. There's nothing so special about a desk. Maybe if
you could rise above your sad contrived obsession and see
it as just another piece of used furniture you could have a
standard life, you could actually live and share with someone else. Maybe then Jennie could stay here forever.

Under the desk he noticed a box. He didn't know why
but he knelt to withdraw it. He didn't know why but he
opened it to look. In the moments after he did a deep change
came over him and the room, over the state of New Hampshire, over the sunny March afternoon. It was as if he'd re-
leased something profound, something infinite, by lifting the
lid—he felt just like Pandora, who had intrigued him as a
child—and his awkwardness, his shame, his contempt for
himself were carried away by whatever he'd let go. As soon
as he saw the writing on one of the cards, the one at the end,
he knew what they were; as he leaned over them and closed
his eyes he could smell their attic resting place and everything in it. Who said she could? he asked himself, what gave
her the right? but he wasn't really angry. Without knowing
all the details he thought he understood the deed, understood why she'd taken them. It didn't surprise him but what
did was that he also—for the first time—sensed their owner.
Her recent presence. He'd never known her, living or dead,
and despite his acceptance of everything she'd had as his
fair (if not appropriate) due and his years spent working,
eating, sleeping in her house he'd had no real image of her,
no true vision. But suddenly she was real. By virtue of the
cards. He'd come searching for one cousin but instead had

found another, had acquired a new relationship he wasn't sure he wanted. As he looked through the cards, inhaling their odor and absorbing their age, a certain type of fairy tale crept into his brain—here was this young princess who had tricked him, despite all his fussy precautions, into un- covering the mirror, the only one in which he was forbidden to look—and he worried the spell he'd fallen under might now freeze him to the spot. He was free to close the box, he found, and to return it to its hiding place, free to stand and move from the room, but he couldn't leave the old woman; that much freedom he didn't have. She'd caught up to him at last and there was nothing he could do. He went out into the hallway and retreated to his bedroom, as if it might give him shelter, but she followed him there, or his knowledge of her did—his knowledge of his own complicity—and he knew the jig was up. It wasn't only Jennie; they had un- earthed the cards together. He was equally to blame.

God help me, thought the writer, this is an odd and fee- ble notion. It was just a box of postcards. They weren't even mailed to anyone here; for all you know they belonged to the gardener. But he was not so easily convinced.

Please forgive us if you're able, he ventured at last. I think you see we mean no harm.

The nicest tree in the world. That was what the paper
said. She had written the words on a state road in Dublin,
pulled over on her way back to Phillip and the house because they needed to come out, and had recognized then
how important they were. She still recognized that now but
now their meaning, which had formerly been clear. It was
an increasingly common experience in her life, of losing a
thread she'd once held firmly in her fingers. Of benign confusion though not neglect. Lately she'd been frightening herself with moments of profound insight, or clarity, or
inspiration—she didn't know what to call it—that overtook
and overwhelmed her any time, any place, no matter what
she was doing or how she was feeling, though she was always
alone. At these moments she understood, it seemed, what

everything meant, not just her own words and stories, not just whatever was before her but everything: war, death, her family, wide northern lakes, tall buildings, music, sadness, her backpack, Charlie, bread and cheese, and memories of summer camp when she was twelve and thirteen. At these moments she could write, she believed, beautifully and forever, but she had sense enough not to rush to her desk, or to try to. It seemed to her that this condition was not exactly about writing, or for the sake of writing, or even part of it; it was, rather, a product of the work she was doing, an associate or concomitant. She was seeing things fresh because she was writing about them. The new vision started from somewhere within her pages, not without. But she wanted it to help her; along with her relief she was filled with regret, each time, when it passed and she remained as she'd always been before. While it was happening she felt infinite, almost godlike; once it was over she was just plain old Jennie. It was nice to be Jennie but it was disappointing too. She knew it had to do with art and she wanted so badly to be an artist that this clear evidence of progress was, perversely, more discouraging than not, at least at times. I wonder if it will ever last long enough, she thought, for me to get something out of it. If it will sneak over me while I'm working one day and make it gloriously easy. Or will I always feel cramped and close and clumsy when I'm actually creating, when I'm touching pen to paper, and that way—that shining way— only when I'm doing something else, when my writing hands are free?

In those strange and altered moments, as well as others more mundane, she sometimes made notes. She was looking at one now. This example had come in a very disturbing fashion—the sense of needing desperately to pull out her pen growing and growing as she drove anxiously along until she was frantic for a safe place to stop, which finally made itself known—but many, particularly in recent weeks, were on her almost before she noticed them and quickly forgotten once she'd written them down. At first she'd scrabbled around for any piece of paper or cardboard but soon enough she'd smartened up and had found, at a dime store in Keene, a small refillable notebook that would fit in her back pocket. It was so satisfying, so comforting to have it always with her that she'd guessed, after just a few days, that its value lay not so much in paper being handy but in the idea of having it so. Maybe, she'd told herself, the point is not that the words are so precious but that they might be. If you know you won't lose them you relax. All that was certain was that since getting the notebook and slipping it into her jeans she'd been scribbling more than ever, at odder and odder times, and had in fact made use of much of what had come. Perhaps not in important ways—perhaps even in contrived ways, once or twice—but it was gratifying to do and it helped to keep her working. That was what was mattered. You don't rule it, it rules you, Phillip had told her, and the business of the notebook helped her see what he'd meant. You did whatever seemed required and kept on writing things down and meanwhile hoped that in the end it made you happy, or satisfied, or willing to try again.

Her moments, her notebook, her pages and Phillip: these were the four corners of her life now, or the pillars, the irreducible elements. Take any one of them away and what she'd built up would collapse. Most of it was hers permanently, was safe and beyond loss, but not all; it was time, she'd admitted to herself very recently, to secure the final piece. I don't want to marry you, she'd said, but perhaps she'd been wrong. The fact that the idea was so bizarre and impossible (imagine what her family would say!) made it all

the more clear that it was very, very serious. Would I—
would he—have gotten into this position if there weren't
enough good reasons?, she'd asked more than once. If it
didn't run deep? Tracing back her path to where she was
now she could see how purposeful it had been. And his too.
It was no accident, their mutual reliance. It was no passing
fancy. They were filling up spaces long empty, together, and
righting ageless wrongs.

The nicest tree in the world. Those were the words.
But what they meant made no difference. It didn't even matter that she'd written them, in Dublin, or that she held them
in her hand. What was important was her place at this
desk—whatever brought her back to it, whatever trick
worked—and her nearness to him. Seeing him again at the
end of the day. And the effort in between. These were what
she treasured now. She put the notebook in her pocket and
picked up her pen and drew a perfect circle, carefully, in
the very center of the lined white paper before her. She
stared into it and sighed.

She remembers the old men. Not her father; he was young
then. The men who were old when she was a girl. Two of
them in town were missing limbs, which terrified her. For no
obvious reason she is thinking of them and of their clothing,
their habits, their peculiar ways of speech. The way they
talked about the war. Her own Papa revered them; he called
them heroes and held their coats, and made his little daughters curtsy when they came by.

She wonders if she is losing her strength, or her energy
(whatever force keeps her going), if the effort of trying to
accept and understand is proving too great. If she is seeking
peaceful shelter in her earliest years. But it's the old men,

not her childhood, that have come to be with her; she sees their whiskers and their pants legs very plainly, their well-worn shoes and their thick cigars, but not her sisters' pretty dresses, not their dolls and other toys. Something wants me, she thinks with resignation, to ponder on them. Something is bringing them to mind.

If only they knew what had become of the world. If only they knew. Forgive us, she whispers, but she is sure they do not hear.

Willie was almost around the corner when the couple caught his eye. It was one of those times when he somehow knew that a man and a woman were banging each other, even if they weren't holding hands or touching at all, and what's more there was something about them that made him get all excited and picture them in bed. Maybe because they had just come from there, or were heading there, or anyway had it on their brains, he told himself, and it was beamed over to you. Like mind reading, because their thoughts were so strong. He was no lech but neither did he object to a little pleasant daydreaming, if opportunity arose, so he stopped by the battered old mailbox to watch as they went slowly down the street.

The first thing he noticed was how attractive she was. "Delicious," he said aloud, though very softly. If he'd been alone for sure—maybe looking from his car, all the windows rolled up tight—he might have said a lot more. He loved her pretty blond hair and the jaunty way she walked; she was slim and he imagined the man's arms wrapped around her, all the way around, or even under her, holding her, as they did it standing up. Then he laughed. Must be this early warm weather, he thought, that's got me worn-out blood stirring. Maybe more than it should. Oh well, it's better than a video—Sue will get a nice surprise tonight, if she wants it—and it's free.

It was hard to stop watching but he had to. He was standing on the street, in the middle of town, plus she might turn around at any time. That's enough, he told himself, and made his eyes move to the man. So the second thing he noticed was that the man was a good deal older, much too old for a young woman like that, and the third was that it was his customer Phil. Good god, he thought. How did he manage it? Look at her. Look at them. So that's who's been driving his car.

He could tell they were happy. Despite his amazement and his sense of something wrong it made him feel kindly toward them. They were window-shopping like kids. He knew they wanted to hold hands and weren't for appearance's sake and he admired that. He wondered how they'd met. Phil had at least twenty years on her, maybe more—it was hard to tell with him, he was such an unusual guy that you could only guess how old he was, couldn't say for sure—but that must be common, thought Willie, among his crowd. Or what would be his crowd in the city. And it isn't the first time you've heard of such a thing; what about Larry and Eileen? What about Rick and Reba—she's twelve years older then him, for god's sake. Don't act so shocked. But as hard as he tried to be fair, to get over it, and as much as he wanted to approve for Phil's sake, something in him was pissed off. Or at least upset and confused.

His eyes went to her breasts and then to her ass and before he could help it the pictures started up again. He could see a new Phil, a strong Phil, one he'd never imagined, but now it all made perfect sense. Girl like that could have anyone, he told himself; he has to be doing something for her, something powerful. Something worth putting up with his forty-plus body and all the ways it's broken down. Writers were famous, he knew, for fucking up a storm with one woman after another, or at least some of them were. Though it was hard to accept this applying to Phil; it certainly took some getting used to. They were standing in front of Smet's Hardware, near the end of the block, pointing at something on display, and Willie shifted his bag from one arm to the other and waited to see what they'd do next.

That might be my Tip, he thought. That might be my Tip, in a year or two. He watched them round the corner and move out of sight, still apart, never touching each other. They'd been walking in the sunlight, while he stood in shadow. They'd been walking in a world of their own. He waited for a moment more, hoping they'd come back, and tried, very hard, to remember her face, before going on his way.

chapter

31

The man is frightened but defiant. Determined to run. Sutherland can see this even from a distance. Through the years he's been at pains to make a study of the prisoners—to observe what he can about their varied states of mind—in case he should ever become one himself. How does it feel to have your weapon taken from you? To be bullied and mocked? To be in fear of sudden death not by bullet or shell but by whim of total stranger, a stranger whose perspective, from your own point of view, is very nearly bizarre? It is one of those things, he guesses, that you can't know for sure until it happens. He hopes never to find out.

There are as many moods as captives. Some show anger, some humor, some just relief at being out of the fighting, but this rebel in his dirty too-large outfit (to call it a uniform would be ludicrous and wrong) is convinced, it is obvious, that he will never survive, and has decided to make a break when he can. He is young, raised on tales of Yankee cruelty. Or counts himself too important to lie idle in a camp. Whatever his reasons he looks like a runner about to start a race, a frozen rabbit calmly waiting for a man to get near before sprinting into the undergrowth. Sutherland studies him with loathing and with pity; he feels a need to reassure him but that impulse quickly dies.

"Problem prisoner, Sergeant," says Jenkins as he approaches. "Can't get him to properly surrender."

"Ain't that his obligation?" asks Sutherland. "I mean, seeing as we ain't shot him."

Jenkins spits. "He just tells me to go ahead."

Sutherland stands in front of the boy, who stares at the ground. "Listen," he says. "We won't shoot you cold because we're not that kind of people. Some would—on both sides, I figure—but not us. So do right and behave yourself, won't you? Don't try anything foolish. That way we won't have to hurt you and have it on our souls, and you'll make it through to the end of this business and go back to your mama some day."

The boy looks up. His eyes are stones. "What're you doing here?" he asks, in almost foreign sounds.

"Pardon?" says Sutherland.

"What're you doing here?" the young soldier asks again.

Sutherland considers him. "Watching over you," he replies.

Everything is finally ready. Not that there was much to do; his life has become so attenuated, so purposeless, that it consists of almost nothing. To change its direction requires hardly any force. Looking back he sees his very presence narrowing, narrowing, dwindling down to this one spot, this one moment; two feet on the porch outside a closed front door, fingers turning the key, eyes finding the backpack, hands lifting it to carry it to the car. A weight in his pocket that is comforting but strange. If he crashes on the highway or simply takes ill and dies the earth will be unaffected, he knows, he'll be unmourned and unmissed. If he never comes back here no one will notice; his few possessions will fade, evaporate, vanish altogether, and in a month or two they'll rent the place to someone else.

There's nothing left, is what it is. Except what he carries. To face this for even a moment is more upsetting than he can bear. It hardly seems possible—conceivable—to have lost so much so fast; he's always seen himself as free but now he knows what freedom means.

If he's honest, Charlie thinks as he climbs behind the wheel of the Valiant and heads down to Forrest Avenue for a cup of coffee to go, he will admit that he is terrified. He is almost overwhelmed. One way or another the future—beyond the single point he has so carefully prepared for—is a dreadful, daunting prospect. To find the means, somehow, to never hurt her again; quick and bitter or long an uncertain, either way he doesn't know that he can do it. He has laid out his plans but fears their going astray. Talk is cheap but action comes harder. At least there is nothing to hold him here anymore; he knows where she is (he hated lying to her sister, hated, hated, hated it, but once done it was a liberating act, the first of many he supposes) and that, it follows, is where he should be. He will do his level best to put his misery into action. The months of longing and despair, her conjured face, fuel his motions. The calculations he's made, drastic though they are, are all the guidance he has; without them there is nothing to keep him from wandering hopelessly, from giving in completely to his deep humiliation, from accepting what he loathes, what he struggles against, from being judged and sent away.

Calm as he looks, deliberate as he seems as he parks the Plymouth in the lot, walks into the donut shop, orders his breakfast, pays and takes the bag from her hand, he is different inside. He is panicked, he knows, even frantic; he is acting in this way out of grief and desperation. With a weakening mind. Something tells him not to do it (find help, find help, find help) but his legs and arms keep moving. As he leaves the lot and drives to the highway he remembers a story he was told long before, by a friend who'd served in Goose Bay. The man had read an early trader's accounting of a lynx, driven wild by fierce northern mosquitoes—and this a native mammal nearly covered by thick fur—leaping over a falls to its death. I am that lynx, he thinks as he takes the toll card from its slot in the machine and carefully chooses his direction. I am approaching the water, the spray. I am in agony; I am running. No, he thinks, accelerating down the ramp and inserting himself into the early morning flow, it's much worse than that: I've already jumped.

It happens so fast there is no time to think it over. One moment Sutherland is talking to Jenkins, who is frying some bacon, and the prisoner is singing—in that funny, airy voice—a southern song of drink and women, and the next the boy is running. Jenkins shouts and Sutherland shouts and the rebel keeps heading toward the distant springtime trees. Curse me thinks Sutherland as he shoulders and takes aim. Where's the shackle I meant to get? If I had it would

243

have saved him. He hears Jenkins's gasp as he pulls on the trigger, hears the familiar report so close to his ear, sees the slight ragged body stumble and fall. "I don't believe it," Jenkins says. "I seen it but I don't believe it." Ignoring him, Sutherland walks slowly forward—it takes forever to reach the spot—knowing just what he will find. And he does: the boy is utterly dead. Shot directly through the heart. Sutherland is wrapped in a blanket of silence, a blanket of immobility, and when Jenkins and the others approach him and speak (holding back at first, he supposes, to give him a chance to get used to it) he is unable to respond.

"Jesus, why'd you do it, Jack?" asks Jenkins. "You didn't even try to chase him." There are tears on his face. "He didn't know any better."

"Shut up," says DeCroteau.

"You of all people, Jack," says Jenkins. "I never thought I'd see the day."

"DeCroteau told you to shut your mouth," says farmer Shepperd, "and you better do it. You leave the sergeant alone. This boy was just another piece of rebel meat and you know he was trying to kill us yesterday. Maybe it was him who shot Bryant or Fiore. Or have you forgot?" He pushes Jenkins's chest with the flat of his hand. "You leave Sutherland alone."

"Oh, Jesus," says Jenkins, "I got to get out of here." Then he turns and walks away.

Sutherland stands in the middle of the field, studying the blood, while they carry off the body. The others try to stir him but when they see that they can't—just one look is all it takes—they respectfully go. He raises his sight along his stretched-out morning shadow to the tops of the trees and beyond them he imagines the way north, north to his home. That boy was crouching scared under a bush at first light, he reminds himself, when Jenkins went to have a piss, and now he's dead. His mama won't see him anymore. This should make Sutherland angry, should make him despise himself, at the very least should make him grieve, but it doesn't. The child is just another number. Another piece, as Shepperd said. There's nothing left, Jack, he thinks, the sun rising behind him. You've been reduced to a murderer. Less than a murderer. You wouldn't even wait and see; you just wanted to have it over. You did the simplest possible thing.

He reaches for the book and the picture in his pocket. He feels them as they rest there. He starts to take them out and something stops him for a moment, but then gives way. They may as well just lay here in the mud, he thinks, as anything, I got no further earthly use.

chapter

32

.

So this is what it took, thought Jane. I wish I knew her secret.

"I feel just horribly about the whole situation," said Jennie. Her hands were clasped, uncomfortably, on the table in front of her. "I hope you understand that I didn't know you existed until your note came in the mail."

"Of course," Jane told her. "You've already said so. I'm surprised he didn't tell you, though I guess I shouldn't be." The restaurant was empty but for them; in two hours people might start coming in for dinner, possibly people who would recognize them, but for now they were nearly alone. A gray-haired woman sat in the corner, reading a paperback. Two cocktails stood untouched between them, plastic stirrers lying beside. "In any case, Jennifer, I don't understand what difference it would make. I wouldn't expect you to not fall in love with him just because I did it first."

"Is that what I've done? Fall in love?"

Jane looked puzzled. "Haven't you?"

"I'm not sure," said Jennie. "I keep thinking I understand what that means and then someone tells me different." She reached for a stirrer with her left hand and lifted it, turning it in her fingers like a tiny baton. "Please call me Jennie."

"All right."

"My point," said Jennie, "is not what I knew or didn't know but that it makes me feel awful to be causing you pain. It really does."

"I appreciate that but I wouldn't have thought otherwise."

Jane sipped from her drink. Jennie also sipped and made a face, then sipped again.

"How did you find out my name?" she asked.

Jane hesitated. "I shouldn't tell you. She made me promise."

Jennie laughed. "Judith May Haas."

"That's right."

"And then you typed the envelope and had a friend mail it in Portsmouth so Phillip wouldn't know who it was from."

"I mailed it myself. But that's basically it."

"How long were you and Phillip together?"

"A very short time," Jane said, after another hesitation. "A season, really. Part of a summer plus some of the fall. I'm sorry to have to say it because it sounds like almost nothing."

"Of course not," said Jennie. "I can tell it was something."

"It was," said Jane. "It was."

"You live nearby?"

"Yes."

"What do you do?"

"I grow fruit."

"How wonderful," said Jennie. "Have I ever passed your orchard?"

"You may have, but I don't think so. It's sort of out of the way."

Jennie raised her glass and swallowed hard, then again. "I'll bet he liked it there," she said.

"I think he did," said Jane.

In a littered parking lot off the New Jersey Turnpike Charlie sits in his car. He is alarmed to be so sleepy—he had thought himself rested—and is afraid to take a nap because he'll never wake up. He know this is ridiculous, that sooner or later someone would notice and check on him, shake him, but the treat is very real, very close to his heart. Anything, he tells himself, anything can stop you now. Can and will. The easiest thing in the world would be for you to change your mind. The hardest will be to follow through. But you owe it to yourself. Fatigue, hunger, fear, common sense— they're all against you. All you have is your passion. There is nothing to go back for so you must move on ahead.

Families come and go, salesmen and saleswomen, young people like him, on their way to and from the toilets, the fried food, the candy machines. He watches them with envy but no malice; he hopes they'll all be safe by nightfall. He wants them to be happy. Appreciate, he tells them, all the blessings you've received. Try not to let them slip away.

It must never, he thinks, happen again. Never, never, never.

He drifts in and out of sleep or of a not-quite-sleeping trance, waiting for the numbers on the dashboard clock to change so he can start the engine and drive again.

"It's a little bit awkward to discuss him like this."

"It certainly is. We don't really know each other."

"And I've never talked about him with anybody. No one in my life knows the first thing about . . . us."

Jane watched her for several seconds. "It was the same way for me," she said at last. "I suppose that's how it will always be with him." Then she looked down at the table. "I'm sorry," she said. "I know you're hoping for something different."

"I don't know what I'm hoping for. But if we stayed together, yes, it would have to be different."

Weight shifting on a chair. Fingers lightly tapping glass. "Is that a possibility?"

"I can't say for sure," said Jennie. "I've just started to take it seriously."

There was silence for a minute while each finished her drink. The only sound was of traffic on the roadway outside, and of the woman turning pages. Jane picked up a stirrer and used it to push her ice around.

"The fact is that what I really miss is fucking him," she said, very quietly. "More than anything."

"Oh," said Jennie.

"I have no immediate prospects for an alternative."

"I'm sorry," said Jennie.

"I had to wait years to find something like that, which makes it harder to do without. You've probably been having good times since you were fifteen so it may not be easy to imagine what I'm going through."

Jennie slowly shook her head. "Don't be mean," she said. "This isn't my fault and I think you should be nice to me. I haven't done anything wrong."

"I'm sorry."

"And I'm not some little slut."

"I didn't mean to say you were. I would never use that word. I'm just envious."

"I've only had serious boyfriends. All my life."

"That's a pretty short life, dear."

Jennie stood. "I don't understand," she said. "If you have something to work out with Phillip I wish you'd go see him about it. Why are you punishing me?" Her face was pink and her fists clenched. The woman in the corner was looking at them, the book open in her hand. Jane reached across the table.

"I'm sorry," she said. "You're right. I'm handling this very badly. Please sit down and help me figure out what I'm doing here."

Jennie shook her head again and sat. "Since you put it that way I guess I have to," she said.

Jane turned to the corner. "Excuse me," she called. "I think we'd both like some more."

The bright blue Lexus cuts him off. For a moment he's uncertain of what to do. The other bumper passes no more than two feet from his own which is dangerous and irresponsible, he knows, not to mention plain rude. He is filled with a desire to correct the other driver; not to hurt, not to condemn, but simply to educate. He wants to find a way to talk, to converse. But as he steps on the gas and pulls up alongside—the battered white Econoline that was clogging the center lane has finally moved right—he sees a sullen young man who won't look at him. Who is ignoring him. Deliberately pretending not to realize he's there. Anger overtakes all his earnestness, his generosity, and he wants to stamp and shout. Damn you, he thinks, there's a person here too. Why would you ever do something like that? Why would you show such contempt for the rest of us? His eyes go back and forth between the road and the Lexus as they slowly gain speed but the young man won't budge, won't look, won't even give him the satisfaction of dropping back or pulling ahead, though the highway is now clear both in front and behind.

He is tempted to take hold of his burden; he is tempted to cut everything short. No. No, he tells himself. Too many hours of thought, of preparation, have gone into his plan, too much investment to throw away. Do not become what you dread. This fellow-traveler is worth nothing, his very residence unknown, his history unimportant. Charlie does not exist for him, but is everything to Charlie; as little as he has now he continues at the center of his own pathetic life.

That would be stupid, he thinks. Forget about it. You may be crazy but you still aren't dumb.

"You're so pretty."

"I think you're very attractive too."

Jane sipped her drink. "Oh, come on, Jennie. You don't have to say that. I was talking to myself. What I meant was that I can't blame Phillip at all. You're so lovely. Exceptional, really. Not that I think that's why he cares for you—don't be insulted—but he must have been tempted from the very beginning. Especially with you staying in his house."

"I'm serious," said Jennie. "I know Phillip well enough to know he wanted you the minute he saw you. I'm sure he did." She smiled. "To tell you the truth I feel kind of threatened."

"By *me*?"

"Yes."

Jane smiled too. "I don't believe you but it's nice of you to say so."

Jennie looked over at the woman in the corner, then at her empty glass, then leaned closer to Jane. "You and Phillip had a good time together, huh?"

"We did. I'm afraid I didn't even know anything like that was possible until I had it with him."

"Not when you were my age?"

"Lord, no."

Jennie looked down. "Can I ask you something else?"

"Of course."

"Are you attracted to me?" she asked, almost whispering.

There was silence.

"Be honest."

Jane finished her drink. "All right," she said. I will. I am."

Jennie nodded.

"How did you know?"

"Just did."

"Am I that easy to read?"

"It's just something I can see when it happens," Jennie said. She moved her glass around the table. "First time?"

"No," said Jane. "I'll stay honest. It isn't."

A man in a dirty white uniform pushed the kitchen door open and waited for the woman in the corner to look up. She didn't but instead of calling out to her he stepped back and let the door swing closed.

"You're a little high, aren't you?" asked Jane.

Jennie nodded again. "Well, of course. More than a little. I wouldn't discuss it if I weren't." She looked around, then at Jane. "This is so unusual, Jane. I feel so close to you."

"But we hardly know each other."

"That's right."

The woman got up and came over and asked if they wanted another round. Jane nodded and they waited silently until she made the drinks at the bar and brought them to the table, and went back to her stool.

"It helps that I'm attracted to you also," said Jennie.

"Oh dear. Please don't say that."

"It's true."

"Maybe so, but either way it makes me nervous and unhappy."

"Oh," said Jennie. "I'm sorry then."

"It's all right."

"It *is* the first time for me, you know," said Jennie. "I was sure I'd never see another woman this way."

"Especially one old enough to be your mother."

"You said it, not me."

"Don't you think," asked Jane, "that it has mostly to do with the liquor, and with Phillip?"

"So what if it does?"

Jane swallowed. "I don't know. It might be informative to consider it in those terms, that's all."

Jennie's voice rose a little and the woman in the corner looked up, very briefly. "Informative of what?" she asked. "I'm not trying to understand it. I shouldn't even have said it. I'm just sitting here drunk in a peculiar situation because you asked me to meet so we could talk." She raised her glass. "And I still don't know what it is you wanted to talk about."

"I guess you don't."

"Look Jane," said Jennie, "Phillip and I are together now but if you wanted to come over some evening . . . well, why don't you? It would be fun to see what happened."

"You don't mean it."

"We could share him, the one time anyway. I'm sure he'd love it. I probably would too."

Jane put out her hand. "Jennie," she said. "Stop it. Why would you say such a thing?"

Jennie leaned forward. *"Because I feel bad,"* she said. *"Because this makes me feel bad."* She was trembling. "I'm never going to love anyone the way I love that man and now you're telling me the same is true of you. That I'm ruining your life. Isn't that right? Isn't it?" She sat back in her chair and closed her eyes. "This is a nightmare," she whispered.

"Jennie," said Jane. "My life isn't ruined. And if anyone hurt me it wasn't you. You had nothing to do with it."

"Then why am I here?"

"I honestly don't know," said Jane. "Stop acting like I'm in control. I'm not. I made a mistake. We should never have met."

Jennie sat up and reached across the table to touch her hand. "I'm glad we have," she said.

"Forget all about it."

"That's not likely."

"I suppose not," said Jane.

"I'm very upset and I wish you didn't exist at all but I really do like you. I really do. I want to meet you again."

"That's a terrible idea."

"Maybe so, but I do."

"Jennie," said Jane. "I've done a very wrong thing by putting you through this. I should be talking to Phillip as you say, not to you. All these feelings for me are because you're trying to be decent in the face of it. In the face of my poor judgment. I'm going to pay for the drinks now and call a cab to meet me at Phillip's house—your house too, I think, by this time—and drive you there in your car and get out at the bottom of the driveway. And then you're off the hook, OK? Please do pretend I never wrote to you. That you never saw me. Please, please do."

"That's all well and good, but I meant what I said," Jennie told her, very slowly. "I hope you'll come see us sometime." She looked up from her glass. "Nobody has to do anything they don't want to. OK?" Then her eyes filled with tears.

A black mood had taken Phillip. While once used to such
diversions he had gone so long without them that it filled
him with surprise. Worse than surprise; it was a shock that
stirred him profoundly. Hard as it was to walk, as he was
doing, in a curved but steady line, to navigate the forest
floor, it would have been impossible to have kept himself
still, at his desk or in a chair or in the company of Jennie.
He was angry at her without knowing why but that was much
the smaller part; he saw it as the product of a deeper disturbance. Mostly he hated his work. His book. He hated the
fact of being a writer. It was more than just fatigue or accumulated reaction, more than the ennui, the despair he often
felt over the endless tedious process. Something about putting words to paper had enraged him, though he couldn't say

what or at whom. Himself, logically, but it was bigger than that; perhaps also his history, his ancestry, his luck—whatever had caused him to end up this way. Draining himself daily into work that no one cared about. Work of no hard value. Not that people wouldn't read it, wouldn't admire it and be moved by it, but in the end they wouldn't care, not the way they cared about their children and their mortgages. Even Jennie; she would love his art fiercely, almost as fiercely as he did, but in the end it wouldn't matter to her as much as his endearments, as his penis, as his smile.

It's not that it isn't beautiful, he told himself as he strode along the muddy path toward the setting sun. It's not that it isn't important. It's just that it doesn't have to be. If it didn't exist no one would need to invent it. He wished he'd been a doctor like his father, or a cook, or even a sewer man, a latter-day Norton, anything that would have him doing something useful or necessary. His opinion of his own meaning, his significance in the world was most graphically expressed by the nausea that grew in him. Throw it up, he urged himself, go ahead and throw it up. Whatever you swallowed thirty or forty years ago. Whatever disgusting thing lives in there, feeding on your substance, perverting your principal. Throw it up and move on.

He knew he had upset and wounded Jennie as he left her; he could still see her face as he'd hurried out the door. He was ashamed but in some ways unmoved, and reproved himself mainly for not speaking his mind. Get used to it, he wanted to tell her—you've had it too easy since I came to your bed. It's been one big afterglow, one long post-coital cigarette, but the moment is finally over. I'm a difficult man and you'd best be prepared for it, and what's more I suspect you can be difficult too. If we end up preserving the larger blessings we've found—our conversation, our lovemaking, the useful way we share our time—we'll be doing very well. All this niceness and joy has been fun but unreal. Time to walk away from paradise and be like everyone else.

He stopped at a favorite glacial boulder (it was shaped like an Easter Island statue, he thought, or at least like the one in front of the South Pacific restaurant on the highway outside Bradley) and sat on a smaller rock that stood by its side. It was too cold for him to sit but now he felt, though he'd been egged on by furies a moment before, afraid to take another step. He looked at a tiny patch of ice, somehow un-melted, on the stone wall nearby, and pictured again her un-happy expression as he'd pushed his way past. It was mean and vindictive of him, he acknowledged, unfair to her and to himself, to disguise his private anger as the end of their happiness. Of their initial, pure happiness, which they would never have again, no matter how long together. At forty-six he'd be an ass to cut it off too soon; no matter what happened it was the last time round for him. The first as well, maybe, he wasn't entirely sure—it was hard to recall the pleasant early months with Miriam, which made him very sad, and with Andrea and Gina he'd been too distant, sorry to say, or at least too self-controlled—but the last with-out a doubt. He was amazed to sense his mood softening, very slightly, as he remembered her kisses of yesterday, her laughter at dinner in the evening, and while he knew that their innocence was, in fact, on the verge of its departure, he was certain it hadn't yet gone.

And it was crushingly clear that he was upset about his work. About this one book or all of them, the text or the chapter heads, the keyboard or the printer ribbons or the same old view from his same old west window; whatever it was it was the artist not the lover who wanted to transform himself, to strip off his identity and cast it away. Maybe, he thought, she is giving you a reason. A reason to get off of the carnival ride. Maybe there simply isn't room for the both of them; writing or Jennie, you may have to choose. This had the ring of truth but was also enormously frightening because it was the writer, after all, who had fallen for Jennie, and the writer she'd come to care for herself, and he knew that even with her beside him—even feeling as he felt at this moment—he would never be able to stop. He'd be at it until the bitter end. Not that she'd help him quit anyway; she'd be rocked by the very idea. An interesting paradox: to hold on to what you cherish you'll have to watch it change its nature. Or to preserve it, let it go. Take your time as you decide.

He turned to look behind him—the slope to the east was brightly spotted, in places, by the broken orange light that worked its way through the clouds—and was reminded of the Maritimes. Of the park he'd stayed at the June before last, in search of respite and relief. It had come to him suddenly, the desire to escape; on the verge of finishing a difficult book he'd found himself in need of solitude, a solitude greater and more enduring than that which formed his daily life, and had recalled a friend's description of a northeastern Eden from a number of years before. He'd hauled out his atlas and found the spot, loaded up his car and driven there in one day, without so much as a phone call for information, without his manuscript or even pen and paper but with three novels he'd been wanting very badly to read and all his camping and hiking gear, and arrived to find everything he'd hoped for. Everything he'd been led to expect. A place—the whole province—like the world of his childhood, a world he'd said goodbye to long before: not yet crowded, still intact, made of dairy farms and small cities and towns and fresh vegetables sold at the side of the road by people who actually asked how far he'd come, who never wished him a nice day. A clean two-lane highway running through the rolling hills. Plain white village churches with gardens beside.

But the best part, by far, had been the park by the bay. His tent and sleeping bag had never left the Volvo's trunk because he'd discovered, as he drove down the slope toward the headquarters, a cluster of cabins (*chalets* they were called and that was okay with him) that had charmed him, won him over in moments, made him want his dead father—and his dead mother too—to come and join him for the trip they'd never had. Due to the early date and the fact that it was Monday he'd had a wide choice of cabins and the woman at the desk—Janice, it was, a lighthearted person helped him decide by telling him which were occupied and even by whom. She'd seemed to understand his need. He'd been so pleased by the setting, by the multicolored cabins and the pine needles and the view of the water, and by what he'd found inside after turning the key—bare wood walls with a calendar from a hardware store and another from the Boy Scouts, the neat little kitchen with its mismatched plates and cups, the gas heater, the hooked rug, the ancient musty wardrobe—that he'd sat with a mug of instant coffee for half an hour or more, not moving except to sip, just looking around him and at the trees outside his window and the next chalet over and the Adirondack chairs, watching the evening slowly fade.

For four peaceful days he'd hiked and slept and read, his first real vacation in decades. Somehow he'd managed a departure from himself. Talking only to Janice and her husband, covering miles and miles of trails without encounter, driving up and down the coast in the late midsummer light, he'd been carried off by nature in a way that hadn't happened for at least twenty hardworking years. A firm lesson he'd badly needed—creation was the source of all beauty, not his overburdened mind—and had accepted with good cheer. He'd been restored by all the hours without his beastly book, his picky sentences, his frustrated pacings and sighs, wondering more than once why it had taken him so long, and had thought about returning (although aware that if routine it might lose most of its value). But rather than fretting he'd accepted it as the singular experience it was, true serendipity, enjoying it while it lasted instead of killing it with regret.

The tides, much discussed, had been worth the journey anyway. It was rare indeed, he'd mused, to find something you actually had to see to believe. No matter what you'd heard. But there it had been, before his eyes: endless blue at dawn, endless gravel by noon. Boats resting tilted on the bottom at nine but riding high at three. As pleased as he'd been to understand the explanations on the signs even that had been peripheral. For once he'd found himself in awe. There is a power, he'd told himself, standing and staring, you'll never have nor understand.

So why am I remembering this now? he asked as he grew chilly on his rock three hundred miles to the south. Why do I want so to be there again? Alone—without her. That must be what I'm thinking. But why? And how so? And what good would it do?

On his last evening, Friday, with the park filling up, a family had moved into the cabin next door. Coming back from his hike he'd caught the older woman's eye as she unpacked their van, and waved in response to her call; with excellent timing she'd knocked on his door, soon after he'd finished both his dinner and a book, and invited him over. He'd gladly gone with her and accepted a drink, shaking hands with the party—aging parents and their daughter of not quite thirty-five, plus a sister and her own young teenager—before settling himself on one of the beds, unembarrassed by the fact that he'd clearly been recruited as company for Penny, unmarried offspring of Leora and Sal. He'd liked Penny; though not very attractive she'd been warm and funny, with neat hair and clear skin, and as he'd finished one whiskey and started the next, talking with Sal about his business in Fredericton and with Leora about their yearly visits to the bay since Penny was a very small girl, he'd thought with pleasure of kissing her. They'd never stand for her spending the night, he'd told himself, astonished at his uncharacteristic willingness to engage, but maybe I can get her off alone on a walk. I'll bet she's eager as can be.

And then he'd noticed the other girl watching him. Fourteen at most—much too young for any man—she'd been both lovely and intent, staring at his face, silent and graceful on a stool in the corner. He'd thrilled to the discovery and also loathed himself, badly weakened by his unexpected envy, his little desire. Their eyes had met and broken away once, twice, thrice by the time Sal had asked if he would stay for a dinner of grilled steak and lamb. "No thank you," he'd said, "I'd really love to but I've eaten," trying frantically not to look at his host's niece again, putting down his glass and rising, backing all too quickly through the doorway to their puzzled farewells. He'd felt badly about Penny—knowing she had understood the way his mind had run—and had thought more than once about going back, about forcing down a chop so he could have the chance to stroll with her to a spot overlooking the sea. But it was impossible. He simply couldn't have risked being near the girl, risked her looking at him again, risked her mother's seeing what she'd brought into his eyes.

It wasn't Jennie. It *was* the book. It wasn't love, it

wasn't sex, it was the book, the book, the damned book. His buttocks were cold and so was his heart as he felt himself turn against his own begotten child. He stood and took a step or two then stopped on the path in the deepening gloom.

"Sutherland," he shouted. "You listen to me. I want you out of my life. D'you understand? We're through. Don't come around me anymore."

He heard a very faint echo, and the scurry of a chipmunk he'd startled from the wall, but otherwise no reply.

"Sutherland," he begged, much more gently, much more softly, "will you for god's sake leave me be?"

Hello Bertha.
Hello Boy.
There they are.
I've been watching.
You know they're cousins?
Now I do.
Thought I should tell you.
It's worth knowing.
It might be.
The man is cousin to me also.
Another interesting fact.
Perhaps you and I?
I doubt it. But who can say?
Not you?
That's information I don't have.
Then how did you know my name?
I hate to tell you but I've been here for a very long time.
I'm awfully sorry.
So am I.

Flow gently sweet Afton, among thy green braes;
Flow gently, I'll sing thee a song in thy praise;
My Mary's asleep by thy murmuring stream,
Flow gently sweet Afton, disturb not her dream.

His voice slowly grew stronger. Almost hidden at first
by hers, weak and timid (there's a switch, he thought) beneath her easy confidence, it deepened and grew. She
smiled as they sang.

Thou stockdove whose echo resounds from the hill,
Ye wild whistling blackbirds in yon thorny dell,
Though green-crested lapwing, thy screaming forbear
I charge you, disturb not my slumbering fair.

Without an instrument accompanying he felt naked and wrong, but only for a little while; it was as if her beauty, which he'd tried and failed so many times to share, had finally made its way to him, graced him, through the method of her music. She taught him what he already knew but on paper only, in his silent written words, and to find this voice outside himself along with the other—because Jennie sat and sang with him, and held his arm—seemed miraculous reward.

> The crystal stream Afton, how lovely it glides,
> And winds by the cot where my Mary reside.
> How wanton thy waters her snowy feet lave,
> As gathering sweet flowrets she stems thy clear wave.

At last he was as loud and as vigorous as she. Not as tuneful, perhaps, but unstrictured and entire. He looked from her face to the fire to her face again and found himself moved by a strange profound excitement. No more fear. No more fear. He still felt, as sure as anything, the hand cradling his heart. But now its fingers told of joy.

> Flow gently sweet Afton, among thy green braes,
> Flow gently sweet river, the theme of my lays;
> My Mary's asleep by thy murmuring stream,
> Flow gently sweet Afton, disturb not her dream.

Bob thought it misguided and she really couldn't blame him. She was very hard put to explain it herself. But something called to her—called, beckoned, persuaded, urged, seduced, coaxed, it didn't matter how she put it—and she guessed the time had come to concede to intuition, or at

r. c. binstock

least to go along for the ride. What possible harm? Perhaps her daughter would be annoyed that she'd arrived without warning, or perhaps her nephew would. Perhaps one or both would be elsewhere. No great loss regardless. She was prepared to turn the rental car around and head back to the city for any good reason, in fact for any reason at all; she had the resources, as it happened, to stake some money and some time on a single whimsical chance. If it ended up being just a visit to Boston that was all right with her, but she suspected it wouldn't. She knew they would welcome her sooner or later. And something deep within her told her sternly to go, to go, and she was well inclined to listen.

Best to leave the house now, before her husband got home, and avoid another argument. She could call him from the airport. She carried her small gray suitcase out to the car and paused to look around—at the wide grassy yard in which Amy and Emily had first learned to cartwheel, at the pool in which Jennie had first learned to swim, at the apricot tree—before getting inside and backing carefully to the street and then driving away.

It isn't the wound so much as the fever. It isn't the hole in his ribcage so much as the pain in his head. They all offer reassurance but he knows he's lost at last. Lost the gamble he can't even remember taking, it was so long ago. He feels regret, now and then, for the grief it will cause Martha, perhaps one or two others, and for the child he never had, but beyond these misgivings there is mostly relief. The strain of waiting for this—of trying to avoid it but not knowing how—has been terrible, almost inhuman; he gladly gives up his place in the elite, the blessed untouched, and joins the thousands of his fellows. Better a wound than pneumonia, he

266

thinks, or worse, or doesn't matter; what's to choose between this fever and a stroke at eighty-three? Either way it's an end.

He knew he finally saw the truth. Who could have told him that a life, four decades, so many springs and summer and falls, could ever come down to a single pure moment of recognition like this? He's been so stupid. Staring at her with deep affection, with a devotion that for once he felt no need to disguise; giving himself as freely as he could imagine— as freely as he'd ever wanted to—without saying a word. He was glad she wasn't frightened. But there she was, staring back, the same triumph in her eyes, no doubt the same ache in the chest, the same wild eagerness to leap on and devour him that he had for her, holding back just as he was because the happiness of putting it off another instant was so deep (if impossible to bear). It was just a passing moment no matter how long it lasted; they were poised on the border of a different existence. They were ready to begin. Once giving in to their excitement, once embraced, they could never return to this threshold. Better to know it as well as they could. To have it to feed on for the rest of their lives.

Was it true? Was it really? He briefly faltered. He was uncertain. But then his joy came flooding back.

Not that either of them had expected it, ever; their astonishment was nearly as great as their desire. They looked at each other with wild surmise. Another painful aspect, another treasure to remember—the way they'd both found so much more than they'd asked for. More than they knew they could. Twenty-four years, sad history, a continent between them, but in the end it worked the same: contentment rediscovered in an unintended place. And accepted with wonder and regret.

The night is dark and deep as he drives the rural highway. He hasn't seen a route number for half an hour or more. He understands that this may be his fault, not theirs—perhaps he failed to notice the signs for the same reason he left the interstate, a reason he can't begin to find the edges of, never mind lay out in full—but still he needs to know. He accepts that wasting time, getting lost, arriving at his destination that much later was a part of his plan, an unannounced part, but he can't help feeling anxious. Maybe I'm farther off track than I realize, he thinks. Maybe this isn't Massachusetts anymore; maybe I'm in Maine. His geography is excellent but no match for the forces at large in his head. Panic, panic, panic, don't panic; shut up shut up shut up shut *up*! Time to stop the car, to find someone, anyone to exchange a few words with, to remind himself again that he is still a human being. But it's the middle of the night in the middle of nowhere and he can't see a light, never mind a place to stop. He isn't sure what to do. Shut the car off and sleep? Go on foot? They'd find him dead in the morning, dragged down by wolves or bears, lying in the forest long miles from the road.

Then he rounds a downhill curve and discovers salvation: a crossroads complete with flashing light and destination signs, and a gas station and diner. Inside he sees the counterman wiping things down, clearly ready to close if he hasn't already. Why's he still open? Maybe a late celebration? Charlie parks the car, leaps out, tries the door and to his relief finds it unlocked, walks in.

"Closing up," says the man.

"Any coffee?" asks Charlie, who has already seen half

a pot on the burner, the orange light glowing. "I'd love a cup to go."

"Long drive?" asks the man, dropping his rag on the counter, moving slowly to the coffee machine, lifting a foam container.

"Yeah," says Charlie. "Too long. But I caught some rest today.

The man looks at him, then starts pouring again. "Ain't no concern of mine." he says.

When the cup is full Charlie asks for another. When both are ready the man puts covers on—after gesturing toward the milk and sugar and watching his customer shake his head—and sets them net to the register. "Buck thirty," he says.

"Need directions," says Charlie.

"Where you going?"

"New Chatham."

"Not much more than an hour. Just stay right on this road."

The fever breaks. He is astonished but pleased. He should be grateful to the Lord but instead he is smug in a small silly way like the time he won a dollar on a footrace, or when they issued him new boots that really fit. He should be offering up thanks but instead he is wondering when they'll bring something to eat. He understands the implications of a wound in the abdomen but he is ravenously hungry. Must be going to live, he thinks, if I'm so hungry. Dead man has no such interest in food. How long has it been since I was shot anyway? Maybe it's healed enough. Maybe it never got my stomach in the first place. He knows he isn't going to die but feels that if he doesn't eat he will quickly be insane. He looks around for an attendant but the ward is very quiet and he sees no one moving. Without trying it he knows he is too weak to stand. He is afraid to raise his voice. What will I do, he asks himself, just lie here and starve? Damn them for leaving me this way.

The enters the room with great caution, very slowly. As if she fears tripping over something in the dark, though of course it won't happen. This was papa's room, she thinks. And Mama's too, long ago. As she watches the bed and re- members her parents what used to be her hand flies to her mouth, to the site of her mouth. There might be children, she thinks. He's not too old. They might have children. They could be Papa and Mama, so many years ago.

But you're here, she tells herself, for a very different reason. You have knowledge to share. She approaches the bed. Around the left where the girl is; she shrinks from the man. She leans over and looks at the face on the pillow. So sweet. So relaxed. She is sorry to disturb her but knows it simply must be done. Wake up! Wake up young lady! She tries her best to shout, tries to grab hold and shake, but none of it works; she finds herself without power. The girl contin- ues to sleep.

Wake up young lady! Won't you please wake up, wake up!

Oh my goodness, she can't hear me.

Without knowing what had roused him Phillip struggled out of sleep. He had questions to answer. As he forced his eyes open he found her beside him and it wasn't a dream, it was real; to wake to her presence instead of empty bed made him lie there and weep. All those years, all those years. All those lonely, lonely years. Here was an opportunity, he knew, to get his life back to even, to outweigh all his regrets with enormous good fortune. To never be sorry about any of it again. As he wept he felt a broader and heavier sense of loss, curiously, than he had ever known before, which was saying a great deal, and for a short but frightening time he thought it would tear him in two. His mother, Carla, lovers, friends, the work he'd never gotten right; all the second chances he'd ever wanted and been denied gathered round him in the dark, pressing on him, so he could feel of them and know that they would not disturb his peace. Wanting what I once had, he thought, as if I'd never had it; that's all over with now. I have her and she me, which is enough to ease the burden. As a writer he felt it was contrived, artificial, almost a caricature but as a man he knew a clear chance when he saw it. A chance not to be missed.

"Stay with me," he told her. "Dearest Jennie, please stay." She couldn't hear him—he hoped she couldn't hear him—but there would be time in the morning. All he had to do was wait.

"You're going home," says the colonel.

"I'm not," says the soldier.

"You are. I swear. The moment you're well enough to leave."

Sutherland frowns. "Where are we, sir?"

"Do you really not know? Have you been so very ill? In any case it doesn't matter. I can arrange for transportation."

The man in the next bed—the one who lost both hand and leg, but on opposite sides—is watching and listening. Sutherland turns and takes care to speak quietly.

"What about you?" he asks.

His colonel smiles. "I'll be just fine, Jack. Don't worry about me. The war is nearly over. I'll be joining you soon."

"If the war is almost done why should I be given leave? I've come this far."

"Too far," says the officer. "When I saw you down, all bloody, it scared me worse than I can say. As God is my witness, Jack, I knew you had to be taken care of. I could see your wife's face, plain as your own, asking me what happened to you. I knew then you'd come to the end of your run."

Sutherland draws a deep breath. "They tell me, sir, that you carried me off."

"With help from others, yes."

"Appreciate it."

"Gladly."

They sit in silence, watching the attendants make their way down the aisle with water and bread. There is noise everywhere—grunts, groans, sighs, curses and angry words, metal on metal, pails striking the floor—but it is the most muffled noise, the most secret noise that Sutherland has ever heard. In the corner stand three doctors; he watches one turn to another and violently shake his head.

"Listen, Jack," says the commander. "When I'm back you'll come to my red-brick house, down on Fairmont street by the cat-tail swamp, and drink good wine with me. That is an order."

Sutherland looks but says nothing.

"By God I'm glad we saved you in time. I'll never forget you. Never."

The man is trembling with emotion; out of shame he averts his eyes.

"Agreed, Colonel, with pleasure," answers Sutherland. "Done and done."

This time she thinks she can manage it. There's only one in the bed and the light's a little brighter. Or the darkness not so strong. At least it seems that way to Bertha. But that means dawn is coming on and there is little time to waste. It took her forever to think it through, to find her way. The message is still unconveyed. She does her very best and believes for a while that she is making steady progress but then feels harsh despair. The woman is no more wakeful than when she first arrived.

Don't you remember? she asks. I think we met, in fact I'm sure of it. My father knew your father. And we were customers of yours. I'm almost sure I watched you play. There is a stirring in the bed.

He comes in tears. Forgive us, oh God forgive us. Having stopped the car to sleep only miles from his goal he is awakened, to his grief, on the same road but in daylight, the same path to an ending he can no longer abide. Except there's nothing else to do. Any path, any option is hopeless; he knows he should make use of the least harmful one, the most brutal briefest one, and steer at full speed for an abutment or a tree, but his courage repeatedly fails. Never to hurt her, a voice whispers, or anyone ever; that would do it. Never again. He unfastens his seat belt, even makes a run or two on the longest, straightest stretches, but he can't. He detests himself. In your pocket, says the voice, in your pocket, in your pocket, so much easier that way. But he knows it isn't true.

So now he's driving to New Chatham to buy his break-fast, to ask his questions, to find the house, to do what he came for. He has no choice.

What's that? asked Bill. Out of dreams of loaves and fishes something brought him wide awake. His alarm would soon be heard. In it's silence he strained to listen. After a moment the sound again. Could be Dad, he thought, and wanted to call. But instead he held his peace.

The doorbell rang. She rolled out of bed, grabbed her robe, looked at him with a puzzling kind of fragile adoration, went quickly through the hall and down the stairs to answer it. It was important not to wake him. When she opened the door the cold air froze her feet and she wished for her slippers, but they were next to the bed.

"I'm sorry," said Jane. "I know it's very early."

"You're here for Phillip," said Jennie.

Jane shook her head. "I'm here for you."

Taking hold of Jane's elbow and pulling her inside, Jennie shut the door. It was still chilly in the hall—she'd have to get those slippers soon—but much better without the wind. She folded her arms and waited.

"We need to talk," said Jane. "More, I mean. More than we did. I think I can explain."

Jennie smiled. "Explain what?"

"Not much" said Jane, smiling too. "Not much more than before. I still don't know what I'm doing here. But I'd appreciate it if you'd come out with me."

"Are you sure? I felt we were lucky to do so well last time."

"Probably," said Jane. "I know it seems ridiculous. But I'd appreciate it. I think it will be worth your while." She held out a pink and white blossom. "In apology," she said.

"All right," Jennie answered, looking briefly at the flower, which Jane placed gently on the table. "Let me go and get dressed. You want coffee?"

Jane shook her head. "We'll get it in town," she said. She watched the other start toward the stairs and reached out her hand.

"Leave him up there," she said. "I don't want to see him now."

As she threw on her sweat suit and socks Jennie watched Phillip's face. She couldn't tell whether he was asleep or just pretending. It was past time for him to have risen.

"Phillip," she whispered. "I'm going out now. I'll be back later on. I'll see you at lunch, maybe, or if not then at dinner."

He was absolutely still. Sleeping, she thought, he must be sleeping. Otherwise he'd answer me.

She paused on her way. "I do love you," she said without turning, "I'll be back," and then went on down the stairs. There was the sound of a heavy door, closing, on an empty hallway, and finally silence again.

Two cars pass on the road, in the early morning light. The driver going east fights the sun in his eyes.

That was Jane, he told himself. Very quiet but it was her. What was she doing here? When did they meet? He was confused, hurt, frightened, almost slapped in the face. One wild development after another; he felt, for the first time, that he might not keep up. He wondered what they were saying and was made a little anxious by the thought of shared secrets. He wanted, he found, to believe they wouldn't do that but didn't know if he could.

Remain calm, he thought. Do take a breath and stay calm. Nothing's threatened by their talking, by their being together. They were somehow put in touch; Jane's understandably upset. For what it's worth you deserve to feel badly about her—you should, now that this chicken's come to roost—but she can't tell Jennie anything new. Anything that would do damage. And she can't possibly bear you ill will; angry, yes, bitter quite possibly, but she doesn't wish you harm.

As he made himself coffee he felt serenity returning. In fact he almost had to laugh. Little Phillie, of all people, at the center of a quarrel. That was a humorous change. He didn't actually believe they were fighting—more like poking fun at him, he guessed, though he hoped it was relatively mild—but even the idea of his having two mistresses in one place at the same time was enough to set him chuckling. From lonely boy to lover boy, he thought. No one who knows you would believe it.

He was halfway up the stairs with a mug and carafe in hand when he saw the absurdity of it. He would never be able to get anything done until Jennie had come home. All right, he asked himself, as he dressed in the bedroom, how long do you have? An hour at least, maybe two, maybe more. And if she gets back before you that's all well and good; she'll see how much you cared, how much it disturbed you when she suddenly went away. He knew the thought as unworthy and tried to push it from him—it was not a time to start on that kind of tit for tat, not just because Jane (a third party after all) had come knocking at dawn—but a very slight sense of advantage, of righteousness in being hurt by Jennie's unnatural departure, clung to him no matter what he did. Oh well, he thought, if you marry her it won't be the last time. There'll be plenty of reasons for both of you to be aggrieved, goodness knows. What is it they always say? Just don't go to bed mad.

The plane had almost landed—the sky bright pink over the wing and over the flats that once were water and shoals, and deep harbor beyond—when Carla thought she heard a cry.

As he went words dame. Words he'd been seeking for a week or maybe more. Something urged him to go on but could not overcome all the force of his habit, not that he really wanted it to, and he gracefully turned and went up to his study. I won't even take my jacket off, he thought. I'll just write all this down. It was an effort but he kept his hand away from the computer. It'll still be there this afternoon, he told himself, after you've seen Jennie and you're both reassured. The book—the goddamned book—can wait now. There's a lot more to life. Everything, finally, in its proper rightful place.

The doorbell rang. Again? he thought. Twice in one day? Unheard of at this address. Perhaps Jennie had forgotten her key and he'd left the door locked. Or she had Jane with her and wanted permission to bring her in. He patiently finished the last of his phrases, refusing to be distracted into losing anything, then set the pen carefully on the desk and went quickly down the stairs.

A young man stood on the stoop. Behind him were the naked trees.

"Where's Jennie?" he demanded.

"She isn't here," answered Phillip, and cursed himself for it—for saying anything at all. What a cowardly way to be.

The man was staring. "This is my house," Phillip told him. "What do you want?"

There was silence between them. A cold wind blew into the hall. He wanted to step outside and pull the door shut behind him but the other was in the way and it seemed unwise to push and shove. Hard as it was he stood his ground.

"What do you want?" he asked again.

The young man turned—Phillip got a last good look at his unshaven cheeks and throat, at his moist, red eyes, at the ragged army jacket and the stain on his gray T-shirt and the faded black jeans—and went down the walk to his dirty, battered Plymouth, parked two inches behind the Volvo. Phillip prepared to call the police. This man is dangerous he thought with sudden fear. Stay calm, stay very calm, remember what he looks like. He's very, very dangerous, could do anything. Look closely at the car, get the plate, tell them exactly where you are so they can find him on the road. Then the young man turned around.

It was the loudest sound he'd ever heard. The brightest light. The most horrible pain. The world spun and crashed and he heard a stricken sob.

Heartbeat. Heart-beat.

And the world went out.

His fever is back and he dreams of the prisoner. DeCroteau shoots to kill and he leaps in between.

Are you crazy? shouts Jenkins. But the ball passes through him and goes right where it was aimed.

*   *   *

She would weep if she could but she can't; she would do anything for him, for the girl, for Kate, for anyone anywhere but she can't. All she can do is remember. It's the only thing she's capable of. It's all they've left her.

You saved one of them, she thinks. That could be what was intended. Or maybe you failed him. But it's all over now.

She sits on the stoop and waits for the end. Free at last. There is nothing to hold her. I could go on to Boston, she thinks, anytime. Or to Chicago, or London, or to Paris or Rome.

Was that my doing? Was it me? Because I judged them and was angry? Because I loved them anyway? She is upset, she is distressed by the thought that she never had a choice. That she was used as a tool. I'm who I am, she thinks, and you made me come back here. I had to care; it was my nature. I'm who I am. Once you chose me it was certain I would look on them that way.

The wide world. Paris France. I could do it, she thinks, it's just a question of time. I wonder what on earth I'd see.

"Did you know there was an island here?" asked the man. "An island in the marshes?"

"Right here? You're kidding."

"Right here," he said. "The water went that way and that way and that, and it was all swamp behind."

She made a sour face as a truck bellowed by. "I can't imagine anything more different from what I'm looking at now."

"I know," he said. "Amazing, isn't it?"

The bright springtime morning sun fell through the lunchroom's plate glass window, its neatly painted letters throw-

ing shadows on the cloth and on the slowly wilting flower.
The women looked at each other.

"I wonder how Phillip is," said Jane.

He saw his final moments and accepted them with only the
slightest regret. He knew no trace would survive but that
was as it should be. Goodbye Martha, he whispered, goodbye house on Franklin street. Goodbye all. With God's grace
I hope and pray.

The darkness descended. His sense, his feeling
dropped from him. His body narrowed down to nothing and
he flickered and expired; he vanished with all his needs, all
his fears, all his memories, as if he'd never been.

Carla felt an odd excitement as she drove the two-lane highway, then turned at the boarded-up summer snack stand and
went over the old truss bridge and down through the valley
into the town. The day was warm, much warmer than she'd
expected, and the sun very brilliant: even New Hampshire
was turning green. She was happy to be where she was, a
little to her surprise, to be going where she was going. She
was happy to feel so certain of the way, for someone who'd
never been, to feel so confident of her welcome for reasons
hidden and undefined. As she went slowly through town and
passed the people standing and walking on the sidewalks
and crossing the street she admired their easy relaxed pos-
tures, their familiarity with one another, the simple elegance
of their storefronts and public buildings; when she saw a
young family that reminded her of her own—two little boys
and a girl running ahead of a couple who were clearly in

love—she wanted to wave and just barely held back. It was a place where she might live someday. She knew she never would but she admired it just the same.

Careful not to go too fast in the open stretch after the red brick school (it was perfect for a trap) she climbed the gentle rise toward the old village green and its companion the large white proud-steepled church, all peace and quiet dignity. She could tell that this had once been the center, before they'd built the mill down in the valley she'd just passed through. The houses were very grand. There was a legend about the church, her daughter had written; the men putting up its steeple were supposed to have heard a musket fired in Concord, Massachusetts, nearly fifty miles away, on a similar warmish April day in 1775.

A mile beyond the green she passed the road to the state park and then searched for and finally saw the small abandoned firehouse that Jennie had described, the landmark for her destination. Aside from that more recent account she'd heard about it long before, in a restaurant in the city, and had for some reason remembered it over the many obstacled years, not just remembered it but made and saved a picture of it that was very close—no, remarkably close—to the reality that now greeted her. How lovely it would be, she thought, slowing her car, feeling great longing and warmth, to put her arms around her nephew in his own home at last. How nice it would be to see Philip again.